Words Composed of Sea and Sky

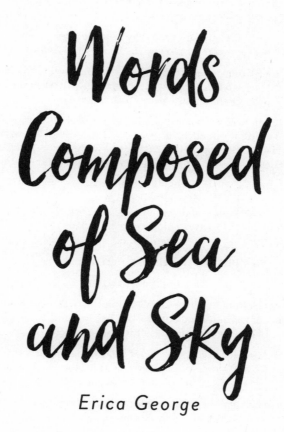

Words Composed of Sea and Sky

Erica George

RP|TEENS
PHILADELPHIA

Copyright © 2021 by Erica George
Cover copyright © 2021 by Hachette Book Group, Inc.

Running Press Teens
Hachette Book Group
1290 Avenue of the Americas, New York, NY 10104
www.runningpress.com/rpkids
@RP_Kids

Printed in the United States of America

First Edition: May 2021

Published by Running Press Teens, an imprint of Perseus Books, LLC, a subsidiary of Hachette Book Group, Inc. The Running Press Teens name and logo is a trademark of the Hachette Book Group.

The Hachette Speakers Bureau provides a wide range of authors for speaking events. To find out more, go to www.hachettespeakersbureau.com or call (866) 376-6591.

The publisher is not responsible for websites (or their content) that are not owned by the publisher.

Print book cover and interior design by Frances J. Soo Ping Chow
Cover Photographs copyright © Getty Images

Library of Congress Control Number: 2020939734

ISBNs: 978-0-7624-6820-1 (hardcover), 978-0-7624-6822-5 (ebook)

LSC-C

Printing 1, 2021

For Emily,

whose words continue to inspire bravery

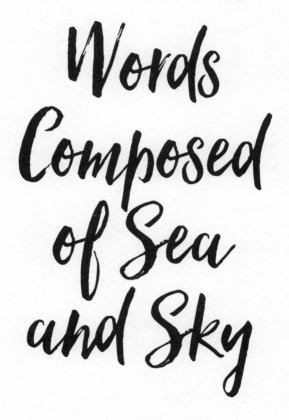

Words
Composed
of Sea
and Sky

CHAPTER ONE

MICHAELA

present day

I f I'm being honest, I've imagined countless scenarios in which one could meet the perfect boy in the most romantic way.

Take number seventeen on my list: the run-in at a bookshop among the shelves, stealing glances between the spines of classic books. Then, of course, there's number twelve: being caught unprepared in the rain, standing under the wilting pages of a newspaper that I just so happen to be carrying, and he comes to my rescue with an umbrella. And perhaps my personal favorite, number one: standing in line at The Good Bean, my local coffee shop, waiting forever to order my favorite muffin, the double mocha, only to find that the most charming stranger has ordered the last one. He realizes that this muffin holds the key to our lasting relationship and offers it to me.

I like the last one best because I get the cute boy *and* the muffin.

Narrowly escaping being plowed down by the cute boy in his navy-blue Audi convertible on my way to pick up my little sister from school was decidedly *not* on my list of ways to meet the perfect boy. Admittedly, I could have avoided the entire situation if my earbuds hadn't been in, and if I wasn't obsessing over the best way to broach a particularly touchy subject with my mom and stepdad once I got home.

I don't hear the car coming because my playlist is too loud, full of angsty, contemplative music to make me feel brave enough for when I get home. It's only when I notice one of the parents on the sidewalk in front of Bayberry Elementary School waving her arms in the air hysterically that I pull out one of my earbuds. The screeching of brakes behind me makes me whirl, catching a glimpse of the Audi swerving to avoid me, running up the curb, and careening into the fire hydrant. Frothy white water spews heavenward, glimmering in rainbows on its way back to the earth.

I remain in the middle of the street, gawking at the scene. The driver, a handsome boy with porcelain doll skin and curly chestnut hair, grips the car's steering wheel and hits his forehead against it dramatically.

"You almost ran over my sister!" Mellie, my sister, screams beside me, grabbing my hand with her free one and trying to maintain her grip with the other on what looks to be a papier-mâché whale.

"She was in the middle of the road!" he yells, struggling to unbuckle the seat belt and open the door at the same time.

I stand there, blinking, trying to comprehend the fact that if I hadn't taken out my earbud at the last moment, I might be dead. The boy stands in front of me now, his fingers raking through his shiny hair, his eyes taking me in.

"You okay?" he asks.

"I'm okay," I assure him. "Your car is decidedly less so."

He almost laughs until he turns to see his crumpled grill and bumper. Then his shoulders slouch and he curses under his breath. "But you're okay, so that's . . ." He sighs. "That's what's important."

I've never seen this boy before. He doesn't go to school with me, and he seems so much more mature, so much more collected, than boys my age. Maybe he's in college. Or maybe he's one of Highland's part-time residents, spending summers on Cape Cod and the rest of the year someplace else.

I haven't exactly played out this scenario in my head, so everything I do from this point forward is just improvising. I reach around to my messenger bag, stuffed with end-of-the-year assignments, random poetry books that littered the bottom of my locker for most of the year, and my trusty notebook, still somewhat fresh and filled with blank pages ready for my summer musings.

"You should take my information for when the police

arrive." I scribble down what I think is important: my name and cell number. Then I offer it up to him, my hand lingering between us, his eyes studying the paper for a moment.

"Thanks," he says, taking it with his pointer and middle finger and offering me a tight smile as he turns back to his car.

"Sure thing."

"Mack," says Mellie from beside me, yanking my hand and tightening her grip. "Let's go. I have to show Mom my whale!"

"All right, Mellie. Chill out." I glance down in time to catch her rolling her eyes and swiping her bangs out of her face.

The boy remains focused on the Audi, the khaki-hued leather interior getting soaked by the hydrant and the gathering crowd of parents and teachers growing agitated over the fact that he was driving so recklessly around little kids. None of this seems to faze him.

"Come on, Mack." Mellie pulls me down the street toward home.

———

When we get back to the house, Mom is already inside, unpacking groceries from her shopping trip and watching the little kitchen TV on mute. Mellie plows through the back door, unhooking her backpack from her shoulders and depositing it on one of the kitchen chairs. "Hey, Mellie-bear," Mom says, leaning down and kissing the top of my sister's head. "How was World Ocean Day?"

"Exquisite," says Mellie, emphasizing the *t* and shoving her right whale into Mom's hands. "Just like I knew it would be. All the teachers told me that the day wouldn't have gone as well if I weren't so responsible and helpful."

"Took the words right out of my mouth." Mom's standing at the stove, monitoring a pot of water that starts to boil softly. "And how was your day, Mack?"

"Fine," I reply.

"Mack almost got run over," Mellie announces.

"What?" Mom's face blanches, and she strides across the room, her hands suddenly on my shoulders. "What happened?"

"I'm fine. Mellie's making it sound worse than it was. A guy swerved to avoid me and hit a fire hydrant."

"Mack gave him her number."

"Oh my God, Mellie," I say, sliding into a chair beside her. "Don't you have some homework to do?"

"I only have a noun worksheet to do," says Mellie, her feet tucked up under her knees on the chair. "I already finished my reading during workshop this morning."

This is it, I think. This is my chance. My sister has literally placed the opportunity at my feet. I take a deep breath. "Speaking of workshops—" I start.

But before I can continue, my stepdad's voice interrupts. "Got hot dogs for dinner, Grace!" Russ stomps up the back-porch steps, a brown paper bag in his arms.

5

"I wish you would have texted me," Mom calls out the screen door.

Russ pauses on the deck before coming inside, raises his key fob, and locks his Dodge Durango. "Why?"

"Because I picked up stuff to make meatloaf."

I groan simultaneously with Russ, which causes us both to regard one another in surprise.

"No meatloaf," I beg, pulling my notebook out of my messenger bag. I start my homework, a creative response to an article we read in class about who, what, or where we call home. I write, changing a few words I had written during fourth period, then I add several more.

"It's too hot to turn on the oven, Grace," Russ adds. "I'll grill some hot dogs." He stands next to Mom at the counter and kisses her cheek, then heads in my direction.

Instinctively, my hands crash down on my words, hiding them from his view. They're still too close to me, too new, to share with anyone, especially Russ.

"I wasn't looking," he says, holding his hands up in surrender. He pauses at Mellie and kisses the top of her head, then eases past the kitchen table to the pantry, where he rummages around for all of the important hot dog condiments.

Feeling like it's safe to review my work, I lift my hand just a little bit and read my poem to myself.

there are no secrets in this house
thin walls
open doors
few rooms
no space
to clear my thoughts
get them down on paper
out of my head
stolen moments
of peace
solitude
words tucked away
and hiding in plain sight
so that the only one
who hears them
is the shy fox
who trotted all the way
from the woods
from the marsh
from the sea
just to listen
maybe my words don't even exist
unless the fox is there to hear them
someone to notice them
notice me

I smile at my small accomplishment. My English teacher will like it. She's basically the only person I let read my poems because my grade kind of depends upon it. Other than that, they're just for me.

Mom and Russ meander about, getting ready for dinner, trading stories from their day. Mom works at a day care center, and Russ owns our town's most affordable fried seafood establishment: the Shellfish Shanty. He comes home almost every day smelling of burnt oil. After I work a shift waitressing there, so do I.

"You want a glass of wine?" Mom asks, bent over and searching in the fridge.

"Get me a beer instead." Russ pauses. "My good beer."

The good beer is expensive and comes in bottles, and Russ drinks it only on special occasions. I know that's my signal, the cue that both my mom and Russ are open to a conversation. They've both had good days at work, and they're mellowing out with an afternoon drink. It's now or never.

"Hey, guys?" I ask, shifting in my chair and retrieving my folder from my bag.

"Hmm?" Mom pours herself a glass of wine and leans back on the kitchen counter.

"So, I was talking with my guidance counselor . . ."

"Who?" Russ asks, realizing he's a part of this conversation, too.

"Her guidance counselor," Mom replies.

"She thinks that my writing is strong enough to get into Winslow College of Fine Arts."

"Where's that?" Russ asks.

"Just north of Boston," I reply.

He nods because he likes the in-state price tag. It's a good start, and I'm spurred on by his mild but rarely won enthusiasm.

"She told me about this retreat they're having in the fall," I continue, pushing my blue folder across the kitchen table and opening it for them. "It's for prospective students, and you bring your poetry portfolio and have access to all of the professors. They give you feedback, and you stay on campus, and you get to see what dorm life is like, and eat in the cafeteria, and—"

"How much?"

I meet Russ's eyes. "Um . . ." I tap my finger against my lips. "Lemme check." I try to buy myself some time by pretending I don't know the exact number. I search for some kind of form to show him so I don't have to say how much.

Mom is busy riffling through the program guide, nodding at several of the lectures I'll be able to attend. I pause for a moment to appreciate that I have a pretty mom. She's much prettier than Russ deserves, and he should really take that into consideration when deciding on whether I can go to this workshop in October.

Besides, if I get accepted to Winslow College, then I'll be dorming there, away from here, and Russ will get what he's always wanted: my mom and Mellie to himself. *His* family.

"Here, the price should be on this sheet," I say, standing and handing it to him.

"Whoa!" Russ hoots, setting down his beer bottle on the table and dramatically raising his hand to his forehead. All the better to make his point. "Twelve hundred dollars, Mack? For a weekend?"

"A *long* weekend," I say quietly. "It's technically five days."

He drops the paper to the table, retrieves his bottle, and paces out to the deck.

Mom lifts what he was just reading and raises her eyebrows, her mouth parting before she even speaks. "Michaela," she says. "That's a lot of money."

"You can convince him," I whisper urgently, gripping her wrist. My eyes dart to Russ's figure on the back deck, opening the cover of the grill and attempting to light it. He curses when it doesn't happen fast enough.

"Baby, I'm not even sure if *I'm* convinced. What if you just applied to the college like everyone else? Is this retreat necessary for admission?"

"It's not *necessary*," I reply, "but if they see my writing ahead of time, if they know what I'm capable of, then I'm more than just grades and extracurricular activities, right? I'm a writer, a poet, someone worthy of their school."

She's quiet, which means I still have a chance to convince her.

"Mom," I beg, squeezing her hand. "It's Dad's school."

She presses her lips together, closing her eyes. "I know that."

"I have to go."

She squeezes my hand. "I'll talk to Russ. Maybe they have payment plans."

Squealing, I hop up and down and peck her cheek with a kiss.

She lifts a plate of hot dog buns and presents them to me. "Take this out to Russ. You know he likes the buns toasted."

"Okay," I reply, taking them from her and heading for the screen door. On the deck, I search Russ for any indication of a changed mind. No such luck.

"Oh, good," he says when he sees me. "The rolls I like."

I nod and turn to go inside.

"There are lots of places to apply to for college, Mack," Russ says once my back is turned.

My shoulders droop as I reach for the door handle.

"Places that don't just specialize in words and feelings. Places that'll get you ready for a real job, the real world."

The hot dogs sizzle on the grill.

"That's not—" I try to explain. But it's useless. He's not going to get it, so why waste my words on him?

I pass through the screen door, letting it slap closed behind me.

"Hey, Mack?" says Mellie from the table. "Is freedom a noun?"

"Yes," I reply, lowering myself into the chair beside her.

"But it's not a person, place, or thing," she protests.

"It's an idea." I sigh, resting my chin in my hand.

She seems temporarily satisfied by this, then snaps up her head from her worksheet and pulls her backpack over to the table, searching frantically for something. When she finds it, a black folder with a shiny gold star, she breathes a dramatic sigh of relief. "I thought I lost it! My pride and joy."

"It's a folder," I say.

She places her hand on my arm. "Not just any folder. It's a Third Grade Student Star folder. Not every third grader gets one. I've been waiting all year for this." She kisses its glossy exterior.

Mom deposits two glasses of iced tea in front of us and says, "You're sweating. Drink something cold." She runs her hand over my ponytail and smiles. "Your hair always gets so golden in the summer. You look like your dad."

I try to smile, but this is the last thing I want to hear right now—that I look like my dad. It's true, and I want to go to school for what my dad went to school for. It shouldn't be this difficult.

"Come and get your hot dogs!" Russ announces, carrying the platter through the back door. "Get me the sauerkraut, Mack."

Wordlessly, I cross the room to the fridge and find the Tupperware container of sauerkraut.

"Oh," says Mellie, "I almost forgot. We got this in school today." She presents Russ with a green form decorated with clipart leaves and twigs.

"What is it, baby?" Mom asks from the stove.

"It's a nature camp for July. All my friends are going."

Good luck, Mellie, I think. *Russ isn't exactly in the giving mood today. You should prepare yourself for the real world. Maybe pick up a shift at the Shellfish Shanty over the summer instead.*

Russ studies the form, then nods his head. "All right, I'll fill it out. When does it need to be back by?"

"Next week," says Mellie, taking the green paper from Russ.

Peering over her shoulder, my jaw practically drops. "It's eight hundred dollars!" I squeal.

Mom closes her eyes and pinches the bridge of her nose but says nothing.

"Why is spending eight hundred dollars on summer camp for Mellie perfectly fine, but I can't go to the poetry workshop weekend?"

"Because it isn't twelve hundred dollars, Mack," Russ says, turning away from the table and helping Mom get the dishes out of the cabinet. "And it's for an entire month, not a weekend."

"An extended weekend!" I say, standing.

"Michaela, we have to pay a sitter to watch Mellie on the days that you're working at the Shanty during the summer. This is probably cheaper than that."

"Ridiculous," I mumble, grabbing my journal and a pen and shoving them into my messenger bag.

"Come on," Mom says, placing a hand on my shoulder. "Let's have dinner, then we'll talk about it later."

"I'm not hungry." I shrug away from her touch and head for the back door.

"Michaela, where are you going?" she calls after me.

Before I can reply, Russ says, "Let her go."

I'm out the screen door and down the steps before I hear anything else.

There's a path that winds from the end of the yard, far in the back, behind the black-eyed Susans that Mom planted after Dad died. I'm the only one who knows about it. Sometimes I'm afraid I'll be caught, that Mom or Mellie or Russ will find me as I weave among the buttery yellow flowers, but no one ever does. I pluck one of the blossoms and tuck it behind my ear.

And I run.

I thunder across the blanket of fallen leaves left over from last autumn, the broken twigs, the sandy dirt, and I wonder if the animals, the only other travelers I've ever found out here, wonder where I'm going. If some soft-eyed deer or a darting fox marvel at the girl who runs so fast. Running to nowhere. Running until her legs are on fire, her lungs burning.

When I break through the branches, the beach heather of the cliffs stretches out before me, and beyond that, the sea, bright and blinding and forever. I stop, squinting up at the sky, then bend at my waist, sucking in breath after breath.

Henry David Thoreau said that here, at the tip of Cape Cod, you can put all of America behind you. But I think he forgot that the best part of being here is knowing that the rest of the world is before you. That the sea can whisk you along wherever it decides to go. There's something grounding in that. Something that keeps me still. Something that makes me stay here, at the tip of the world, the start of everything. The start of whatever I want.

I glance over my shoulder, still panting, the trees shrouding my path home. Taking the black-eyed Susan blossom from behind my ear, I pick the petals. They fly away on the wind.

CHAPTER TWO

MICHAELA

present day

T he center of Highland nestles within the curve of the bay. Narrow side roads split from Main Street, edging along the marsh, and the little cottages, with their glowing windows and brightly painted doors, cling to one another as the town gently bleeds into the tall seagrass and scrub pines of Cape Cod. With my messenger bag slung over my shoulder, I follow the cobblestone sidewalk past little restaurants, the white clapboard church on the hill, and its gated cemetery with jagged, tilting headstones that jut out from the rocky soil, so grimy with age that the names of the dead are difficult to read. The captains' houses rise before me, most of them exquisitely restored and all of them immaculately maintained. It's like walking back through time.

The early evening sun is still high in the sky, but it's losing its grip, slipping slowly down to the horizon. A full moon waits on its haunches just above the canopy of the trees. Before me, the old theater buzzes with young actors, trading memorized lines and anxiously waiting for their auditions.

I'm only interested in finding one person, though—the only person I know I can vent to. I stand on my tiptoes, searching for her familiar face. "Chloe?" I call.

"Over there," replies a boy beside me, pointing to the steps leading up to the theater. Chloe faces the park across the street and pounds her chest forcefully with her closed fist, reciting some soliloquy. The golden light of the setting sun casts a glow on her warm brown skin.

"Thank you," I throw over my shoulder as I dart toward her.

"What are you doing here?" Chloe asks when she sees me; and after she's studied my face for the briefest moment, her second question is, "What happened?"

"It's what *isn't* happening. Russ won't let me go to this poetry workshop in the fall at Winslow College, but he lets Mellie—"

"I don't have time for all the details, but I don't doubt you've just experienced an epic injustice, and I want to know more later. Come here." She gathers me in a hug as best she can because she's a little shorter than I am, then pushes me away and points across the street. "Meet me at the park at eight, okay? Auditions will be over by then, and we'll get ice cream together."

"Okay," I say with a nod, tucking a loose piece of hair behind my ear. "Good luck."

She squints at me.

I cover my mouth, the sudden realization of my mistake gripping me. "I mean, break a leg!"

She nods approvingly.

I make my way across the street, but a park is lonely when there's no one there. The playground is empty except for two middle school kids on the swings, staring at their phones and not speaking to one another. The benches are deserted, and the pedestal of what will soon be a statue of our town's local hero, Captain Benjamin Churchill—better known as the Highland Whaler—feels painfully solitary. They're erecting it in honor of the 160th anniversary of his death at sea. After being eaten by a whale. Or swallowed by a whale. Something to do with being ingested by a whale. Anyway, it's morbid.

I don't sit; rather, I keep moving down the street until Highland's town center melts behind me. In the distance, Cape Cod Bay sparkles in the coming twilight. The bay is a beacon, and I never feel half so forlorn near the water. Crossing the sandy, worn pavement of Beach Plum Lane, I cut through the near-empty parking lot and kick my flip-flops off at the top of the dunes.

The tide is far out, but inching back in, and I can see the silhouettes of couples walking the tidal flats, shadowed by the bright glare of the setting sun. A few people wade in the shallows, baskets on their arms, digging for oysters. I situate myself in the sand, knees up, resting my journal against my bare thighs. My pen clicks open, ready for whatever words are about to spew out of me. And they're angry words. Hurt words.

Stupid, selfish, ignorant.

This doesn't make me feel any better. Dwelling on all of Russ's annoying qualities only makes me fixate further on the wrong inflicted upon me this afternoon. Instead, I let my eyes settle on one of the oyster people. The one closest to me is tall, and he wears a baseball cap and high rubber boots. Every so often, he bends down, retrieving an oyster from its hiding place, and tosses it into his basket. He's a shadow, darkened in contrast by the sun's blinding corona behind him.

I pick him as my subject, someone I don't know, someone I can make up as I write.

> *At the start of the season,*
> *every oyster is ripe and ready for plucking.*
> *Too comfortable from a winter*
> *of languishing in their cold sea bed.*
> *They don't anticipate his*
> *rubber boots*
> *wire basket*
> *the hidden shucking knife*
> *or his rough hands*
> *that sift through gloppy sand until he happens*
> *upon a shellfish.*

When I look up from my writing, the boy is significantly closer than he was before, bending over the shallow ripple of a wave. "You sketching me?" he asks without looking up.

"Kind of," I reply. "I'm writing a poem about you. And oysters."

He finds one, lifts it from the bay, and drops it into his basket. "Oh, yeah? I didn't think oysters were worth writing a poem about."

I close my journal, my pen marking the page. "Everything's worth writing a poem about."

He moves deeper into a tide pool. "Do you come down here just to write?" His back is to me, and his voice is carried away by the breeze, but I still manage to catch what he says.

"I usually write at home," I reply, wrapping my arms around my knees. "But I had to get out of there today."

"Everything okay?" he asks.

"With what?"

"At home?" He stands up straight, and I think he's turned toward me because I can hear him better, but it's hard to tell in this light.

I rest my chin on top of my knees and sigh. "Do you ever get so frustrated by a person's inability to understand what you want? Like, you think you're saying something clear and obvious, and yet the person is so completely dense that they miss it?"

"Sometimes," he replies. "Like when you really want tacos for dinner, but instead it's leftover dried-out spaghetti?"

I lift my chin and breathe in sharply through my nose. "Sort of, I think?"

"Like, who wants leftovers when you could have tacos?" He bends down again, plucking an oyster from the sand.

"It's a little more complicated than that," I murmur. "My stepdad and I don't get along."

"Ah," he says. "That sucks."

"He honestly believes that he treats me and my half sister the same, but it's not true. I don't even think I can blame him. Mellie is his. I'm some other man's daughter."

"Did you tell your mom how you feel?" he asks.

"No," I say glumly.

"What about your real dad?"

"He's dead," I reply.

The oyster fisherman stands up straight, one of his broad shoulders tilting downward, and he shifts the basket from one arm to the other. "I'm really sorry. That was shitty of me to ask."

"You didn't know."

He plods toward me, the gentle splish-splash of the tide pool relaxing my whole body as the water parts with each of his steps. When he's only a few feet away, I look up, his prominent jawbone and deep brown eyes clear now with the dipping angle of the sun.

I just unloaded my family issues to Finnian Pearce. Finnian Pearce, the star pitcher of our unbeatable school baseball team, the Highland Whalers. Finnian Pearce, who throws an eighty-three-mile-per-hour fastball. Finnian Pearce, over whom every single girl I know fantasizes. Finnian Pearce, Russ's nephew Ryan's best friend, until death do they part. *That* Finnian Pearce.

I groan. He plops down beside me, lifting his knees and resting his elbows on top.

"I shouldn't have said anything," I say quietly, trying to shift my journal off my lap and into the sand on the other side of me.

"No, it's cool," he says. "I mean, I'm glad I was here to talk."

Well, this evening has gone down an unwieldy path. It's one of those moments where I'm not sure if I should go on pretending like we actually know one another, or if I should introduce myself, because why would Finnian Pearce actually know who I am? Michaela Dunn, writer of poetry by the bay. Even Ryan, my pseudo-cousin, hardly acknowledges me (which is a daily blessing).

"I'm Michaela, by the way," I finally force myself to say, but the tail end of my words fades into the breeze.

"Yeah, I know," he says. "Mack. You're Ryan's cousin." He pauses. "Well, his uncle's . . ."

"Yeah, I'm Russ's stepdaughter," I finish.

He leans back a little, a grin taking hold of his mouth, and extends his right hand. "Finn Pearce."

I laugh, taking his hand and letting him vigorously shake mine. "I know who you are, Finn."

"We had world history together sophomore year."

I did not, in fact, remember that.

"You sat diagonally in front of me. Asked me for an eraser cap once."

Oddly specific detail to remember. But to keep him from feeling awkward, I smile down at my toes, curling them into the damp sand, like I totally remember this scene.

"You don't remember," he realizes.

I purse my lips together and shrug apologetically.

"The eraser was hot pink, and you told me that you liked a guy who wasn't dictated by stereotypical gender norms."

Nodding, I pull my hair over my shoulder and twist it loosely between my fingers. "Sounds like something I would say."

He stares out at the bay. "I won't tell Ryan what you said, if that's what you're worried about."

I exhale through my nose, my shoulders relaxing.

"It's not his business. I get it."

"Thank you," I say softly.

We sit silently for a little while, and soon the sun dips behind the edge of the bay, a spit of orange puncturing the sky before it disappears for the night.

"Well, can I read it?" he asks.

"Read what?"

"The poem you wrote about me."

I guffaw, then cover my mouth in embarrassment. "Read my poem?" I ask him. "The one I just wrote? No."

"Why not? It's about me."

"I didn't know it was you. I guess it's more about oysters."

"Let me read it, then."

"Absolutely not." I slap my hand down on the journal beside me, and Finn leans back on his elbows.

"I'll let you try one of my oysters."

"No thanks," I reply.

"Free of charge." He sits up quickly, digging deeply into his rubber boot and retrieving his shucking knife. His right hand shuffles around in his oyster basket, the shells clattering together. "You have to try one. They're the best. Wellfleet oysters are world renowned."

"I know, but . . ." I watch as he wedges the knife between the oyster's shells, then pops it open, almost effortlessly. He detaches the flesh from the shell but lets it rest inside and offers it to me.

"But I . . ."

His eyes widen. "You what?"

"I've never had an oyster outside of a restaurant."

His hand still offers the waiting oyster. "Where do you think those oysters come from?"

"The bay."

"Exactly. This is basically the freshest oyster you're ever going to eat."

"But there's no cocktail sauce," I murmur.

"Sorry, I'm fresh out. Come on, try it."

I press my lips together.

"Okay, how about this?" he suggests. "I'll have one with you. Deal?"

I nod, taking the oyster from his hand, and he pops open another.

"All right, let's do this," he says. He taps his shell to mine. "Cheers."

"Cheers."

We slurp our oysters back, and I laugh as saltwater trickles down my chin.

"You got it!" Finn discards his empty shell in the sand beside him as I wipe the dribble off my face. "It's good, right? Better than a restaurant?"

"Better than a restaurant," I admit. "Thank you."

"No problem."

"Hey," I say, handing him back my empty shell. "It's almost eight. I told my friend I'd meet her after auditions."

"Better get going, then." Finn hops up and wipes his sandy hands on his pants. He reaches down, offering to help me up from the dune. "I hope things go better with your stepdad," he says as he pulls me to standing.

"Thanks for listening."

He nods and smiles. "See ya, Mack."

"Bye," I say with a wave, clutching my journal to my chest.

Finnian Pearce is, quite possibly, the most cliché guy in Highland for a girl to have a crush on. I decided this a while ago, and as I traipse across Beach Plum Lane and head into town, I'm convinced of this. Between the uniform, the rumors of his "speedball" worthy of a Bruce Springsteen song, and those chocolate-colored eyes with the longest lashes unfairly bestowed upon a boy, there's no questioning my certainty. Girls who crush on Finn have no imagination, no sense of romance, no creativity when it comes to the perfect guy.

But then again, none of those girls have ever watched him shuck an oyster. I dare a peek over my shoulder, and he still stands on the beach. He waves once. My breath catches, and I wave back.

I shake off the light-headed, heart-pounding feeling and find my park bench, positioned directly in front of the pedestal for the statue dedication. I lift my feet from the ground and rest them on the edge of the bench, then prop my journal against my legs once more. My pencil point conjures tiny dots along the lined paper, but no actual words; I stare at the empty pedestal, wondering what a statue dedicated to a whaler would look like. Or why this guy is even worth a statue. It's not like he died in a war. He died killing an animal that's now federally protected.

I've heard the stories, of course. Captain Benjamin Churchill was only eleven years old when he went to sea; he distinguished himself, rose through the ranks, and was the captain of his own ship by the age of nineteen. There are even rumors that, secretly, he was a poet. That's the part I've always liked best— the idea that at night, when the rest of his crew was asleep, he snuck down to his berth and wrote lines of sonnets, maybe to his lover, by the light of his whale oil lamp.

But that's not the Highland Whaler the rest of the town reveres. His face, now reduced to a cartoon image, graces the sign at the local mini golf course, and farther down Route 6, he can be found advertising the freshest scoops of homemade ice cream on the Cape.

I lean back, sighing, and I think that's when I notice the advertisement, the little sign beside the pedestal. I immediately recognize the insignia of Winslow College of Fine Arts.

Jolting off the bench, I whip out my cell and take a picture of the information. I stare at the image, then slip my phone into my back pocket and dash across the street.

At the theater, the actors are trickling out the front doors, fervently whispering to one another about how the auditions went. I hop up and down, stand on my tiptoes, searching for Chloe. She exits the theater, arm in arm with another girl, and they're laughing hysterically about something. When she sees me waving like a lunatic, she motions for me to join them.

"What's up, mama?" Chloe asks.

"This," I say, shoving my phone in her face.

"Too close, too close." She grabs my wrist and pushes it farther away, her mouth moving as she silently reads the advertisement. "I don't think I get it. You want to write a poem about the Highland Whaler?"

"I want to go to the poetry workshop at Winslow College, and it just so happens that they're hosting a competition for local students to write the dedication poem to be included on the pedestal of the Churchill statue. The winner gets a scholarship to the poetry workshop this fall. I wouldn't even need Russ's help if I won this!"

"It's all falling into place," says Chloe with a sage nod. "Yes, you must invoke the Highland Whaler. Only *he* will get you to Winslow College."

"But what do you know about him?" Chloe's friend asks.

I smile weakly. "Only that I really like the peanut butter fudge crunch ice cream he makes as his Friday special."

"There's a start," says Chloe.

CHAPTER THREE

MICHAELA

present day

Chloe and I stand shoulder to shoulder, our books clutched to our chests as the rest of the Highland High School students clean out their lockers for the end of the year. It's the last full week of school, and while the seniors are taking advantage of the tutorial period to study for finals, the juniors are finished, and there's not much to do.

Except stare at the mural of the Highland Whaler painted above the gym doors.

"Why do you think they chose him to be our mascot?" Chloe says. "His heroic spirit? His brooding demeanor? His strong, chiseled jaw?"

"I don't know," I reply. "But I need to find out." Pulling my journal from my messenger bag, I jot down a list of questions:

1. *Why the town's fascination with a young man who died over a century ago?*

2. What makes whaling worth celebrating?

3. Is there something about him that would appeal to twenty-first-century readers?

I sigh.

"I wish I could help you," says Chloe, her hand on my shoulder. "But I'm not exactly meant to be anyone's literary muse." Her eyebrow twitches up with a sudden spark of inspiration. "What about Mr. Fink? You know how he loves Cape history. I bet he'll have ideas of where you can start."

I bite the inside of my cheek. "I guess so."

"Go see if he has tutorial now. Scoot on down there." She swats my butt in the direction of our science classroom.

"What if I'm taking up the time of someone who actually needs help in his class?"

"You're stalling. Ask to talk to him later, then. What am I, your mom? Go!"

I start weaving through the usual hallway crowd, looking back only once to have Chloe blow me a kiss. I pretend to catch it.

Mr. Fink's lab is always humming with people at work, and when I walk in, there are at least a dozen students working with him on their final projects. Mine's been done for a week, so when he sees me lingering in the doorway, he offers me a questioning look.

"I'm just here to . . ." Unfortunately for me, my attention

and words are snatched away by Finnian Pearce sitting across the room, slouched down on his lab stool, one hand on the laptop keyboard, and the other trying desperately to keep his nodding head upright. He rubs his eyes awake and finds me staring at him.

Then he smiles.

"Mack?" Mr. Fink prompts.

"Oh, right. I was wondering if I could talk to you, maybe after school? I have something I'm working on, and I'd really love to ask you some questions."

"Let's talk now. Give me a minute, and I'll be right over." He motions toward the empty stool next to Finn's.

He doesn't realize that my feet are now officially cement. I can't bring myself to take a step, to get any closer to him. Finn watches, waiting for me to take my seat, then realizes that all his binders and his bat bag are in my way.

"Sorry," he says, expediently clearing the spot at the lab table.

"Thanks," I say quietly, regaining control of myself and slipping onto the stool beside his. I glance down at my outfit, and I wish I had taken the time this morning to pick out something a little classier than black leggings, an oversize long-sleeve T-shirt from the Shellfish Shanty, and my scuffed Converse sneakers. I pull my scrunchie, releasing my sloppy bun, and run my fingers through my hair.

Finn steals a quick glance in my direction, straightens up on his stool, and starts typing. I retrieve my journal, open it and press down on the crease, then lean to my right as casually as possible so that Finn doesn't think I'm purposefully trying to block his view.

After a few minutes, Finn clears his throat. "You trying to finish up your final project, too?"

"Nope," I reply. "I handed in mine last week."

"Oh." He starts tapping his foot. "I'm almost done with mine. Just putting on the finishing touches."

"Cool," I say, eyes glued on my journal.

"Did you, um, get your grade yet?"

I turn to face him, closing my journal and suppressing a grin. "Yeah, I did. Ninety-seven."

His eyebrows practically hit the ceiling. "Wow. Wasn't ready for that one." He turns his laptop toward me to show off his slides of glacial erratics. They're very colorful and annotated with lots of different fonts.

"Very nice," I say with a smile and a nod.

"The goal is to dazzle him with my impeccable slideshow design skills."

"I think you've got that down." I reach back into my messenger bag and retrieve my anthology of Romantic poets. I open to where I left off and continue to read, hoping that spending some time with the professionals will inspire something to finally appear on my blank page.

"What are you reading?" Finn asks.

"Lord Byron."

He scoffs.

"What?" I ask.

"I dunno. That guy seems like such a tool."

"He is not!" I practically shriek, then, realizing the volume of my voice, I slouch a little deeper on my stool. Softly but adamantly, I continue. "He's one of the greatest poets in history."

"He can write good poems and still be a tool."

"He was sensitive and easily distressed."

"I think," says Finn, clicking away at his laptop, "in the words of my English teacher, he was *highly romanticized*."

It's my turn to scoff.

"I mean, look what you just did," Finn goes on. "You don't even know the guy, and you put thoughts and feelings into him."

"I *inferred* the thoughts and feelings."

"Mmhm."

I tap my pencil on my journal. "What?"

"Nothing," he insists with a shrug.

I settle into my book, my eyes darting between the poems and my own blank page in front of me. Somehow, it's now impossible to think of anything worth writing about Captain Benjamin Churchill. A person I'm going to have to put thoughts and feelings into. To infer them. Why did Finn, a person I inferred was a brainless jock, have to go and be rather profound and insightful?

"Mack?" says Mr. Fink. "Come on over."

I gather my things, stuffing them into my bag, and follow him back to his desk. He pulls up a worn, mustard-yellow chair for me to sit in.

"What's up?" he asks. "You saw your grade on your final project, right?"

"Yeah, I saw it last week. I'm really proud."

"You should be!" he says with a nod, then shuffles a few papers before him, stacking them on top of one another and securing them with a binder clip.

"I'm actually working on a new project," I say. "A summer project." From my bag, I retrieve my phone—a contraband item, but I know Mr. Fink won't mind that I have it on me, because it's me. I scroll through my pictures until my screen displays the advertisement for the poetry contest hosted by Winslow College.

Mr. Fink puts on his reading glasses. "Ah, Captain Churchill! One of my favorite local legends. You're going to write a poem about him?"

"I thought maybe you could fact-check it for me?" I ask. "Give me some feedback?"

"What about this: How about you work on your poem all summer, and at some point in August, we'll meet at the Shellfish Shanty? I'll give you my feedback in exchange for a free lunch."

I smile, breathing a sigh of relief. "I can do that."

Before any plans can be made, a yelp goes up across the room, and a girl leaps to her feet, staring down at her overturned water bottle that has spilled its contents across her laptop.

"Mack," says Mr. Fink, "do me a favor and run down to room four-oh-six. There are rolls of paper towels in the back closet."

"Got it," I say, dashing out the door.

I bolt down the hall and duck into 406, locating the back closet. Behind the tall door, the paper towels are on the top shelf, far in the back. I curse under my breath, examining the room and figuring out what my options are. There are a few chairs stacked in the corner, ready for summer cleaning, and I start to take one down.

"I got you," says Finn from the door. He crosses the room and plucks a roll of paper towels with ease before I can even move.

"Thanks," I say.

Holding it out of my reach, he says, "So you're writing a poem over the summer?"

"Were you eavesdropping?"

"No." He pauses. "Actually, yes. But not very well, because I didn't hear the whole thing."

I don't want to tell Finn about the poetry contest. I'll feel exposed, and I've already felt too much like that with him already. "I'm working on a project over the summer. For a college application. Mr. Fink's going to help me."

He looks crestfallen, and I realize I don't like being the cause of this.

"Why?"

He shrugs. "I qualified to take a remediation class over the summer."

"Summer school?" My eyes widen.

"No, not summer school. A remediation class. I didn't fail English. I just came ridiculously close to failing. And Coach says if I don't bring my grades up, I'm off the team, and let's be real, nobody wants that."

"Of course not," I say, even though prior to this moment, I couldn't have cared less about our baseball team.

"I was kind of hoping that maybe you'd be able to help me. Because you seem like you've got your shit together."

I think this is a compliment, so I nod.

"Is that a yes?"

"I don't think—"

"Please, Mack. I'm already embarrassed that I have to be in the class. And I'm embarrassed I asked you for help. But I can't get kicked off the team. There's too much riding on this summer. Please?"

He is remarkably difficult to say no to.

"Okay," I cave.

He tosses the roll of paper towels to me with a hoot. "Up

here, Mack." His hand is high, waiting for a resounding slap from mine.

I have to hop a little, but I give him the high-five he wants. "All right, you can give me your number when we get to Mr. Fink's. I left my phone there."

"Thanks."

"You can thank Bounty for this."

He grabs the paper towels from my hands. "Thank you, Bounty," he says, and kisses the plastic wrap.

"You're weird," I inform him, heading toward the door.

"But refreshingly charming," he calls after me. "You have to admit."

I do have to admit. Just not aloud.

CHAPTER FOUR

MICHAELA

present day

I write in my father's office.

Or at least what used to be my father's office. Now it's an amalgamation of office, guest room, and Mellie's playroom. There's a full-size bed; two baskets full of Mellie's stuffed animals call the closet home. At the far end of the room, my dad's desk sits tucked away near the window, a single lamp illuminating the tiny corner, and a picture of him and my mom holding a toddler-size me presides over where I work. We look happy in this picture. Dad's laughing at something and staring lovingly at Mom. That's basically my memory of him, considering I don't have any of my own—him holding me and laughing, my mom's hand running through my hair's blond ringlets.

But this isn't the easiest place to write. It can't contend with the family that I share this house with.

"Mack, Mack, Mack, Mack," Mellie says with every jump on the bed behind me. "Mack, are you listening?"

"I can't help but hear you, Mellie."

"My teacher," she says with a hop, "says that's not—" she lands on her tush "—the same as listening." She's on her feet beside me, in a perfect gymnast's salute, like she's just done a back handspring for a panel of judges.

"I know, but I'm trying to write."

From down the hall, I hear Mom's vacuum sucking up dust bunnies and the occasional hairpin. "Feet up, girls," she says over the roar of the machine when she appears in the doorway. "Gotta get this clean before Monday."

"What's Monday?" shouts Mellie.

"I can't hear you!" Mom says over the roar of the old vacuum.

"Monday!"

Outside, the screech of Russ's saw sends me right over the edge. He's constructing a do-it-yourself fort with his brother and Ryan, and they've been slicing wood all morning.

"That's it," I say, slapping shut my journal and clicking off the lamp. "I'm out."

"Where are you going?" Mom calls over the vacuum.

I bend down and press the power button on the vacuum, silence swathing the room in a soothing wave. "For a walk," I say, calmly closing my eyes and taking a deep breath. "I need a walk."

"Don't forget you have a shift tonight at the Shanty from six to ten."

"I won't forget," I assure her, grabbing my messenger bag and tossing my journal and two favorite pens inside.

Once I'm outside, free of the cacophony that is my family, I start to head toward town, down the dusty beach road I live on. But I'm pulled in the opposite direction by the scuffling of small paws near the brush. The sound is too soft to be a coyote, but too big to be a rabbit or a chipmunk. I follow the noise through the sun-dappled woods until the trees break into open grass.

A rusty red fox with black paws and black-tipped ears darts out toward the sandy sloping cliffs leading to the Atlantic, and I breathe in the salt air. This is a much better place to write about someone who might have walked these very paths, out past Highland Light, which reigns over the land like a stately queen. The fox pauses on the dirt path before me, checking over his shoulder, as if beckoning me along.

I follow him obligingly. He leads me past the beach plums, through the milkweed and the marsh elder, and down to where the deer make their beds at night, near the inlet. The water is shallow, with gentle ripples, soft cries of sea birds, an occasional gannet flying overhead, and about a mile out, the Atlantic crashing along the shoreline. Above me, on a high cliff scaled only by a singular wooden staircase and the occasional squawking seagull, the Whaler's Watch Inn presides over the entire landscape.

There are lots of old houses and inns in Highland, and each boasts that Captain Churchill once slept there. The Whaler's Watch, however, is the only one with a distinct possibility of this being true. Before it was an expensive inn with ocean views, it belonged to Mr. Ebenezer Pearce, Benjamin Churchill's uncle by marriage.

I plop down in the middle of the path, surrounded by black-eyed Susans and buzzing bees, and I begin to jot down what this place is. Hundreds of years of history, thousands upon thousands of whispered rumors carried away on the wind, and a legend so elusive that I wouldn't be able to recognize him if he were standing right in front of me. Maybe for that I need to go to the Whaler's Watch, to breathe in the history for myself.

I trek across the grasslands, down to the muddy sand at the base of the bluff overlooking the inlet. There's a narrow expanse of water I need to cross before I make it to the wooden stairs ascending the cliff. I could take off my shoes and wade through the water, but then I'd be too wet to speak to anyone at so fancy a place as the Whaler's Watch. Even now, I spy a girl standing on the back deck under a canopy of black umbrellas, folding napkins and watching me, and I feel like I'm on display.

Finding a place where the water just trickles through the reeds and grass, I muster up my courage and take a leap onto an island of sand and mud in the middle. I make it, but my balance is off, and my journal goes flying into a bank of damp sand.

"Shit!" I mutter under my breath. I make one more leap to the other side, retrieving my journal from the ground and wiping it down with the corner of my Edgar Allan Poe T-shirt. The "Nevermore"-quothing raven is now officially covered in grains of sand.

Up on the deck, the girl who was folding napkins comes to the balcony, leaning on her elbows and smiling. "You okay down there?"

"Yeah," I reply, thumbing through the pages to make sure my work is still in once piece. "Crisis averted."

"Come on up." She nods toward the building. "I'll get you a glass of water."

I climb the wooden stairs, and when I get to the top, I turn back, staring out over the inlet and toward the ocean. The waves batter a thin strip of sand, and farther out, a sailboat floats by, its sails puffed and flapping in the afternoon breeze.

"Here you go," says the girl, placing a glass of water on one of the wooden tables and next to it a carafe in case I want more. "I'm Brittany, by the way," she continues, extending her hand.

"Michaela," I reply, and we shake hands.

Brittany is young—maybe in her mid-twenties. She has dark hair twisted into a knot on the top of her head, and she's wearing a half apron with two big pockets and long apron strings that are wrapped twice around her waist and tied in front. "What were you doing down there?" she asks.

"Writing," I reply, taking a long gulp of cool water. "I was trying to find some inspiration."

"Well, you've come to the right place," she says, motioning toward the ocean.

"I was actually on my way here—to see if I could find out something about the Highland Whaler."

"Huh," she says. "He supposedly stayed here, you know. Whenever he was last in Highland."

"I thought maybe if I occupied the same space he once did, I'd be able to figure him out. I'm writing a poem about him for the statue dedication in the fall. The one in the park."

"Oh, right!" Brittany says. "For the poetry workshop retreat at Winslow College."

"Yeah," I say, impressed she knows what I'm talking about.

She shrugs. "My little brother goes to Winslow College. Well, he's actually my half brother. Same dad, different moms. My mom owns this place. I help her run it, and Caleb is here all the time, too. Both our families are still really close."

"Thanks so much for the drink," I say after taking one last large gulp of cool water. "I'll let you get back to work."

"Do you need a place to write?" Brittany asks. "Because down in the sand doesn't sound particularly comfortable. But maybe that's just me."

"Where else is there close to the inn?" I glance around at the empty tables on the deck, wondering if I could possibly snag one off in a corner, just to be here and near the ocean.

"Inside the inn," she says, her hand on the door to one of the dining rooms. "It's almost five, and the early birds will be here any minute. This deck is gonna get crowded. But there are lots of little rooms you can tuck yourself away in. If you're writing about the Highland Whaler, then you should at least walk the same halls he did, right?"

"Thank you," I say, following her through the glass door and into the dining room. As we travel the hall, I notice small dining rooms, each with its own fireplace.

"This place is so old, we couldn't actually knock any of the walls down to make one big dining room," says Brittany, like she can read my thoughts. "I kind of like it this way better, you know? It has more character."

I nod, poking my head around a doorway. The room is laden in shiny, dark wood, polished brass, and miniature replicas of whaling ships. There's even an old harpoon over the fireplace. We cross into a main foyer, and the center hall steps turn wide. A boy appears at the top of the landing.

"Caleb," says Brittany, smiling.

Wordlessly, he trots down the steps, hands in pockets. His face seems familiar. I know him, but I don't know from where. Once he's standing in front of me, I try to place his expression.

A table at the Shellfish Shanty? The halls at school? Strolling through town? When I'm walking Mellie . . .

Mellie. In front of the school. On the street. In his blue Audi. With water gushing from the fire hydrant. I glance out the window at the inn's parking lot, and there it is: the near-perfect piece of German engineering that almost ran me over and its perfectly repaired front end.

"Caleb Abernathy," says Brittany, stepping back to reveal more of me, but I only want to shrink into myself. "This is Michaela. Michaela, this is my brother, Caleb."

"Hey," says Caleb with a nod.

"Hi," I reply. "We've met, actually."

Brittany smiles. "Oh, yeah?"

I try to keep my fluttery insides under control because Caleb doesn't seem to remember. "It had to do with a fire hydrant."

Caleb's expression doesn't even flinch. "Oh, right. Sorry. I guess I was distracted by the damage to my car."

Awkward, but understandable. I try to be as removed as he is from our chance encounter, but he's difficult not to stare at.

Caleb Abernathy is entirely different from any boy I've ever met. His skin is like ivory, his eyes a pale, thoughtful blue, and his dark, messy curls keep falling across his forehead. He wears a loose button-down shirt, khaki pants, and boat shoes that look like he's about to step onto a yacht. He's exactly what a writer should be—artistic and aloof, probably thinking the most profound thoughts right now, even as I ogle him awkwardly. His mouth twitches as he takes me in. Maybe he's trying to figure me out, too.

"Michaela is a writer, too," says Brittany. "She's doing some research on the Highland Whaler."

"Cool."

I clear my throat, tucking a lock of hair that's fallen free from my ponytail behind my ear.

"She's interested in Winslow College," continues Brittany.

Caleb presses his lips together, nodding, his hands still in his pockets. "I like it there."

Turning back to me, Brittany gestures toward a little room with a table and chairs and low shelves that only come to my waist. They are filled with old books. "Sometimes my mom sneaks in here to get some paperwork done, but I know she won't mind if you sit for a little while, soaking in the ambiance."

"I've gotta run and mail this package for your mom," says Caleb, grabbing a puffy manila envelope from the hostess station and his Audi key fob from a hook on the wall. "I'll be back in a few. Nice to see you, Michelle."

"It's Michaela," I say, but he's out the door just as an elderly couple enters for dinner service.

Brittany stands at the door. "If you need me, I'm around. I'm on tonight until eleven."

In all the excitement of actually getting to write in the

Whaler's Watch, I forgot that I had a shift at the Shellfish Shanty. "I won't be here too long," I tell her. "I have a shift tonight, too."

"You work at a restaurant?" she asks, plucking a few menus from the hostess station. She smiles at the couple who wait patiently for her to seat them.

"My stepdad owns the Shellfish Shanty."

"That place is amazing," she says.

"A regular dream come true." My laugh comes out breathy and awkward.

Brittany leads the couple to the back porch, then joins me again in the little office. There are huge, multipaned windows in the back of the room that look out over the inlet. "Come back whenever you want. I'll let my mom know that you'll be joining Caleb as one of our authors in residence."

"Really?" I ask. "I can write here whenever I want?"

"Sure. I mean, this is the kind of place that inspires stories and poetry, right? Someone has to write about them." She pauses. "Other than Caleb." With that, she disappears around the corner.

I seat myself at the table, pressing down on the crease of my journal, and I start to describe my surroundings: the old, sweet smell of polished wood; the damp air that infiltrates the building from the sea. I keep writing with one eye on the clock that's shaped like a helm, and about twenty minutes before I need to be home to don my Shellfish Shanty T-shirt, I close up my journal and sigh.

The Whaler's Watch is significantly more crowded now, and there are other waiters and waitresses carrying trays of cocktails and appetizers from the kitchen through the halls and into the dining rooms or out onto the deck. Brittany stands at the hostess station, a phone secured between her ear and her shoulder, and her nodding has a frazzled element to it.

"Okay," she says. "Yup, okay. I'll do my best." She slams the receiver back in its cradle.

"Everything okay?" I ask.

She looks to the ceiling and closes her eyes. "I just had two girls call in sick for tonight. I'm going to have to cover their shifts."

I glance around. There's a cluster of waiting patrons at the door. "Can I do anything for you before I leave?"

Her eyes snap open, flooded with relief and gratitude. "There's a basket of fresh towels just around the corner," she says, pointing. "Can you bring them up to the rooms on the second floor? Two towels for each room? No one's in them right now, but you can knock just to be sure."

"On it," I say.

I lift the basket and carry it up the staircase. There are six rooms in all on this floor, three on each side of the hall, and a closet at the very end with its door ajar. Brittany was right; all the guests are still out for the day. I leave a neat pile of towels at the foot of each bed, and when I reach the end of the hall, I give a little sigh of satisfaction. There are three towels left over, so I open the door to the closet to put them away.

Only I'm not greeted by rows of shelves, but rather a flight of stairs. The late afternoon sunlight drips down from the top of the shallow curve of the staircase, and I try to peek up, not actually climb the stairs, but I can't help myself.

At the top, the staircase opens into a small room surrounded by windows that are framed in twinkle lights and shelves filled with books. The Atlantic stretches out before me, the roar of the waves muted by the inn's walls. In the far corner, a messy desk faces a window. I shouldn't be here, but I can't help from entering farther.

I run my fingers along the spines of the books until I reach the desk, papers scattered everywhere, old diaries and letters mixed with recently typed and printed pages. I shuffle them so that I can see a few more. Stories from the Highland Whaler's time at sea, anecdotes from when he was just a little boy. It's difficult to imagine an eleven-year-old on a whaling ship among men, sailing around the globe, facing possible death at any moment. Young kids are supposed to be at home with their family, or in school, learning, jumping in the tide pools, collecting shells. Playing baseball.

I quickly shake the image of Finn on a baseball mound

from my thoughts. There's no room for Finnian Pearce here, not when I've found the writing hideaway of a boy one hundred times more contemplative and introspective than any baseball player could ever hope to be. A boy who cares about the past, one who knows that words matter, one who reads books and hangs twinkle lights and writes with the lure of the Atlantic coursing before him. One who goes to Winslow College.

Something stops me—something that forcefully pulls me from reveries of a boy I don't actually know. A worn leather journal sits precariously on one of the bookshelves beside me, tied closed with a leather knot. I lift it, my fingers itching to pull the cord. I glance over my shoulder. No one knows I'm up here, and I figure Brittany is too busy to wonder where I've wandered off to. If I open this, maybe I'll know Caleb Abernathy a little bit better. Maybe it'll provide me with something to say the next time I see him instead of mumbling like an idiot. I pull the knot loose and the pages fall open.

But it's not Caleb Abernathy's journal. Not even close. The pages inside are dried out and stained, the beautiful penmanship faded with time. On the first page, I read the inscription:

Leta Townsend, 1862

I flip through the pages, scanning the entries casually. She had sisters and a little nephew, and she lived with her parents, and she even wrote a few poems. Some of the paragraphs are too faded to read, too worn away to make any sense. I turn one more page, and my eyes fall upon something I can't ignore. A poem. It takes up an entire page and is signed by the author.

Captain Benjamin Churchill.

Call it history, call it a haunting, or ghosts, or phantoms, or shadows. But I can hear her whispering in my ear.

Leta Townsend wanted me to find this.

I can't steal the journal from the room, but I need to know whatever Leta Townsend knew about Benjamin Churchill, because it's bound to be more than I do. Quickly, I pull my phone from my back pocket and start taking pictures, page after page. As many as I can in whatever time I have.

It's only the sound of a car chirping while being locked that makes me stop. In the back parking lot, Caleb steps away from his Audi and shoves the key fob into his pocket. I close Leta Townsend's diary, re-tie the leather cord into a neat knot, and place it on one of the bookshelves, then race down the stairs with my extra towels before anyone knows I was ever up there.

CHAPTER FIVE

Leta

Summer 1862

lift my face to the afternoon sun, and the sea breeze whips by me, tangling my hair, causing my skirts to flap about my calves. I breathe it in.

"I am the ocean," I say, eyes closed. "I am the clouds in the sky. The seagulls, coasting on the wind. I am a—"

"A loon," says my sister, Caroline, from behind me. She plops down in the sand, plucks a piece of seagrass, and is now intently studying it. "A complete and total loon. Mother will be cross if we skip sewing circle again today. And we're already late."

"You have no imagination," I say, facing the sea once more. In my hands, I grip a bottle and a letter, rolled tightly into a scroll that can fit through the neck. Once I cast my words to the ocean, the only thing that awaits me for the rest of the day is the tiresome company of sewing circle. This moment needs to last for as long as possible.

"It's not that I don't have any imagination," says Caroline, "it's that it isn't quite so well-developed as yours. Besides . . ." she stands now, skipping down the dune to be by my side "—it's morbid to write letters to a dead man."

"It's poetic, and it's the only way I can reach him now. My words floating along the sea until they come to the place where the sky kisses the water. That's where they'll find him."

Caroline rolls her eyes. "You didn't even know him."

"I did, too," I insist. "I went to school with Captain Benjamin Churchill."

"Not for very long. He must be several years older than you."

Benjamin Churchill, the boy who has occupied my childhood memories and now my imagination, is dead. Of this I am certain.

Fairly certain.

I'd prefer to be more certain, but there are few assurances in life, and I'll take what I can get. Really, there's only a smidgen of doubt.

Benjamin Churchill left when he was eleven. The story goes that he packed up his belongings one warm night in June and boarded a coach headed to New Bedford. He was going to start a new life because there was nothing left for him in Highland. No parents, few friends, and the only sibling he had was an older brother who was employed as a whaler.

So he left. I can't blame him, and I don't miss him. I hardly knew him; Caroline's right. Once, I recall, and I make sure to tell my sister, he picked me strawberries on a church outing. The ones that grew on the far side of the hill. It was a spot, he claimed, that only he knew, and the strawberries there were the sweetest.

And another time, in school, he pulled one of my braids. It was during math, and I was trying my best to concentrate, and he was trying his best to distract me. I've never held with the notion that boys who like you and want your attention treat you poorly. I whipped around and smacked him across the face.

His cheeks turned bright red, particularly where my hand had made contact. He left the schoolhouse and never returned. I don't think he liked school very much to begin with, and I suppose my actions gave him more of a reason to leave.

That's my memory of him now. The boy who always leaves, is departing, is gone.

I curl my letter to him into the glass bottle, cork it, and then toss it into the Atlantic Ocean. Like I always do. I tell Benjamin Churchill everything. The words I cannot share with anyone else. I tell him my secrets, my wants, my desires. And he never tells. In return, he lets me write poetry under his name.

A wave claims the bottle for only a moment, and then it floats and bobs out to sea.

"Caroline," I say.

"Hm?" she replies.

"I have something to show you."

"What's that?"

I retrieve a folded note from the pocket of my apron, and I hand it to my sister. "Read it."

She flattens the paper and scans the words.

Dear Captain Churchill,

We are pleased to inform you that your collection of poems will be published this fall in our quarterly journal. We thank you for your submission and look forward to more of your writings.

Sincerely,
Maxwell T. Jacobs

"Leta," says Caroline. She grips my shoulder, staring at the words, as though if she lifts her eyes they might change and prove to be a lie. "Is this true? Are your poems going to be published?"

I nod emphatically, and Caroline leaps into my arms.

"Leta, this is the most wonderful news!"

I grip her shoulders and push her to arm's length. "Caroline, you can't tell anyone. Not Mother, not Father. And certainly not your husband. He's a hopeless gossip."

"He really is," Caroline agrees. "Don't worry. My lips are sealed."

If Benjamin Churchill ever knew he was a writer of fine poetry to be published in *Alden Quarterly Magazine* of Boston, I wonder what he'd think. I wonder what kind of poems he'd write. I've taken great care to imagine Benjamin Churchill the way he ought to be. The way he would have been had he lived past his teenage years.

"Thank you, Benjamin Churchill," I whisper, then I blow him a kiss toward heaven.

Caroline and I link arms and head up the road leading into the little village of Highland. Sewing circle is being held today at Mrs. Mildred Budd's house, and it's situated closer to the bay, away from the harsh, icy winter winds of the North Atlantic.

But it's May now, the frightful weather far behind us, and as we enter Mrs. Budd's house, the air is still and stagnant.

"There they are!" cries Mother. "Heavens, girls, I thought we'd lost you. You see, Mildred, I told you they were coming."

"Simply delayed," says Caroline with the confident air that comes with being the prettiest sister, well-married, and situated in a house that everyone envies. She breezes past the other ladies and takes her place at Mother's side. She encourages me to join her. And I do, albeit reluctantly. "But really, who can resist this weather we're having? Leta and I took a detour by the lighthouse."

I could slap her.

"The lighthouse!" Mrs. Budd croons. "For the weather, you

say?" She casts a glance in my direction as though I'm so painfully obvious that she feels sorry for me. "Was Elijah Pearce at home?"

Caroline realizes her mistake. "No, we didn't see him. I mean, we were hardly even near the lighthouse."

My face burns as their discussion hisses and whirrs about me.

"Oh, look at her!" says Mrs. Budd, elbowing her eldest daughter. "Look how she blushes! It won't be long now before we hear wedding bells."

"Elijah is my friend," I say weakly. But these words don't matter. I can defend our friendship until sunset, and Mrs. Budd and her ilk will continue to spin tales about us till dawn.

"Really, Mildred," says Mother, her eye practically twitching. "I believe my Leta will make a better match than the keeper of Highland Light."

Now I'm flustered by two simultaneous and yet altogether different conclusions.

I do not want to marry Elijah Pearce. Of that I am fairly certain. I'd prefer to be more certain, but there are few assurances in life, and I'll take what I can get. Really, there's only a smidgen of doubt.

And even if I did, how dare Mother make it sound as if marrying Elijah would be a punishment? Elijah may be poor, but he is honest and gentle. He's my friend.

He's my best friend.

I venture a glance over at Mrs. Charlotte Pearce, Elijah's aunt. Benjamin Churchill's aunt, too. She has no idea any of this is going on. She can hardly hear these days. The letter hidden beneath the neckline of my dress feels awkward, and it jabs at me.

Part of me feels guilty, surely, for benefiting from the dead. For stealing Benjamin's name and using it to my own advantage. But it's difficult for a young woman to have her writing taken seriously, let alone published. It's been so much easier since I've begun using the name Benjamin Churchill instead of Leta Townsend.

Even his name sounds more serious than mine. What's more domineering and demanding of attention than a church on a hill, after all?

His aunt tells the story of his death at almost every dinner party and usually at sewing circle (but not today, and I can't determine whether to be grateful or exasperated by this).

And it's always the same. She never forgets one detail. The great Pacific Ocean was placid the day he died; the sperm whale that Ben had harpooned, however, was anything but. Churchill's whaleboat was tossed heavenward in a great, foamy spray, and then plummeted back down into the hellish jaws of the leviathan. Nothing was left but splinters.

I always try to comfort Mrs. Pearce, remind her how brave and intrepid Benjamin Churchill must have been to face the wild determination of an enraged whale, and at so young an age, too. But she gets a far-off look, as if she can see her nephew on the sea, the grim reaper always peeking over his shoulder.

"I heard that we finally have a new minister coming to Highland," says Mother. She raises her eyebrows as if she expected this but is still dissatisfied. "After waiting for so long, I suppose we should be grateful."

At last, the conversation has diverted from the topic of Elijah Pearce.

I sigh, trying to distract myself with my sewing, but for every stitch I make, I feel I need to pull two out and start over. It's mind-numbing work, and I'd rather be tucked away in my garret at home, writing a new poem.

A little boy's voice interrupts the hive-like hum of the sewing circle. "Mother, look!"

My oldest sister, Susannah, glances up from the quilt she's been working on. "Theodore, what have I told you about running through houses with muddy shoes! Apologize to Mrs. Budd."

Teddy stops short, almost falling over, and in his right hand, he clutches a small jar. "Oh, I almost forgot," he says and dashes out into the kitchen. He calls from the door, "I'm sorry, Mrs. Budd."

"I didn't think he'd be a bother," says Susannah, apologizing to the women of the sewing circle. "But I had no one to watch him today, and . . ."

"He isn't a bother," I say, but Susannah ignores me.

She continues, "I wish he had someone to keep him entertained."

The other women all nod sympathetically, as though Teddy is the unruliest little boy who ever did exist.

"I'll entertain him," I say, dropping my sewing.

"Leta, dear," says Mother, tugging at the sleeve of my dress.

"It's no bother." I smile, and before she can say another word, I'm out the parlor door, free and untethered to enjoy the afternoon with my nephew.

Teddy waits for me in the kitchen. He's small for a boy of eight, finely proportioned, and prone to illness. He always has dark circles under his eyes, like he needs more sleep than he gets. But his mouth is turned up in a hopeful smile when he sees me in the doorway.

"Aunt Leta!" he cries, hopping up from the table. "Look at this jar."

He holds it out to me, and I admire it accordingly. "It's a very fine jar," I tell him. "What will you use it for?"

"My adventure today," says Teddy, "will take me down to the beach in search of clamshells."

"Would you mind if your aunt joins you, or is this a solitary adventure?" I ask.

He grabs my hand in reply and pulls me out the back door. Breaking from the house, we trot down the sloping hill. The sky is an almost unnatural shade of blue, and there's not a cloud to be found. I can see the water now, glittering below the sun, as I reveal the shell I've wrapped carefully in my handkerchief. "Look at this piece I found for you yesterday."

Teddy grabs the sliver of purple shell from the palm of my hand, and his mouth forms a perfect little "oh" of admiration. "Let's fill the jar, Aunt Leta," he says.

"We can certainly try," I call as he surges ahead of me, down the dunes and into the surf. He splashes through the gently lapping waves, waiting for them to retreat and reveal the treasures of the bay.

"And then we can look for blackfish!" he calls back to me.

"Not too loud," I warn him. "When we look for blackfish, we only look to admire. But if the men should see . . ."

"Then they soon will expire," Teddy finishes for me, digging into the sand and plucking a clamshell from the damp grains.

Teddy likes to rhyme things with me. He says it's how he helps me with my poetry. Sometimes we make it a competition, to see who can come up with the cleverest rhyme. He came up with this one, though I'm not certain he fully grasps the reality of it all. That groups of blackfish are driven up on the shore and slaughtered for their meat and for their oil. He's never seen it, the way the clear water of the bay runs red while the whales that remain writhe in anticipation of death. If I have it my way, Teddy will never know.

"I have a secret for you, Teddy," I say. "You promise to keep it?"

He's pulled from his hunt for clamshells and gallops toward me, extending his pinkie. "I promise, Aunt Leta."

I grin down at him, our little fingers entwined. "My poems are going to be published in a quarterly magazine."

"Aunt Leta!" he cries, grabbing both of my hands and jumping up and down. "It's what you've always wanted."

"It is," I agree, and I can't help but be swept away in his enthusiasm. I jump, too, and he beckons me to follow him in his frolicking in the waves.

Part of me knows that Susannah and Mother will be cross when they see us return to the sewing circle, soaked through and flushed from exertion. But the other part of me is careless. I chase Teddy through the shallows and across the flats, and back up into the dunes. Sprays of sand erupt from his feet.

"You can't catch me, Aunt Leta!" he taunts over his shoulder, but then he disappears along the side of the dunes. He practically drops out of sight.

"Teddy?" I call, pausing to catch my breath.

His little head pops up among the sharp grass, and I know this expression. He's mortified. "I'm so sorry," he says.

"Teddy," I call again. "Who are you apologizing to?"

He glances over at me and then points downward. "To him."

"Who?" I ask, my hands finding my hips in a posture of authority.

A young man sits up, his back covered in sand, but otherwise well-dressed. "To me," he says. He stands, brushing off the sand from his legs. "No harm done," he assures Teddy. "I've sustained worse injuries."

"I'm sorry," I begin, shaking my head and coming closer.

He turns to me, lifting a bag and a case that's shaped to hold a fiddle. "You too, eh?"

"Are you from around here?"

"I am," he replies, grinning at me.

He really has the most arresting smile. I'm suddenly at a loss for words, and this rarely happens to me.

"You are?" I say. "Because I've lived here all my life, and I don't recall ever seeing your face before."

The man runs his fingers over his short hair and an excess of sand sprinkles across his shoulders. In his right hand, he holds his coat, and he drapes it over the opposite shoulder, securing it with his finger. He has eyes of a mercurial color, a shade and tone that shifts with the cloud coverage, with proximity to the water, and I think he's teasing me, though I can't be sure why.

"*Seen* my face?" he says. "Look a little closer." He leans toward me, pointing right above his chin. "I can still feel the sting of your hand across my cheek."

I step back and almost lose my balance.

"Do you know me now?" he asks. He edges around us, gathering his rucksack and heading toward town. "I'm Benjamin Churchill," he calls over his shoulder.

I stand there, jaw slack, watching as he walks away toward Highland.

Damn that smidgen.

CHAPTER SIX

MICHAELA

present day

This," says Mr. Fink, motioning to the fish tank near the window, "is my finest specimen yet."

I blink to make sure I'm seeing things correctly.

But it's Chloe who raises her hand.

"Yes, Chloe?" he says.

She takes a breath. "Mr. Fink. Is that a lobster? With one claw?"

"It is!" he says. I can't see his lips, but the thick gray mustache that covers most of his mouth moves up and down like a puppet whenever he speaks. "*Homarus americanus*! Or as I affectionately refer to them, the lice of the sea." He lovingly sends kisses to the creature.

"That's gross," I say under my breath.

"I was at the local grocer," Mr. Fink continues, pacing the length of his science lab. "I overheard one of the customers complaining because this particular crustacean had lost a claw, no doubt in battle, and therefore she did not want him. I wondered who would. Then I realized, I would. It was me!" He points to himself enthusiastically. "Now he's our class pet."

"How do you know it's a he?" Ryan asks from behind me.

"I can't tell for certain," says Mr. Fink, "but I have a hunch." He squats down to look the lobster in the eyes through the tank's glass wall. "There isn't a humane way for this little fella to die, and I thought it was my duty as a scientist to enlighten my students while keeping him alive."

"Thanks, Mr. Fink," says Chloe, slouching down on her stool.

"Next year, if you take honors bio with yours truly," Mr. Fink continues, removing his glasses and cleaning them with the hem of his shirt, "we'll be delving into the diverse marine life of our coast. Seals, sharks, mola, right whales, and humpbacks. I'm actually anticipating an exciting visit from a colleague of mine."

"Is this colleague a marine mammal?" Chloe asks.

"Of course not. Marine mammals don't move efficiently on dry land."

"Of course not," she says and nods.

"No, my colleague at Boston University. She's working on a study of bowhead whales off the coast of Canada. It will be an enlightening discussion, and I look forward to sharing it with you."

The bell rings, and a building-wide cheer erupts from every room. It's the last day of school, and everyone is headed to the beach. Except me, of course. I'm the lucky girl who gets to work a double shift at the Shellfish Shanty to start off my summer. Luckily, Chloe is working the double with me, so I won't be entirely alone.

The Shellfish Shanty presides at the top of the pier just on the outskirts of Highland, its gray cedar shakes weathered from harsh New England winters. Fishermen come in from the bay with their fresh catches, and tourists park far down the street and enjoy the scenic walk through town in order to snag a picnic table and eat their meals in the company of our three resident seals who swim along the side of the pier, begging for scraps like blubbery sea dogs.

By the time Chloe and I get to work, the lunch crowd is in full swing, and Russ is already in the kitchen helping the fry cooks and barking orders at the waitstaff. We head to the back room, changing out of our school clothes and slipping on our mandatory black T-shirt with "Shellfish Shanty" written in a jaunty font over the cartoon face of a grinning clam.

"Now that you're the resident writer at the Whaler's Watch," says Chloe, popping her head through the collar of her shirt and pulling her hair free, "are you gonna cut down on your shifts here?"

"Can't," I reply. "Russ would lose his shit."

"Well, did you at least write anything decent while you were there? Or were you too busy sizing up the eye candy?"

"I wrote something," I say. "But it was after."

"After you left?" She stares at her reflection in the little mirror hanging on the wall, applying an extra coat of mascara and stretching her free arm out behind her. "Gimme. Let me read. I can tell you whether I think it's worthy of a statue. I'll give you a dramatic reading of the poem and everything."

"It's not ready yet," I reply.

"Party pooper."

"Check my teeth," I say, giving her a forced grin.

"All clean. Gum?" She pulls a fresh pack from her apron pocket.

"Gum."

Tossing me a piece, she closes her eyes and savors our last few moments of peace, made even more valuable by the distinct roar of teenage-boy laughter coming from out on the pier.

Someone knocks on the door with an impatient cadence. "Girls? You decent?"

"Decent!" I call.

Russ opens the door. "Let's get out there. We have a big table of baseball players waiting." He thumbs toward the longest wooden picnic table on the pier, and there they are, several members of the baseball team dressed in their practice jerseys. Ryan is at the head of the table. The team does this sometimes:

grabs the biggest table at the Shellfish Shanty, orders massive platters of fried food, then plays baseball on terribly full stomachs. It's usually the same group, too: Ryan, two outfielders, Matt the catcher, and Aidan at shortstop. Only this time, they've brought their star pitcher along. Finn sits across from Aidan, studying his menu. I can't decide whether this makes waiting on them better or worse.

Chloe groans dramatically.

"Guess that means you, Mack," says Russ, and he lets the door bang shut behind him.

"It was me last time!" I whine.

"But you don't have Ryan Spencer following you around like a weird little reject puppy," Chloe protests. "Please, Mack? I don't know how many more sarcastic remarks I can launch in his direction only to have them fly over his head."

"Chloe, they're the worst to wait on, and you know it. You bring them plate after plate of food, and the tip is total shit. I got two nickels, a paperclip, and a lint ball last time." I turn to leave it at that, and I'm almost out the door, when Chloe gives it one last attempt.

"I'll split my tips with you today if you do me this favor!" she yelps.

I pause, hand on the doorknob. "Half your tips?"

"Yes." Her eyes are wide with desperation.

"From the whole night?"

"The whole night."

This could be worth my while. Chloe is everyone's favorite waitress. She's cute and cheerful, and she's much more engaging than I could ever hope to be. She tells me it's all an act, because all the world is a stage, but I know she's just being modest. She's honestly that much fun, even when she's just bringing people food.

"Deal," I say, and before she can change her mind, I'm out the door, my pen shoved securely behind my ear and my pad in my apron pocket. I pull my ponytail extra tight and prepare for battle.

"Big Mack!" Ryan shouts. "Are you our waitress today?"

Finn glances up from his menu and straightens in his seat.

"I pulled the short straw."

"What about Chloe?" Ryan asks. "Where's she?"

"Her nerves couldn't handle waiting on this group of troglo- dytes, so I told her I'd do it."

"Trogla-what?" asks Ryan.

"Troglo—" I try again. "Never mind. Can I get you guys drinks?"

They go around the table, telling me their beverage of choice, and I head back to the kitchen to start filling their foun- tain drinks.

Chloe's there, loading a tray with cups of hot New England clam chowder for one of her tables. "You know, I think it might be worth waiting on that table for all the wistful glances Finnian Pearce is sending your way."

"What?" I snap unintentionally, and I hope my tone is hidden by the rattle of ice cubes cascading into the glasses.

"Finn," she says. "When they told us he was moving back here two years ago, I couldn't get that string-bean kid from elementary school out of my head. All limbs and big ears. But now." She fans herself, and her accent transforms into something very southern as she pretends to clutch a set of pearls at her neck. "Well, I do declare, he is a *dream*."

Chloe's right, of course. Finn was pathetically skinny and awkward when we were little, his hair always too long, but it's like living inland transformed him. He's still tall but with all lean muscle and an intense, dark gaze. His hair is buzzed short now, too.

"He's all right," I say.

Finnian Pearce, no matter how dreamy, is not at all romantic. He's typical. Common. He's a jock who likes to sweat and throw balls across fields. He hangs out with Ryan and his band of merry dimwits. Any girl who ever dates him will always be *his* girlfriend, and the first thing anyone will ever ask her is, "Doesn't your boyfriend throw an eighty-three-mile-per-hour fastball?"

Finn's girlfriend definitely wouldn't discuss history, or poetry, or politics with him. He'd be too busy practicing or working out, and he'd have absolutely no interest whatsoever in Captain Benjamin Churchill or how he may or may not still be relevant today.

"Just all right?" Chloe balks. "You're obviously blind. You need help." She twirls out of the kitchen and back into the cheerful June sunshine.

Once my tray is laden with drinks, I head out and distribute them among the boys, then stand back as they take long gulps. Before they're done ordering, I'll have to get them fresh ones. "What'll it be, guys?" I ask, my pen hovering over my pad expectantly.

"You know what I always get, Big Mack," says Ryan.

"Don't call me that."

"Oh, come on," he says with a grin. "Everyone calls you Mack, and we call you Big Mack."

I feel Finn's eyes on me.

"Stop, Ryan," I try to say as firmly as possible.

"I didn't do anything," he insists, still finding this enormously funny.

"Ryan," says Finn.

He stops laughing and looks up.

Finn's eyes are focused and intense. "She said stop calling her that. Be cool."

Ryan swallows audibly, then reaches for his Coke and takes a long swig. "I'll have the double cheeseburger, please," he says.

I jot this down, then glance up once, quickly, to silently thank Finn. He smiles and looks down at his menu.

I go around, writing down each order, and when I arrive at Finn, he pauses and flattens the menu on the table. "What's your favorite thing here?" he asks me.

The other players exchange glances.

"Me?"

"Yeah, what would you recommend?" Finn leans back in his seat and crosses his hands behind his head. He has very broad shoulders. Probably from throwing fastballs.

"I like the, um . . ." I try to answer, but my brain is foggy. "I like the fried oysters." I realize too late what I just said. What I might have just implied about the first time we met, and how Finn might take it.

His face softens, and he tries to hide a growing smile as he sits forward, handing me the menu. "Yeah, me too."

"Okay, then," I say a bit breathlessly. "Be back in a few. Need another round of drinks?"

"Yes," they all chorus, then resume their hum of sporty conversation.

Back in the kitchen, Russ grabs my attention, thrusting stacks of napkins into my hands. "Do me a favor and refill the napkin dispensers at the condiment station."

"I'll do the drinks for the guys," says Chloe, swooping in.

I situate myself at the condiment station, shoving napkins

into the empty dispensers and trying to sneak peeks over my shoulder at the baseball players' table. Finn isn't watching, though. Of course, he's not watching. He's busy hanging with his friends. He wanted a lunch recommendation from me. Nothing more than that.

"What's wrong?" murmurs Chloe, appearing beside me.

"What? Nothing's wrong. What do you mean?"

"You're sweating, and you keep looking at the boys of summer over there. What happened? Do they need a smackdown?"

"No, nothing's wrong, I swear."

Chloe stills, her head tilted down and her voice even quieter than before. "Don't look; act casual."

"What?"

"I said act casual. Finn's coming over."

"He probably wants a napkin."

"He probably wants you!"

"You're insane, I—"

"Hey, Mack." He's right behind us now.

Chloe and I spin simultaneously, plastering smiles on our faces. "Finn, hey."

He fiddles with his fingers, not exactly looking me in the eyes. "Um, I was wondering if you wanted to get together tomorrow?"

My mouth opens but no words come out.

"Remember, you said you'd help me with English?" He looks

up, and his eyes plead with me a little. "I thought maybe tomorrow we could meet at the library or something and go over our plan."

I blink and regain my composure. "Tomorrow," I repeat.

"Is great," Chloe finishes for me.

"On the contrary, it isn't great," I correct her. "I'm babysitting my little sister."

"That's cool," says Finn. "Maybe I'll just stop by your place? Text me the address." He pivots and heads back to the table.

"'Text me the address,'" Chloe repeats. "You didn't tell me you have Finn's phone number. You little sneak!" She keeps hitting my arm.

"It's nothing," I insist. I take the tray of drinks from her and make my way to the boys' table. "It's nothing," I say again over my shoulder, just for emphasis.

But her arms are crossed over her chest and she's smirking at me, which makes me feel like it's decidedly something.

CHAPTER SEVEN

MICHAELA

present day

There's a boy here!" Mellie screams from the living room.

"God, Mellie," I mumble. I push myself away from the dining room table and cross the living room to watch Finn get out of his car, a blue Volvo station wagon that must miss the nineties. "I'm helping him with English."

"I want to sit next to him," Mellie announces. "He looks like he smells good."

"Whatever makes you happy, girlfriend."

Mom is at work all day, and Russ is busy doing inventory at the Shanty, and because Mellie's camp doesn't start for another week, I lucked out in being her babysitter for the day. Now I get to share Finn with her. I open the front door before he has the chance to ring the doorbell. He's standing there holding a gift bag.

"Hey, Finn," I say, leaning against the frame.

"Hey, Mack."

"Is that a present?" Mellie asks, poking her head between my arm and the door.

"For you," says Finn, extending the bag in her direction. "I thought I'd get you something to do while Mack and I work."

Mellie's eyes are like saucers, and she reaches out for the gift, but he snatches it back before she can get a grip.

"Unless you don't like coloring."

"I do, I like coloring!" Mellie insists.

"Awesome," says Finn, and he lets her have the bag. As she digs through the tissue paper, he continues, "I'm Finn, by the way."

"Mellie," she says, clutching the box of one hundred assorted colored pencils and a coloring book. "Come inside and color with me." She pulls him in and slams the front door closed. It makes the china in the hutch rattle.

Lifting his backpack, Finn follows Mellie to the table and takes his place beside her. She slides her notebook in his direction, and he nods approvingly.

"I'm writing a story about a mermaid and a unicorn, and their babies will be narwhals."

Finn raises a skeptical eyebrow.

"These colored pencils will be perfect for illustrations."

"Obviously," says Finn.

"So, where do we begin?" I ask, sitting opposite of the two

of them. "Poetry? That's my strong point. I have some antholo-gies, so maybe we could pick two poems each and analyze them together?"

"Okay," Finn replies, and he takes my offered book of Romantic poetry. He begins paging through the chapters, in search of something that strikes him. Everything should strike him. It should be impossible to choose.

"Hey, Mellie?" I say.

"Hmm," she replies, working diligently on her coloring. She sits on her knees in her chair, her feet tucked under her butt. She's concentrating so hard that the tip of her tongue pops out from the side of her mouth.

Finn lifts his head from his poetry.

"Are unicorns usually blue?" I ask.

"Doesn't matter," Mellie says. "Besides, cerulean blue is my soul color."

I close my eyes. "Your what?"

Huffing, Mellie sits back. "In school, all my friends took the crayon quiz. It told us what our soul color was, and mine is ceru-lean blue. It means I have to do all of my work in that color from now on, so I can be true to my soul."

"But Mellie," I try to protest.

"I saw you do your writing in pink gel pen," says Mellie, and I stop talking.

"Can I take the quiz?" Finn asks.

"Yes!" Mellie whips up her head from her story and dives into her backpack, which she has yet to unpack from school, searching for the quiz questions she needs to ask Finn. "Okay," she says, pulling out her ponytail and then putting it back up. "First, I need to know where you would go on vacation. The ocean, the mountains, the city, or the desert."

Leaning back in his chair, Finn considers this, tapping his chin. "Definitely not the city. And I live by the ocean, so I'll go with the mountains."

Mellie checks this off on her sheet. "Next, what's your favorite food out of these options? Garden salad, tacos, cheeseburger, or chicken parm."

"Oh, that's a tough one."

While they contemplate the finer questions in life, I give my journal a flip through and settle on a draft of a poem I've written. I tried to channel Leta Townsend, to view things from her perspective:

> *Any words you ever said*
> *were because of her.*
> *When the sea swallowed you whole,*
> *it never bothered to spit back*
> *anything of any value:*
> *thoughts, words, stories.*
> *It cleaned the flesh from*
> *your bones,*
> *fashioned toothpicks from your ribs,*

ripped your tongue from
the safety of your closed mouth,
but left your name
whole
intact
complete
for a town to claim
and concoct stories of your valor
to give a football team
or a mini golf course
or the ice cream parlor
(maple walnut, mint chocolate chip, strawberry.
The strawberries grew
on the sunny side of the hill,
you picked them for her
once.)
A name
for a girl to use,
to fasten her words, to keep them afloat
because words
she had
when you
did not.
And a name
you had
when hers was
not enough.

Behind us, the kitchen's screen door slaps open, and Russ clomps in. I frantically glance between Finn and Russ, but Finn seems completely unperturbed. Meanwhile, I'm trying to think of excuses for having a boy in the house while no adult is home. *He was starving, so I thought he could have a snack.* No. *I found him on the side of the road, and*—okay, he's not a cat. I can nix that one.

"I guess I'll have to go with chicken parm. I eat a lot of cheeseburgers, but chicken parm is a classic, am I right?"

"A classic," agrees Mellie. She glances up from her scribbles. "Hi, Daddy."

Russ squeezes in between the chairs and the wall. "Hi, baby girl." He plants a kiss on her cheek.

Finn stands, extending his hand. "Hey, Mr. Spencer. I'm Finnian Pearce. I play baseball with Ryan."

Russ doesn't even flinch. He shakes Finn's hand vigorously and claps him on the shoulder like they're old buddies, then grins. "Oh, I know you. You're the phenomenon who throws an eighty-mile-an-hour fastball."

"Eighty-three," I mutter.

I should have known that sports would bring them together. No excuse needed when you've brought home the star pitcher for the Highland Whalers. Finn is the exact guy that Russ would want to see me with. Athlete, roots practically leeching into the Cape Cod soil, pleasantly predictable, and *not* Caleb. Finnian Pearce is a one-way ticket to mediocrity, which is just the kind of guy Russ would feel comfortable around.

"What are you two working on?" Russ asks, leaning over the table.

Um, excuse me? When has Russ ever cared what I was working on?

"Poetry," I reply. "Basically, everything that's over your head."

Russ grumbles something and wanders away into the kitchen in search of a cold beer and then to the recliner in the basement, where he watches every possible channel ESPN has to offer.

"Okay, next question," says Mellie. "Pick your favorite animal. A dog, a horse, a dolphin, or a monkey."

"Dog, no doubt," Finn replies. He turns the page of his anthology of Byron and clears his throat. "He only wanted to know what we were doing."

Finn doesn't know the dynamics here. Finn is new. I give him the benefit of the doubt. "He's always finding something to pick at," I say. "And he's pretending he's interested because you're here working with me."

"Yeah, but . . ."

"No," I reply, but I don't even look up from the anthology. "You don't know him."

"And one last question," says Mellie.

With a quiet sigh, Finn turns from me and back to my sister. "Shoot."

"What's your idea of a perfect date? Fancy dinner out, a concert, cooking at home, or a sporting event?"

"Sporting event," says Finn.

"That can't be your answer," I say.

He tilts his head to the side and smirks. "Only it is."

"That's *your* idea of fun. A date should be something you both want to do."

"Like analyze poetry?"

My heart almost stops.

"Oh, my gosh!" Mellie cries, holding her quiz up in the air. "You won't believe this, Finnian Pearce, but your soul color . . . is . . ."

"Cerulean blue?" he guesses.

"Cerulean blue!" She claps. "We're soul mates."

He offers her a high five. "Must be."

"What about these?" I ask, pointing to two poems for Finn's consideration. I only ask out of a sense of obligation, because I told him I'd help him, but I know what he'll say. He won't care which poems we analyze because poetry doesn't matter to him.

"Looks good," he replies as his phone dings beside him. He glances down and reads the text. "Shit."

Mellie and I both study him. "What is it?" I finally ask.

"I, um." He stands, packing up his things. "I need to go to the Maritime Museum."

"Is there a nautical emergency?" I snicker at my own joke, but when I notice he's not laughing, I ask, "Is everything okay?"

"Yeah, I need to cover a shift there. My aunt owns it, and she has to run out for a bit. She doesn't want to close the museum while she's gone."

The Highland Maritime Museum is situated in a little cedar shake building that used to belong to the lighthouse keeper before Highland Light became automatic. Now it holds a bunch of nautical plunder found along Cape Cod's coast: some pirate treasure, a few letters, and lots of knots. Like, plenty of rope. It isn't exactly a bustling example of commerce.

"But we didn't even—" I begin.

Finn interjects. "You can come with me. No one's gonna be there. There's lots of space to review notes."

"You should go," says Mellie, coloring in her mermaid with cerulean blue. "I'll tell Dad you left."

"All right," I agree, closing my journal. "Let's go."

"I'll drive us," says Finn. "Your house will be on my way home, anyway."

"Mellie," I say, "finish your story. I'll read it when I get back."

"Aye, aye, captain." She even salutes me.

"She's the best," says Finn with a chuckle.

"A regular laugh riot," I mumble as I cross the lawn and climb into the passenger seat.

Beside me, Finn buckles his seat belt and starts the engine.

"Here we go," he says as the Volvo crunches down the driveway. After a minute of driving, he clicks on the radio and begins sorting through his preset stations.

"I didn't know your family ran the Maritime Museum," I say.

He nods and settles on a classic rock station.

"I thought you only moved back recently."

"I guess it was almost two years ago," he replies. "We moved back from Wareham to help my Aunt Becky take care of the museum. She's on her own, and money is tight."

"Oh," I say. And I'm quiet for the rest of the ride. So is he.

Several hundred feet from the cliff, the lighthouse presides over the North Atlantic. It's the kind of place that makes you feel as if the ocean goes on forever. After we park in the gravel lot, I get out and walk to the observation deck. It's like sensory deprivation and overload all at once. The rush of the wind and the roar of the waves drowns out any wayward thought I might have, and the sea is pale and gray, the late afternoon sun far behind us.

When I turn back down the path, Finn stands at the door to the museum, tossing his keys up into the air and catching them without even looking. I wait for him to ask me what it was I was doing.

Instead, he says, "Sometimes I stand there, too." He opens the door and allows me to go first.

"I'm sorry," says a lady behind a cash register. "We're about to—"

"It's me, Aunt Becky," says Finn, stepping behind me. "I'm here. You don't have to close. This is my friend, Michaela. We're gonna work on some poetry together while you're out."

Aunt Becky sags with relief. "I didn't know if you'd be able to make it," she says, coming around the side of the counter and running her hands through her short, graying hair. "I got a call from the bank, and I'm not sure if I—"

"It's okay," says Finn, and he wraps his arms around her. She's a tiny woman, and he's pretty tall. She practically disappears in his hug.

She pushes him away and swipes at her eyes. "You're right. It's okay." She digs deep into the pocket of her jacket and pulls out her keys. "I'll be back in a little bit, but if it gets to be six, lock it up for me. You know the alarm code?"

"Got it memorized," says Finn, tapping his temple.

She smiles briefly then looks at me. "It was nice to meet you, Michaela."

"You too," I reply as she slips through the front door.

Finn meanders over to the cash register and drags a stool up on the other side. "For you," he says.

But I'm already off exploring the museum. There isn't much to it—only one room of displays, along with some newspaper clippings, pictures of people from hundreds of years ago. I read the explanations of how the lighthouse used to be run and about the men who ran it. Like Elijah Pearce. I pause at his photograph. The boy from the lighthouse. It's in black and white, but I can tell that his hair is light and so are his eyes. He has a pleasant expression and holds a cane between his two legs.

"Are you related to this guy?" I ask.

Finn peers over my shoulder. "Yup. My great-great-great-grandfather. He took care of the lighthouse and fought for the Union during the Civil War."

"That's amazing," I murmur.

"What is?"

I catch myself, not wanting to get into too many details about the diary I've been reading. "I've been trying to write a poem and to figure out how to make the past relevant. It kind of struck me how we're standing in the lighthouse that your ancestor ran more than a hundred years ago."

"We Pearces are of robust stock," he says, puffing up his chest.

"You make it sound like you're coffee."

He sighs. "Coffee sounds pretty good right now."

Returning my gaze to Elijah's photograph, I say, "You don't look like him."

"Yeah, well..." He slouches back on his stool. "People marry, get more genes mixed in there. You and Mellie don't really look alike. Do you look like your dad?"

I snap my head to attention. "Russ is not my dad."

"I know," says Finn. "You told me. More than once. I only meant . . ."

He must interpret the way my shoulders freeze, my mouth hardens into a straight line.

"I'm sorry," he says.

"Me too." I finally take my seat on the second stool and begin sorting through my messenger bag for my book of poetry. I empty the contents: pencils, pens, Post-it notes, my journal. "I think I forgot the anthology," I say.

"These your poems?" Finn holds my journal in his hands, thumbing through the pages.

I automatically wrench the book from him.

"Whoa, there."

"They're not finished yet. Really not ready for anyone to read." I try to get my heartbeat under control.

"Okay," he says. "I get it."

I slip the journal back into my messenger bag and grab my pencil. "Where were we?"

"Before or after you lost it?"

My voice grows quiet. "I didn't lose it. I'm . . . protective. Of my poems."

Finn buries his nose in his book for a while.

"What about Benjamin Churchill?" I say softly, trying to mend the bridge I might have burned moments ago.

"What about him?"

My question suddenly feels absurd, like paste in my mouth. But I ask him anyway. "Do you think the rumors about him writing poetry are true?"

Finn shrugs. "Maybe. There's not a lot of information to go off of."

"You don't have anything here in the museum about him."

"Much to Aunt Becky's disappointment." Finn closes his book and stretches his arms over his head. "Aunt Becky is obsessed with Captain Churchill. She wants to find indisputable, physical evidence that he ever stayed in Highland so she can put it in the museum. Make it a tourist attraction, because he's kind of like a ghost, you know?"

"Do you think she'll find what she's looking for?" I ask, unspoken hope saturating my voice. "Like a poem?"

"Nope." Finn jots something down in his notebook. "But she'd want to find a poem. A poem would make everything feel kind of real."

"She doesn't have anything?" I ask. "Not one thing about the Highland Whaler?"

Finn sighs. "She has one thing. Like, literally one. Come here." He stands up, his stool scraping painfully across the worn wooden floors, and he leads me over to a glass display case, pointing to a faded letter from Benjamin Churchill and sent to someone he refers to as "my love." Some of the sentences are clear and crisp, while others are too difficult to decipher, smudged with dirt or faded with age. But what I can make out rocks my imagination.

"My favorite line is this one," says Finn, pointing. His finger lands heavily on the glass protecting the letter.

I hope that when people look for something that is left of me, all they'll find is you. "That's my favorite," Finn says again. "The way he looks ahead and wonders how he'll be remembered, knowing that it depends on someone completely outside himself." He laughs and rubs the back of his neck. "I think he must have loved this person."

"But he never says it," I point out.

"Sometimes you don't have to."

I take a deep breath, a wave of his scent suddenly bombarding me—deodorant and sweat and laundry detergent. My shoulders relax, and I keep reading. "That's nothing," I say. "Look at the last line. It's . . ." But I can't finish what I want to say. I can't accurately explain how this sentence is art, as clearly the author wasn't even trying. *"It must be a powerful thing, this bright and boundless sea, to blind me to your love for me."*

I repeat it, murmuring it aloud. One sentence that is so much like a poem.

"But there's no context," says Finn. His voice is dark and solid in the tiny room. It anchors me in the present.

"But it sounds like poetry," I try. "Is your aunt gonna have to close this place?"

"Maybe."

He won't look at me now, but I want him to. I take out my phone and open to my pictures of Leta Townsend's diary entries.

After I got home the other night, I read as many as I could before my eyelids began to droop. I didn't want to read them all at once. I wanted to savor them, make them last, in case I couldn't get back to Whaler's Watch for the rest of them. But I read enough to know that when everyone in Highland thought Churchill was dead, he actually came back.

There's Finn's physical proof. Maybe not the pictures, but the actual book at the Whaler's Watch Inn. But part of me is selfish. This diary is my guarantee that my poem will be different from the rest. It's what will set me apart from everyone else. It's what will make Winslow College take notice of me. If the proof of Captain Churchill is sitting in this dinky little maritime museum, then the power of my poem is gone. I'm not ready to let it go. Not when I haven't figured out the whole mystery.

"This place really depends on the tourists," says Finn. "And how much interest they have in the people who came before us. I guess we'll have to wait it out and see, you know?"

I nod. "Yes, I guess so."

"Sorry," he says, and he smiles a little. "That was a bit of a downer."

I reach out and touch his arm, which is already tan from baseball season, and I even surprise myself. I don't think I anticipated this boy to be so invested in the Highland Whaler. I didn't expect to share this with him. "You can't always be the positive one, right?"

He smiles at this. "Thanks for listening."

"And now," I say, heading back to my stool, "to really lift your spirits . . . more Byron!"

"You're the worst."

I grin. "You asked for my help this summer. There's no going back now."

CHAPTER EIGHT

Leta

1862

Elijah Pearce keeps the lighthouse, and on a Thursday morning, like any other morning, I can expect to find him there, tending to his duties. His job isn't a glamorous one, but necessary, and he's never wanted to be anything else. He's as reliable as the light he protects.

When I find him, he sits at the base of the lighthouse, mending a tired-looking fishing net and singing to himself a song about whisky or beer, or some libation he rarely indulges in but prefers to sing about.

"My lady Leta," he says without looking up.

When we were small, he could never seem to get my name right. It always ended up coming out as "lady." Now it's his joke.

"What brings you up this way so early?"

"A dinner invitation," I reply, trying to speak and catch my breath from my hike up the hill.

"Can't say no to that," says Elijah. He bites off a line of string and spits it out beside him.

"And it's extended, of course, to your Aunt Charlotte." I pause, staring out at the sea behind us. "And your cousin, Captain Churchill," I add.

His hands still working to weave the rope, Elijah replies, "He's not my cousin."

"Then what is he?"

Elijah shrugs. "My cousin by marriage, I guess? He's the nephew of Aunt Charlotte, her brother's son. And I'm the nephew of Ebenezer Pearce. I'm related to my uncle, and he's related to his aunt, and we were only brought together because my uncle and his aunt married."

"But still," I say quietly.

Elijah goes back to his netting. "He's not my cousin."

"It must be so fascinating to be related to such a person," I go on, ignoring Elijah's exaggerated sigh. "One of the most famous captains in the world, sailing the high seas, visiting far-off ports."

"Reeking of boiled whale blubber," Elijah mumbles.

I'm quiet for a moment, taking a seat beside Elijah on the overturned rowboat. The breeze carries two crying gulls over our heads, and the methodic crash of the waves and the weaving of the rope lulls me. I lean against his arm. "If Captain Churchill wrote poetry, what do you think he'd write about?" I ask quietly.

"If he what? Poetry? Ben?" Elijah laughs so hard the net,

now perfectly mended, slips from his lap and onto the ground between his feet. "He wouldn't. I can't even pretend to put words in his mouth. Leta, you have such an imagination."

"Elijah," I say, relinquishing my seat and standing before him.

"Yes?" He finally looks up, squinting because I stand before the sun.

"I write poetry."

"That's lovely, Leta, but I know that," he says, standing and lifting his net. He admires his handiwork, checking to make sure all the necessary parts are mended. "You've always had a way with words. Is that really why you've run all the way up here?" He smiles. "Did you write me a poem? Is that it? You've written a love poem, and you'd like to recite it for me?"

"Elijah, please, this is serious."

"I should say so." He has subtle blue eyes and sandy hair, and there's always a bit of scruff on his cheek. It gives him an impish demeanor. "After all this time, you're harboring feelings like this for me? I'm right flattered."

"Oh, Elijah, I'm worried."

His face drops a little bit. "About what?"

"My poems have been published. I'm published, Elijah."

He drops the net and barrels over to me with an embrace. "Leta, that's fantastic!"

"Yes, it is," I admit into his shoulder. He smells of fresh air and salt and sweat. With slight reluctance, I pull away. "But that's not what I'm worried about. Elijah, I didn't publish the poems under my name. I was afraid the publisher would be hesitant to put them in the magazine because I'm a girl. I made up a pen name—a man's pen name."

Elijah is clearly trying to follow along, bless him. He wants to help, except he doesn't know what it is with which I need help.

"I wrote them as Benjamin Churchill," I say. "And now he's back."

Elijah takes a long, deep breath. "Do you think he'll be cross with you?"

I play with the loose cuticle of my forefinger.

"Don't do that," says Elijah without even looking at my hand. "You'll make yourself bleed."

"But I'm nervous!"

"I don't think you should be," he says, hauling up his net and hoisting the little rowboat upright.

Above us, seagulls coast on the ocean breeze, squawking to one another, then diving below the cliffs to chase the retreating tide.

"He won't find out anyway. Who's to tell him? You won't, and you know I won't."

"I know," I admit.

"Even if he did find out, I don't think he'd be angry. He isn't like that."

"Isn't like what?"

Elijah thinks for a moment. "Well, in order to be angry, you have to care, don't you?"

I nod.

"I don't think Ben cares about anything or anyone."

I dart forward, standing at the opposite end of the boat and making sure that Elijah is looking directly at me. "You don't know that. He may be your cousin, but you hardly know him! He left when he was eleven, and now he's back. He's practically a ghost, Elijah."

He nods. "You're right about that. We all gave him up for dead. It hit Aunt Charlotte the hardest, I think. She was practically a mother to him."

I plop down on the steps to the lighthouse door. "That's tragic."

"Are you going to write a poem about it?"

I glance up, and he's grinning ear to ear. I stand and punch him in the shoulder.

"You're cruel to me, Leta. Cruel." He pretends as if I've truly injured him.

"Yes, well," I say, shaking out my sore hand. "If I really hurt you, I'd never forgive myself." I lean on his shoulder as I free a pebble from my shoe. "I'll see you at dinner?"

"Wouldn't miss it," he says.

An invitation to the Townsends' house is the epitome of all dinner invitations in Highland and most of the Outer Cape. My father and mother seldom hold parties, but when they do, they spare no expense.

Rarely did any guest realize how intolerable a dinner party here actually was. My mother sits to my right, wearing the latest fashion and asking far too many questions of the guests. She does so in such a manner that they have no idea she's prying for any information or gossip she can use at church or at the sewing circle. This onslaught of questions is only ever interrupted by her reminding me to sit up straight, then turning, regretful, to the guests as if to apologize for my lack of decorum.

She'll say, "She's a pretty thing, I know it, but such a dreadful lack of posture."

But tonight, she has nothing to say to me. I'm wearing the exact dress she picked out in the morning, my back is ramrod straight, and I eat my chowder in delicate ladylike sips.

Mother beams proudly in my direction and finally turns her attention to Mrs. Pearce and Elijah, who are seated across the table. She clears her throat. "Do you think your nephew will be joining us soon?"

Mrs. Pearce, an elderly woman and hard of hearing, glances up at Mother. "Oh, I would think so. He's a free spirit, that Ben. Always has been since the day he arrived on my doorstep!" She turns to Elijah. "Don't you remember, Elijah, how Ben would get lost out on the dunes for hours as a little boy?"

Elijah nods and smiles, then swallows another spoonful of chowder.

"Well, he's damnable late," says Father, pulling out his pocket watch and checking the time.

Mother touches his wrist to silence him. Luckily, Mrs. Pearce didn't hear any of it.

Teddy sits to my left, and he chatters on about the shells he found at low tide today. His mother sits silently beside him, trailing her spoon through her soup but never actually eating any. Susannah's husband, however, encourages her to take a bite.

"Caroline," says my mother. "Did you get that fabric you liked for the Crawfords' ball?"

"That party is weeks away," I say.

Both Caroline and Mother regard me with wide eyes.

"Yes," says Mother. "That's enough time to have a new dress made. You may want to consider having the same done, as you're getting a little thick around the edges."

I lift my spoon, stare her down, take a heaping portion, and shovel it into my mouth.

"Charming," says Mother, dabbing her lips with her napkin.

A scuffle of feet near the doorway brings all our attention away from our plates.

"Is that him?" Teddy whispers to me as Ben appears beside my father's chair.

"In the flesh," I reply.

"He's very intimidating," says Teddy.

There's no denying that Benjamin Churchill is tall and solid, and a puckish expression constantly tugs at his lips. He gives the overall impression that he knows more than you do about almost everything, and you're lucky that he's even gracing you with his presence.

"Hello, Aunt Charlotte," says Ben, leaning over and kissing his aunt's cheek.

"Captain Churchill," says Father as Ben sits, unfolding his napkin and placing it across his lap.

"Captain Townsend," he replies.

"How pleasant of you to join us this evening. I daresay we were all waiting with bated breath for your arrival."

"My apologies," says Ben. "I was detained in town. Greeting old friends and the like."

"He's a good lad," says Mrs. Pearce as Ben lifts his spoon and begins eating his chowder. "He's always been a good lad."

"Thank you, Aunt Charlotte," Ben says dutifully.

"Mr. Churchill," Teddy pipes up beside me.

His spoon hanging in midair, Ben's eyes raise until he finds Teddy's. "Captain," he says. He slurps his soup and swallows. "Captain Churchill."

"Oh," says Teddy, shrinking slightly into himself.

My skin prickles and my mouth begins to burn with all the words I'd like to launch at him.

"Well?" says Ben. "What were you going to say?"

"Um, I only wanted to know where your ship last sailed to."

"We were hunting sperm whales in the Pacific."

"That's far," Teddy whispers to me.

"Indeed, it is," I agree. "Far enough for *Captain* Churchill to have forgotten his manners."

Ben chuckles and takes another spoonful of soup.

"Well!" says Mother, her spoon clanging to her dish. "Where must our main course be? I think I'll go and check on it."

"I've seen whales before," Teddy continues, though his tone is slightly less enthusiastic. "Like the blackfish in the bay."

Ben nods and takes another bite of chowder. "Blackfish. They have the finest oil, which is good for watches. Mr. Nye would pay a pretty penny for it."

Ben suddenly turns his attention to me and begins, "Tell me, Miss Townsend, what have you been doing with your life since I left?"

I want to ignore him, but unfortunately, *my* good manners never fail me. My heart begins to pound, and I don't dare venture a glance across the table at Elijah. He'll undoubtedly be waiting for my reaction, but if he thinks I'm going to admit that I've been secretly writing poetry under Churchill's name, then he doesn't really know me at all.

"There's plenty to do in town," I say. "Enough to keep me entertained and content."

Ben snickers.

"If you don't think so, then why return?" I say in a harsher tone than I intended.

"Highland is a beautiful place, I grant you that," Ben says. "But whether it's entertaining, I still need proof."

"I'm sure that when you've been to so many ports of call around the world, Highland would seem rather dull," says Caroline. She reaches out and touches his arm. "I would love to hear some of your stories after dinner."

Her husband is too busy tearing off hunks of bread and sopping them in his soup to care that his wife is flirting with the guest of honor. Not that I blame her, because if I had to be married to old, fat Fred Chilton, I'd flirt with Churchill, too.

But circumstances run in my favor. I only need to get through dinner with him.

———

Almost everyone has left.

Mrs. Pearce was tired, so Elijah offered to take her home. Susannah claimed a headache, so they left as well. I depart the drawing room, leaving Father, Fred, and the illustrious Captain Churchill discussing Confederates.

Besides, my little garret at the end of the house is the perfect place to spend an evening in peace and quiet, especially after having written countless poems under the name of a man who has turned out to be a witless pig.

That was harsh, as pigs are pleasant creatures, and I forget the circumstances surrounding a whaling captain. A ship is no place to cultivate fine manners and acceptable etiquette. He's only just returned home. I can give him another chance.

I begin lighting candles in my private nook, only enough so that I can see the words I write before me. I begin jotting down thoughts, and it makes me feel like a silly, starry-eyed girl.

"I hope it wasn't me who forced you into hiding up here in the attic."

I practically lurch off my seat to face the voice that's followed me across the house and up two flights of stairs.

"Captain Churchill," I say. "What are you doing up here?" He climbs the steps toward me, one hand on the railing.

"I wanted more entertaining company," he says, peering around the room. He rubs the stubble of his chin. "And you went this way."

"You shouldn't be here," I say.

"No, I shouldn't. But here I am." He smiles. "What do you do up here that's so interesting?"

"Nothing," I say, slamming shut my diary.

"Looks like something."

"It's nothing," I repeat.

He nods, taking the last step and turning the corner around

the banister. "There is lots of storage up here," he says. "Trunks of your fine, lacy things?"

"Really, Captain Churchill," I say, "do I look like the kind of girl who keeps trunks of fine lacy things and useless garments that impede any movement?"

"All girls do," he says. He pauses to observe me. "But maybe not you."

I turn back to my diary, reclaiming my pen, but I can't seem to put anything down on paper. I can't seem to tear my thoughts from the man behind me. He pulls my hand from my words.

"But I've decided you're not like other girls," he says.

My mouth has now refused to produce spit, and my tongue feels like a wad of cotton. It doesn't feel like a compliment. It feels like he's trying to convince me of a feeling I've never entertained. "Oh, how flattering," I say. "You've only been in my company for an evening, and you've managed to formulate a conclusion on my character. Well done."

He chuckles, and I hear his feet on the steps once more. "Good night, Miss Townsend." He climbs back down.

"Leta," I call to him.

His head reappears. "I'm sorry?"

"You may call me Leta. You always used to."

He nods and smiles. "Good night, Leta."

CHAPTER NINE

MICHAELA

present day

A storm gathers over the ocean, whipping the waves into a frenzy, their frothy whitecaps trampling the shoreline. But I'm safe here, in a tiny room at the Whaler's Watch, a soft lamp glowing upon the shiny oak table as the rain pelts the window. I sip a steaming mug of tea because the storm has brought cool weather and gusty winds. The old walls shudder with thunder, but my pen presses to the paper of my journal and nothing is stopping the words today.

> *In the eye of a storm,*
> *you can almost forget that just outside the safety*
> *of the clear and open sky*
> *the air still, the sun bright,*
> *there are forces at work*
> *thunder and lightning*
> *raging winds and the sharp shrapnel of rain*
> *that threaten to tear you apart.*

The deck is closed to diners, and behind me, I can hear the quiet murmur of conversation floating down the hall. There aren't many people here between lunch and dinner, especially because the view isn't half as lovely from inside. Those who have braved the weather quietly nibble their food or sip their drinks, their tables dimly brightened by a single candle tucked deep inside the glass walls of a mason jar.

It feels like we all found our eye of the storm.

A soft knock interrupts my daydreaming, and I turn to find Caleb lurking in the doorway, the shadow of the hall falling over half of his face.

"Hey," he says with his signature nod. He runs his hands through his hair, then flips it back and out of his eyes.

"Hi," I reply, lifting my right foot from the floor and wrapping my arms around my knee.

"Have you seen Brittany around?" he asks. "She told me she needed me to run out for something, but she never said what."

I shrug. "No, I've been writing in here for the past hour."

He steps into the room, the golden light of my little lamp illuminating his features. High cheekbones; sleepy, thoughtful eyes. He looks like something Michelangelo would have painted—an angel on the ceiling of a cathedral.

"You writing a poem for the statue dedication?" he asks.

"Mmhm," I reply. "I'm trying, at least. Haven't really come up with anything yet that sticks."

"That's cool," he tells me. "I go to Winslow College."

"Yeah, Brittany mentioned that. Do you like it there?"

He shrugs. "I like it better than Princeton."

My eyes grow wide. "You went to Princeton?"

"Nah," he says, leaning against the table and crossing his arms over his chest while simultaneously rolling his eyes. "My mom wanted me to go, though. I actually wanted to take a gap year, travel the country. Winslow College was our compromise."

"And you study writing there?"

"Creative nonfiction."

Creative nonfiction sounds so much more serious than poetry—so much more elevated and official.

"I'm actually writing about the Highland Whaler now. One of my professors is mentoring me."

I lean back in my chair. "Why the Highland Whaler?"

Caleb shrugs. "It feels like I grew up with his ghost," he replies, his eyes coasting upward, and then he turns to look behind him as if he almost expects to see a phantom of Benjamin Churchill roaming the hall. "Something omnipresent and pervasive, but not easy to hold down. I'm giving it my best shot to make him real."

Literally the most romantic thing a boy has ever said. It takes everything in me not to swoon.

"Brittany and her mom said I could write here. Well, upstairs."

"In one of the rooms?" I ask. I hate pretending not to know something. It makes me feel itchy.

"Kind of." He turns and inclines his head toward the hall. "Come on."

I get up, pushing the chair back under the table with a low groan of the legs against the wood floor, and I follow Caleb up the stairs and down the main hall of the second floor, until we get to the door that looks like it belongs to a closet. I breathe so deeply my lungs stretch and burn. This is worse than just pretending not to know something. This is pretending not to have *been* somewhere. Not to have *seen* something. It's all kinds of secrets tangled into one.

"Watch your step," Caleb warns, leading me up the curving staircase until we reach his attic writing room. "This is where it happens," he informs me, spreading his arms wide. He crosses the room to his desk, gesturing to the scattered papers.

"Do you have any books on Captain Churchill?" I ask, taking a hesitant step closer.

"No," Caleb replies. "Nothing about him specifically. I'm using some primary sources from other whaling captains to make a few of my scenes in the Pacific as realistic as possible. I might even try my hand at writing a poem for the statue dedication. Really work my creative muscle. My professor is the one running the contest. He's a native of Highland, and he's obsessed with Churchill."

My throat tightens. If Caleb is going to write a poem for the contest, then he has access to Leta's diary, too, if he only thinks to look for it. He'll know just as much about Benjamin Churchill as I do. I sneak a glance at the bookshelf. Her diary sits just where I left it.

I try to laugh it off. "Yeah, but you don't need the workshop weekend as a prize. You get whole semesters at Winslow College."

Caleb faces the window. The storm over the Atlantic is calming now, the sky at the horizon brightening. "But to have something carved in stone, you know? Being certain that what you have to say matters and is going to outlast you? That's worth it."

His expression wordlessly informs me that he won't be dissuaded.

"Hey," he says suddenly, turning like he just remembered I was still in the room. "If you're interested in going to Winslow College, you should come to the party my friend is having next Friday. She lives in Chatham, and a bunch of us are getting together."

"You all go to Winslow?" I ask.

"Most of us."

A party with a cohort of worldly, wordy intellectuals, including the dashing and pensive Caleb Abernathy. A vision flashes through my mind of college students smoking cigarettes and swirling glasses of red wine around a fire pit overlooking Nantucket Sound, exchanging verbose philosophies and discussing politics and history.

"I'd love to come," I tell him.

"Cool, cool. What's your number? I'll text the address."

"Here, type in yours," I say, offering him my phone.

Outside, the wind howls mournfully, the walls tremor, and from the shelf across the room, a book falls from its place, landing facedown, the pages folded awkwardly.

Caleb chuckles. "I guess we're waking up the ghosts."

CHAPTER TEN

MICHAELA

present day

W hat'd you tell your parents?" Chloe asks as I climb into her black Civic.

"I told my mom that I was sleeping over at your house," I reply. "What are we telling your mom?"

"That we're going to see some artsy movie with subtitles in Hyannis. Genius, right? She'll never question it."

We head down Route 6, past the general store and the place that sells massive pool toys shaped like unicorns and popsicles and pizza until we get to the rotary at the end of Eastham. My phone dings as Chloe takes the exit to bypass the town of Orleans.

Finn texts me, I've finally chosen a side in the great Byron debate.

What is the great Byron debate?

Whether I like his poems.

And . . . ?

I don't like his poems.

I suppress the groan that threatens to escape my mouth.

"Who's that?" Chloe asks.

"Nobody."

"Holy shit, is that Finnian Pearce?"

I glance down at my phone, and he's sent me another text.

Are you ending this convo in revolt?

Talk later.

I'll be at the Maritime Museum after my game. They're doing ghost tours all night, but I'll be organizing the knots.

I smile at this, but don't respond.

"You have a wide and varying taste in boys, don't you?" Chloe says, applying lip gloss in her rearview mirror.

"Don't be ridiculous," I scoff. "And pay attention when you're driving. Besides, I'm not interested in Finn. He's one of Ryan's friends. That automatically negates any hotness he might have."

"Just because Ryan is a turd," says Chloe, "doesn't mean all of his friends are. I mean, look at us. I'm practically a goddess, and you're . . ."

I arch an eyebrow.

"Well, you're plain *adorable*," she says, reaching out and pinching my cheek.

"You're a delight, Chloe. Truly."

"I think Finn likes you."

"Chloe, I'm basically his tutor, that's all."

"Still, he likes you. He likes what he's getting from you."

"He likes Byron?" I ask. "Because that's all he's managed to get from me."

Chloe shrugs her shoulders as we cruise down the remainder of Route 6 in relative silence.

It isn't until we turn off into Chatham and onto Route 28 that she says, "Put the address in your phone and tell me where to turn."

We pass through the center of town and make a right like we're going to Chatham Light, but the house is a little before that.

Chloe's car hums down the dead-end street lined with signs for the interior designers and landscapers that are working on the mansions overlooking the cove.

"Are we in the right place?" I ask. Each house is immense, the yards meticulous, and they all belong on the cover of a New England coastal living magazine.

"Navigation says yes," replies Chloe. She cranes her neck to take in the massive house obscured by a high gate. "I want to be this girl's friend. I mean, she must be the best."

"Yeah, the best," I repeat.

"You nervous?"

"A little."

"Did you text Caleb yet?" she asks.

"Yeah," I say, staring at the screen of my phone. "He says to come around back."

We get out of the car, adjusting our outfits. I chose tight black pants with a silky, ivory-colored sleeveless top tucked in, my long blond hair pulled back and into a high bun. My sandals have a heel that's a lot higher than I'm used to wearing, and I'm terrified that I'm going to roll my ankle. Chloe wears a white dress, her long box braids draped over her shoulder. She's striking. She looks like she belongs here, at a party with college kids; I look like I'm trying too hard.

As we travel the cobblestone walkway up to the house, the low thrum of a bass resonates from the backyard.

"I thought you said red wine and a fire pit," Chloe mutters.

Someone screams, then a splash, followed by the hooting of boys.

"I think I just assumed."

We round the side of the huge white house and come to the gated backyard. People are in the pool swimming, tapping beach balls back and forth, and throwing one another in the deep end. Beyond the patio is the water, shimmering with moonlight.

"We forgot our suits," says Chloe, staring.

A chant of what sounds like someone's name rises up from outside, and the subject is then promptly tossed in the pool. She's wearing a dress, I see, and not a bathing suit.

"It would seem that doesn't matter," I reply.

"You made it."

Chloe and I both turn and witness Caleb Abernathy

sauntering toward us, a slight stagger to his step, his beer sloshing over the rim of his cup.

"Oh, this is classy," mutters Chloe.

I pinch her arm.

"Hey," I say as Caleb gathers me up into a sloppy embrace. He smells like Abercrombie and Fitch and sour beer, and I really wish he'd let go.

"See," says Caleb to the guy behind him. "I told you she'd come. Michaela wants to go to Winslow College, too." He pauses, his eyes roving up and down Chloe. "Who's your friend?" he asks without looking at me.

"Chloe," she says, extending her hand.

"Come on," says Caleb, "we're all friends here." He motions for her to hug him.

"No, thanks," she says, crossing her arms over her chest.

He laughs this off and takes a long swig of beer. Grabbing my hand, he leads me to where the games are set up on the patio.

I check to make sure that Chloe follows, and she lags behind a bit, her eyes darting back and forth along the crowd. Chloe is strong and brave and determined, but she's human, too. And when I take her out of her comfort zone, her insecurities show.

"You have to get the ball in the cup," says Caleb. He sways a little. "Like this." He launches his Ping-Pong ball, and it flies over the collection of cups at the opposite end of the table.

"Drink!" yells our opponent.

He does. He chugs more beer.

"Okay," says Caleb, wiping his mouth with the back of his hand. "Your turn." He hands me the Ping-Pong ball and waits.

I toss it, and it circles along the rim of a cup before plopping into the beer below.

"Yes!" cries Caleb, and he lifts me off my feet. "That's my girl."

I manage to last the game only having to chug one cup of beer, which tasted awful and mostly of pool water. Chloe watches me from the sidelines, her arms crossed over her chest.

"What's the matter?" I ask, handing her a cup.

She shakes her head. "No, thanks."

"Come on," I say quietly, our shoulders bumping. "What's the matter?"

"This party makes me uncomfortable," she says, running her hands up and down her arms. "The people here aren't our friends, and I'm not really interested in changing that, and this isn't a swanky, upscale college party. It's a frat party. It's so awkward."

"I'm sorry," I say. "Wanna go down to the beach and see the water?"

She shakes her head. "Maybe we can leave soon?"

"Chloe!" I cry louder than I had intended. I lower my voice so no one knows we're having a disagreement. "We've only been here for, like, an hour. I think I saw someone bring pizza inside. Let's go get a slice. You'll feel better." I begin pulling her inside.

"No, I'm good. You go have fun. I'll try to make some small talk over here. With this guy, for example." She thumbs in the direction of a guy passed out against the back of the house.

"A little longer," I say. "So Caleb isn't mad."

Chloe hops up onto a stool near the grill. "Well, go on," she says, fishing through her bag and pulling out her lip gloss.

"Pizza first," I say. "And I'm getting you some."

Inside, it's dark and quiet, a reprieve from the antics beyond the sliding doors. I locate a box of cold pizza on the counter and drop two slices on a paper plate.

The back door quietly clicks open, and I know it's Caleb. I know without having to look up from the pizza. He comes up behind me, placing his hands on my waist and breathing softly against my ear. I turn to him.

"Thought I lost you out there," he says, his mouth incredibly close to mine. His eyelids flutter sleepily.

"No," I say quietly, trying to push myself from him, but he has me pinned against the counter. He's remarkably drunk and incredibly close. "I'm right here. Getting pizza." I duck under his arm, taking a paper plate of pizza in each hand, and I motion toward the door.

"Come back in here when you're done," he says.

My brain is frantic to find a reason not to go back inside, because this isn't the Caleb I know from the Whaler's Watch. But maybe I didn't know that Caleb, either. Now all I want is to make some connections from Winslow College, connections that aren't necessarily him.

"I can't leave Chloe by herself," I toss over my shoulder.

Just as I reach the door, a roar of laughter rises from the backyard.

"What was that?" I ask.

"Who cares?" says Caleb, following me over to the door. His nose is in my hair, like he's trying to tempt me to turn into a waiting kiss.

"No, seriously," I say, pushing him away.

He stands back and examines the scene out the kitchen windows. "Wow," he says, and then starts to laugh. "They just threw your friend into the pool. I think she lost a shoe."

"Shit!" I dash out the back door.

Chloe, her black mascara dribbling down her face, swims over to the side of the pool, hoists herself out, and takes a deep breath.

"Are you okay?" I ask, grabbing her hand.

"Fine," she says, wringing out her hair and marching across the paver stones.

"What happened?"

"I was talking with a guy, and I guess he thought it would be funny to throw me into the pool. Fully clothed. Apparently, he's been doing it all night. And for every girl he gets in the pool, some other guy has to drink." She points to a preppy looking kid gulping down a beer. "So I win, I guess."

"Chloe, I'm so sorry."

"It's fine. Let's go home." She begins heading for the gate that leads to the driveway. But I don't follow. "Mack?" she says.

"I don't want to go yet," I tell her, glancing over my shoulder. Caleb stands at the door to the kitchen, beckoning for me to come back inside.

"Are you *kidding* me?" Chloe's eyes are about to explode. "I'm soaking wet, Mack. My makeup is ruined. I want to go home."

"I'll go find you a towel," I suggest.

"No," says Chloe. "You know what? Forget about it. I'm going home."

"Oh, come on, Chloe. Don't leave me here!"

The gate slams shut, and she's gone. My shoulders slump as I cross the patio and rejoin Caleb.

"Look, it's whatever," says Caleb when I'm standing next to him under the portico. "She wasn't having a good time, and she was bringing you down."

"I guess," I say, still staring at the gate, hoping she'll come back.

"Listen. I'm gonna go to the bathroom real quick. Don't go anywhere."

"Okay," I say, almost relieved at my sudden alone time. "I'll go sit over there." I point to an L-shaped outdoor sofa. There's a couple making out in the opposite corner, but I have enough space to myself.

After a few minutes, I strain my neck for a better view into the house. It's hard to see through the glass doors, though; the brightness of the underwater lights in the pool and tiki torches reflect back at me. Resuming my browsing of social media, I think I should text Chloe. My thumb floats over the letters, but I can't bring myself to do it. This was my idea. She knows what I wanted; she knew how much it meant to me. But even now, as I sit here alone on this sofa, waiting for the only person I know at this party to come back from the bathroom, I realize that I'm not having the good time I thought I would. No one wants to talk about college or exchange ideas. No one even notices me when they walk by. I drop my phone on the cushion beside me.

And it buzzes.

Greedily, I open it, secretly hoping that it's Chloe apologizing first.

But it's not Chloe. It's Finn. Again. And he's sent me a picture of a knot on the side of a boat.

We have knots like this one.

Yet another picture of a knot, this one infinitely more intricate than the first.

And this one, the double carrick bend.

I laugh a little and grip my phone tighter.

And who could possibly resist this sheershank?

I reply, **My mind is blown by the diversity in nautical knots.**

I put my phone down, glance over my shoulder to see if

Caleb has managed to find a way out of the bathroom, and when I'm satisfied that he hasn't, I lift the phone again. I stare at the three dots informing me that Finn is writing.

It should be.

He sends me another one, and I ask, Which one is this?

He types, A square knot.

Will you ever run out of knots?

After a minute, he sends me a picture of a knotted rope that's worn at the end.

I'm a frayed knot.

I double over and snort with laughter.

Caleb is still in the bathroom. I decide it might be nice of me to go and check on him.

I step through the slider doors and into the huge, empty kitchen. There's no one around, and the room is in total darkness. Carefully, I tiptoe down the hall—like there are going to be people around, and I don't want to wake them.

"Caleb?" I say when I reach the bathroom door. It's open a crack. "Caleb, are you okay?"

He doesn't answer, so I walk in.

He's not in the bathroom. I check my reflection in the mirror, rub away some running eyeliner, then reapply lip gloss and resume my search for Caleb.

"Caleb?" I call down the hall, poking my head into a room that's used as someone's office, but there's no one there, either.

I move on. "I think I should call my friend. I feel funny leaving things like—"

The final room, a kind of conservatory with lots of leafy plants, hardly hides the fact that Caleb is pressed up against a girl, her shirt on the floor and his hands on an exploratory adventure.

"Oh!" I practically yelp. "Okay, sorry, I'll go." And I retreat down the hall, out the slider doors, across the patio, and through the iron gate to the front yard. I find a little wrought-iron bench and flop down, defeated. This has been a dumb, pointless night. Lifting my phone, the screen lights up once more, this time with a drawing of a ship.

Finn writes, **Schooner or later, this joke will knot be funny.**

Only it is funny. Surprisingly funny, and he manages to make me smile, even from far away. I close my eyes and sigh. Opening Finn's text one more time, I write, **Hey, can you come and pick me up?**

———

Finn gets out of the Volvo, leans his arm on the roof, and marvels at the house.

"Come on," I call over to him. "Let's go. I'm tired."

He doesn't get back into the car right away, and his eyes settle on me. "You look . . ." he begins, but then laughs quietly. "Really fancy. Like, really dressed up."

"Thank you, I think." Behind me, I hear someone approaching, but I figure if I get into the car quick enough, then I won't have to deal with the impending drama.

"Michaela," says the voice.

Or I will. I turn and face him. "Caleb, hey."

"You leaving already?" He saunters over, taking a sip of beer from his red Solo cup.

"Yeah," I say. Behind me, Finn leans on the roof of his car, his eyes narrowed in Caleb's direction, and he doesn't move. "This is Finn."

Caleb nods at him.

"We're about to leave," says Finn.

"Why?"

I open my mouth to speak, but I don't know how to tell him that I hate it here. That I'm so far from myself that it makes my skin feel too tight for my body. Instead, I go with, "Because I want to."

"Is he making you leave?" Caleb asks.

I fumble, trying to figure out what he means. "Finn? Finn never makes me do anything I don't want to do."

"And I don't interrogate her when she's made herself clear." Finn sniffs and straightens his shoulders.

I smile. "What he said."

Caleb laughs, waving us away. "Whatever. Do your own thing."

We both duck into the Volvo, and Finn puts it into reverse, his right hand on the back of my seat, and he arches so he can see out the back window. "I don't like him," he says.

"Well, you don't know him, either." I fidget with the zipper of my wristlet.

"So you do?" Finn asks.

"Not necessarily, I'm just saying. I don't know him that well, either."

Finn is quiet for a while. I feel like I got him out of bed, even though he told me he'd be at the Maritime Museum. He's wearing gray joggers and a worn Red Sox T-shirt. We travel the private road, and then Main Street through Chatham's town center until we're back on Route 28. "Where are we headed?" Finn asks.

"Your house, I guess," I reply, rolling down the window and letting the cool night air blow my stray hair away from my face.

"Yeah, that's not an option."

"Why not?"

"My mom would shit a brick if I brought a girl back to sleep at our house."

"Well, I can't go back to my house," I say, checking the clock. It's almost midnight. "If Russ knows I went to a party instead of sleeping over at Chloe's, he'll never let me out of the house again unless it's to work at the Shellfish Shanty, and I really can't handle that." I cover my face with my hands and sigh deeply.

"Hey, hey," says Finn, touching my knee. "It's no big deal. We'll go someplace."

I stare out at the occasional restaurant or store, but mostly at the dark pine forest. It eventually gives way to the dunes on Route 6, and finally the Atlantic Ocean. We drive in silence for a while.

"Thanks for coming to get me," I finally say. "Even if we're destined to drive around aimlessly for the rest of the night."

"You're welcome," he replies, his hand resting casually on top of the steering wheel. He puts on the blinker and turns toward the ocean. "The museum is still open, you know. Wanna see some knots?" he asks.

"You sure do know the way to a lady's heart."

"Obviously," he replies. "But at least it's an option. When I left, there were still a ton of people waiting in line for the midnight ghost tour."

"We'll be just in time," I say.

Finn is quiet for a moment, and then asks, "Why did you need me to pick you up, exactly? I don't think you went to that party by yourself."

A vision of my soaking-wet best friend flashes through my mind, and I try my best to keep from shuddering. "Because Chloe was my ride, and I let her down, and she left, and the boy who invited me was making out with another girl, and I was all alone."

"Whoa."

"I know."

"That guy in the driveway invited you?" he asks, turning away from me like he saw something out the window. But it's too dark, and the woods are too deep.

I scratch my eyebrow, almost to distract myself. "His name's Caleb Abernathy. You wouldn't know him; he's in college."

"Oh," Finn replies, and as we crest a hill, Highland Light comes into view, flashing across the road for a moment before the shaft of light spans out to sea, guiding the ships away from the treacherous shoals of Cape Cod. Just like it has for hundreds of years. Maybe like it did for Leta Townsend. For Benjamin Churchill.

Finn parks, turning off the engine, and we sit for a moment in the silence. There are a ton of cars here; he wasn't exaggerating.

"All here for the knots?" I ask.

He scoffs, like this is common knowledge. "Of course." Then he turns and looks at me, his eyes soft. "You want in on some knot action?"

"I do," I reply, opening the door and stepping out into the night. Near the water, the air is cooler, and the sky is crisp and clear, dotted with diamond-like stars and accentuated by a full moon.

"Come on. There are so many knots to see."

I smile down at my feet. Somehow exploring all the knots at

the museum in the middle of the night is infinitely more interesting than any college party.

Finn waits for me to walk in front of him, and we travel the gravel path up to the lighthouse. "Aren't you cold?" he asks.

"Not really," I lie.

"You want my hoodie? I've got one in the car."

I shake my head. "I'm good for now."

Inside the Maritime Museum, clusters of people mill about, reading from pamphlets about the natural history of our coast or perusing the little room of souvenirs. Down a narrow hallway, others wait in line to climb up the tower of the lighthouse.

I try to notice the things that I didn't the other day, when Finn first brought me here. I try to see everything through fresh eyes. Old portraits from the nineteenth century line the back wall. I pause at one of a girl, and I smile at her name plaque. Leta Townsend has brownish blond hair and eyes that smiled along with her mouth, and she's smiling at me. Most of the other people in the portraits are staring almost blankly, the expression fixed on their faces like it's part of the latest fashion.

But not her. Not Leta. I turn to Finn. "Do you know who she is?" I ask, pointing. I don't want to let on that I already know who she is. Her words are hidden in my phone right now. I want to hear what Finn knows. I want to hear his interpretation and see if it matches mine.

He crosses the room and smiles when he sees what I'm asking about.

"That's Leta Pearce. My great-great-great-grandmother."

"Pearce?" I ask.

He nods.

"Not Churchill?" I know it's a stab in the dark. But I could have sworn I *felt* it in Leta's words. Benjamin Churchill was the one for her—her rebellion against sleepy Highland and all those sewing circle gossips. Her jump from the tip of the world; the boy she would end up with.

"What?" Finn asks. "You're kind of obsessed with Churchill, aren't you?"

"Not obsessed, necessarily. I've set a goal for myself this summer to figure out who he was. Or why he mattered, I guess."

"Why he deserves a statue in a park?" Finn supplies, standing beside me.

"Exactly."

Finn shrugs. "Come on, let's climb the lighthouse."

"The line's too long," I say. "We'll be waiting forever."

"Come on, now. You know I'll hook you up." He grabs my hand, and I trail behind him as he leads me past the line of people to the base of the stairs. "I'm basically a curator at this place," he says. "I get to skip the lines and act like I'm going to do something official up at the lantern."

"Hello, Finnian," says an older man, standing at the steps. "Here to give some facts up at the top?"

"If you need me to," says Finn, shaking the old man's hand. "This is my friend, Michaela. She's gonna help out tonight."

The man looks down at my feet. "Not in those shoes, she's not."

Bending down, I remove my high-heeled sandals, my feet breathing a sigh of relief, and I give him a salute. "Ready for duty."

"My great-great-great-grandfather, Elijah Pearce, was the lighthouse keeper before he went to fight in the Civil War," Finn says as we climb the curving metal stairs up the center of the lighthouse.

"Yeah, you mentioned him last time," I say. The steps are steep, and every so often, the brick walls are interrupted by a little window, and on the sill there's a lantern or a book about Yankee whaling.

"He was Leta's husband."

"But what about Benjamin Churchill?" I try again.

Finn laughs, pausing to turn and raise an eyebrow at me. "I dunno, what about him?"

"Oh," I say.

"Believe me," says Finn. "If we could link Benjamin Churchill to this little town, maybe find one of his poems, we could put up all kinds of interactive displays. We could talk about Yankee whaling and Provincetown and the tall ships. We could get schools to come here on class trips. All kinds of things." He sighs and hangs his arms on the railing of the stairs. "That's what Aunt Becky has been hoping for a long time. But until then, we've gotta work with what we've got."

We spiral upward, getting dizzier with every step, until we reach the top. I've climbed lighthouses before, and I'm always surprised by how high they are. But I've never climbed one at night.

"Well?" asks Finn. "What do you think?" At the top of the lighthouse, we enter a room confined by glass that offers a 360-degree view. The Atlantic swamps my vision, and I know then how insignificant we are. How for centuries people relied upon something so comparably miniscule to save them from the jaws of Cape Cod's shoreline.

Silently, I stand beside Finn, taking a few moments to let it sink in. "I think," I finally say, "the world is a very big place, and we are impossibly small."

Finn doesn't say anything for a while. But then he turns to me and smiles. "Yeah, I think that's about right."

We're quiet for a moment, taking in the sea and all the stars.

"So, you um . . . ? You and this Caleb guy. You're . . ."

"We're not anything," I tell him. I grip the railing in front of me for balance. "We never were."

"Oh," says Finn. "Good."

CHAPTER ELEVEN

Leta

1862

There is a mark on the floor near the fireplace. One that I must have missed when I last cleaned. But it's difficult to miss a spot when you're down on your hands and knees, brush clutched in soapy hands, scrubbing until your skin feels as if it's about to crack. I can't stop staring at it, though.

"What's wrong?" Mother asks. She holds a good portion of my hair and gives it a swift yank, trying to coerce it into cooperation. "Do you feel ill?"

"Why would I feel ill?" I ask, closing my eyes as she pins my hair into place.

"You're the last of the Townsend girls, Leta," she replies, staring at my reflection in the mirror. "People will expect you to make a good match. You'll need to dance with any eligible gentleman who asks."

"I hope you've prepared a good soaking tub for my bloody feet when we get home."

"Don't be witty, Leta."

"I'll try to sheath my scathing sense of humor."

"That's a good girl," says Mother with a pat on my shoulder. "Men don't like to feel as if their potential wife is too clever. It emasculates them."

I spin in my chair. "If my wit emasculates a man, then I can't imagine that he was much of a man to begin with." Try though I might to stifle them, the words keep their forward momentum. "Besides, that can't be true of all men. Elijah Pearce thinks I'm clever, and he likes me just fine."

Too late. There it is.

Mother laughs quietly. "Elijah Pearce? Of course he thinks you're clever. And he'd marry you, too. What a joke, Leta! If you'd like to marry the lighthouse keeper, say so, and skip the party at the Crawfords'."

"I didn't say that," I mumble.

"Well, then, stop speaking nonsense and get dressed before you make us late. Your father is waiting outside in the carriage." She leaves the room in a flurry of mumbling and exasperation.

Staring at my own reflection, I apply a little more rouge and secure my pearl earrings. I'll show Mother.

Every year, the Crawfords hold an extravagant gathering, one that puts anything my mother ever hosted to shame. Still, she would never miss it, and she would never allow the rest of us to miss it, either.

And when we arrive, it is every bit as decadently tasteless as it is every year. They've hired a miniature orchestra, there are multiple punch bowls, tables laden with food, and everything gilded in blinding gold.

I flap open my fan to appear at ease, but I'm only trying to distract myself from my pinching shoes and to find a familiar face in a sea of dancers. I'm never myself at gatherings such as this. I'm sometimes the girl my mother hopes I'd be, or the girl a gentleman would prefer me to be, or the girl that the other girls wish to include in their company. But I'm never simply Leta.

Until Elijah walks up.

He isn't quite himself, either. He's uncomfortable in the fine clothes Fred has lent him, and he pulls often at his stiff collar on his journey across the room toward me.

"Am I presentable?" he asks, glancing around to see if anyone can hear him. He laughs a little, to alleviate his own anxiety.

"You look quite dashing, Elijah," I say, touching his hand.

"And you, Leta," he says, his eyes roaming downward and then back to meet my gaze, "you always look so beautiful."

"Oh, stop it. You're flattering me so I won't beat you at cards later." I tap his arm with my fan.

"No, I—"

"Leta, dear?" Mother's grip descends upon my shoulders.

"Caroline is over there with the Crawford girls. Why not go and say hello? You wouldn't want to appear rude."

"No, that would be a travesty, Mother."

"Good evening, Mrs. Townsend," says Elijah.

"Hello, Elijah," she says with a soft smile. Mother likes Elijah, deep down. She always has. But if Elijah is going to stand in the way of me and an eligible bachelor of her choice, then Elijah needs to be dealt with. "You understand, don't you?"

"Of course, Mrs. Townsend."

I take my leave of Elijah and cross the ballroom. Caroline greets me with her extended hand.

"You do look quite beautiful, Leta," she says quietly so that only I can hear. There are several girls in this gossipy knot, and they're too entrenched in conversation to be interrupted. "Did you pick out this dress?"

I admire the seafoam green silk and my white gloves. "I did. You like it?"

"It's perfection," she whispers.

"Every year, we have the same discussion," says Eugenie Crawford with a roll of her eyes. "My parents insist we invite him, and I insist that it's degrading."

Caroline takes a deep breath.

"I'm surprised he even has clothes for such an occasion!" another adds.

"Who?" I ask.

Eugenie snickers. "Don't worry, Leta."

"Worry about what?"

Caroline squeezes my hand.

"We all know how *you* feel on the subject," she continues.

My heart begins to race despite my attempt to remain calm. "Perhaps if you informed me of the subject, I could give you an updated account of my opinion."

Eugenie blinks at me several times and snaps her fan open as if consumed by a sudden heat wave. "Elijah Pearce."

I swallow a howling scream, but I maintain my composure. "Are you seriously disapproving of his being here? At a gathering for the neighborhood? Is he not our neighbor?"

"Well, the lighthouse is practically on the other side of town . . ." Eugenie tries.

"It's our lighthouse!" I cry. "It shares a name with the town!"

Caroline squeezes my hand again.

"There's no need to get yourself in a dither, Leta," says Eugenie. "We shouldn't have even mentioned it to you considering your attachment to him."

"I don't know what you're even talking about, Eugenie. I have no attachment to Elijah Pearce. He's been my friend since—"

"You were small," Eugenie finishes for me. "Yes, we know."

The story must be getting old. "In any case, he never bothers anyone."

"But what if he should ask one of us to dance?" another girl asks, lifting her nose as if she's smelled something particularly disgusting.

"Leta will dance with him," says Eugenie. She sniffs and snickers the right amount so as not to be offensive. "She's his staunch defender. Her feelings for him obviously run deeper than she lets on."

"Oh, but Eugenie!" cries another. "If we snub Elijah Pearce, will we offend his cousin?"

My ears prickle at attention.

"I heard that Captain Churchill is supposed to make an appearance tonight, and I would do anything to dance with him. I'm even saving him a spot on my dance card. Look." She presents the evidence.

"I don't think Captain Churchill cares a whit about Elijah Pearce," says Eugenie with an authority she doesn't deserve. "They're not even relatives by blood. Besides, if Captain Churchill is going to dance with anyone, it's me. I'm the oldest, so I get him first."

Caroline squeezes my arm discreetly.

While the girls fight over Benjamin Churchill like two dogs with a bone, I survey the room, hoping to find him, to catch his eye, to encourage him to dance with me first.

But Ben is nowhere to be found. Not on the ballroom floor, not near the punch bowl or the food, not with the old men discussing the politics of war.

Elijah almost takes me by surprise when he appears by my side.

"Did I startle you?" he asks with a smile.

"No, not at all," I assure him.

"If you're not otherwise engaged, will you save me the next dance?" His face is turned downward toward mine, his eyes unable to make direct contact. When he smiles, he shifts his weight from his left to right side.

I know what I'd like to say, and it should be easy to produce those words, but I feel my skin growing splotchy, the blood rushing to my face. I hate being the center of attention. I hate that the Crawford sisters and their friends all think they know what I'm going to do, what I'll say. I hate that my mother thinks she can dictate everything about my life—and this party, and my future. I hate that Caroline feels as if she must support me but isn't sure what exactly it is I want.

I hate that if I had it my way, I would dance with Elijah.

After all the secrets I've told him, the jokes we've shared, maybe dancing with him would be the next logical step.

But I'm too aware of Eugenie's eyes on my back.

"You know, Elijah," I say quietly, pressing my hand to my forehead, "I feel a little faint. I'm not sure I'm up to dancing."

I won't look up. I won't watch his expression drop.

"I think I'll go and take a breath outside for a moment."

"I'll go with you," he offers.

"No," I say, all too quickly. Eugenie giggles behind her fan to her friends, but it doesn't stop me. "No, I'm fine, really. I'd rather be alone. Thank you, though." I finally glance up. His eyes study me, desperately looking for a way to reclaim his words, his offer.

Too late. For both of us.

Outside, the full moon hangs low in the sky, shedding its dusty light on an elaborate row of hydrangea bushes, and I cover my face with both hands. I've broken something, but I can't be sure what yet. Our friendship, his feelings, this entire party? My heart thrums painfully in my ears, and these stupid shoes are absolutely finished. I wrench one off my foot and launch it over the hydrangeas and into the grass.

"Watch your aim, Miss Townsend."

His voice floats out from the opposite side of the hydrangeas, and when I peek over their blooms, saturated in deep blues and purples, Captain Churchill is on the other side, sitting on the ground. There's a fiddle in his lap.

"Captain Churchill," I say slowly, standing before him and crossing my arms over my chest. "What are you doing out here?"

He hands me my shoe. "Avoiding flying footwear."

Wandering around the edge of the bushes, I meet him where he sits. He's hunched over his instrument, his coat discarded and his bowtie hanging loosely about his neck. I try to think of something to corral him into conversation. "I have it on good authority that there are several young ladies yearning for a dance with you."

He snorts. "I'm repairing my fiddle."

"Now?" I ask. "In the dark?"

He looks down at the fiddle, then back up at me as if the answer is so glaringly obvious.

"You brought your fiddle to a party?"

This time, he supplies me with three determined blinks. "As you see."

"I think you find excuses to be unsociable."

"I do," he says, and his fingers move deftly over the instrument. He loosens one of the pegs and pulls out the snapped string. Then, presenting a new string, he glides it through the top hole in the peg, wraps it several times, and lays it flat over the bridge. "And now," he says, his tongue sticking out a bit, "I tighten it." He jumps up in one fluid motion once the string is in place. "And tune it." Producing a bow from behind him, Captain Churchill plays a low, sad song—one that moans out into the night air and strains its melody all the way to the Atlantic.

"Where did you learn to play?" I ask.

"On ships," he replies, the bow drifting over the strings. He closes his eyes in concentration, as if the sudden blindness will usher him back to the sea. "There's little to do on a ship at night. So it would be me, and my fiddle, and the occasional passing whale. I like to think that sometimes I played for them. What brings you out and away from all those admiring eyes, Leta?" He nods to the common room as he stoops and returns the fiddle to its case.

"I'm feeling unsociable, too."

"Disappointing gentlemen all across Cape Cod?"

"Highland, at least," I say with a smile.

"Well, then you've come to the right place." Ben begins to amble down the garden path and out into the high grass separating the Crawford property from the rest of Highland. The hush of the sea is accented by the chirping of toads, the strings of crickets. "I don't dance, either."

I follow him. "Because you choose not to?"

"I never really learned."

"Then let me show you," I suggest, extending my hand. Even as the words dart out past my lips, I know that I shouldn't. I know that Mother would tell me that if I really wanted to secure Captain Churchill, I wouldn't dance with him under a canopy of stars, in the company of trees, with no one to chaperone us except an errant fox that peeks out from the underbrush.

But my offer remains, and he stares at my hand like he can't be sure what to do with it.

"You don't want to waste your time on me," he says, and chuckles under his breath, scratching the back of his head. "I'm not made for dancing."

"That's ridiculous. Everyone is made for dancing." But I'm afraid this sounds more like a plea than the confident declaration I had intended.

"We can hardly hear the music out here," he says.

"Dancing doesn't require music," I say. "It requires counting. Surely you can count."

"I can."

"Then dance with me." I take him by both hands and lead him far out into the high, sharp seagrass, and I guide his hands to where they belong. "One hand goes here," I say, placing it on my waist, "and the other holds mine."

"Like this," he says, studying our joined hands.

"Just like this."

"If I step on your foot—"

"I have a feeling that you'll be surer of yourself once we begin, Captain Churchill."

"Ben," he says. "If I call you Leta, then you have to call me Ben."

"If I call you Ben, you'll dance with me?"

"I can't say no to you, Leta Townsend."

We're face-to-face, our torsos practically touching, and I suddenly find my breath intractable. I begin the count, and with a nod of my head, I lead him across the field in the time of a waltz. Soon, he catches on and takes the lead, and we're galloping through the weeds, extending our arms from time to time, stretching until we're fingertip to fingertip. My hair frees itself, rebelling against the many pins Mother found necessary, and I discard my shoes with no consideration of finding them again.

"You know," Ben begins, his grin contagious, "when I was a boy, I thought that dancing was the most monotonous, soul-sucking form of entertainment there was."

"And now?" My breath comes fast.

"I'm glad I let you convince me otherwise."

"Let me?" I say. A flurry of wings explodes into the air at our approach and disappears amid the night sky. "You had no choice in the matter, I'm afraid. You were going to be my protégée, like it or not."

"And am I a bitter disappointment, Leta?" he asks.

"Your dancing, Ben, is by far the most captivating experience I've ever had at a party held by the Crawfords."

"Then we must do it again sometime."

"It's too bad," I say between breaths, "that their party is only once a year."

"We must find another time, then," he replies, and our dancing slows, the space between us disappearing. "And make more excuses . . ." My hands are upon his shoulders, and his on my hips. Our noses touch. "To be this close."

We share the breath between us.

"Leta!"

Wrenching myself away from Ben, I turn to face Caroline

standing at the edge of the hydrangeas, their deep hue accenting her sky-blue dress. Behind her, a gaggle of girls stare with huge eyes. And following them, Elijah. He walks slowly, as if he's trying to make sense of what he sees.

"Were you dancing out in the wilderness?" Eugenie asks. "With Captain Churchill? Unchaperoned?"

"I was . . ." I reach up and try to fix my hair, but it's too late. It must look ghastly. "This can hardly be considered the wilderness."

"Miss Townsend was teaching me how to dance," says Ben, taking a step forward and blocking me from their scrutinizing observation. "She has been a gracious teacher."

"Well, that's Leta for you," says Eugenie. "She gives and gives and gives."

I push past Ben's shoulder and storm between the girls. "Envy is an awful color on you, Eugenie. But then you've never been known for your good taste."

Behind me, Ben attempts to stifle a snicker.

Elijah follows me, like always. I make a stand, probably offend someone, and Elijah chases me in an attempt to calm me. But I don't want to calm down right now. I want to feel the way my skin prickles, because I'm Leta Townsend, and I did what no one was expecting. I danced, unchaperoned, with Captain Benjamin Churchill. And he's no longer just a dead boy who has lent me his name. He's flesh and blood and sweat and laughter, and he danced with *me*. Not Eugenie, and not any other girl. He danced with me.

"Leta," says Elijah.

He's found me under the stairs inside the Crawfords' house, finding a cushion and pulling down the rest of my hair. I exhale with relief.

Elijah saunters over, his hands in his pockets and his head tilted to one side.

"I'm fine, Elijah," I say before he can ask. And I am. I've never been better. I don't need Elijah to chase after me like some puppy, making sure I'm not pretending to be stronger than I am. "I simply needed a moment without those knowing eyes on me."

"Leta," he says again. "I wanted to dance with you."

If I keep talking, maybe we won't have to have this conversation. Maybe I won't have to own up to the slight I gave him—he who has never let me down.

"And it could be the last time I get an opportunity. Because I'm leaving."

I freeze in place. "What do you mean, you're leaving? Who will tend the lighthouse?"

"I've joined the Union Army, Leta."

My legs propel me upward, and I march toward him. "You can't."

"I did."

"You can't leave Highland, Elijah. What would we do without you? What would *I* do?"

He considers this for a moment, nods his head once, and takes a step back. "Perhaps that's a question best posed to Captain Churchill."

CHAPTER TWELVE

MICHAELA

present day

The Fourth of July has always been kind of a big deal in our neighborhood. We live on a dead-end street, one that has been in need of repavement for a while, and there are only seven houses altogether. Every year, we rotate who's going to host the epic Fourth of July bash, and every year, each house tries to outdo the others.

This year it's our turn to host. Out the window of my dad's old office, I watch as each family arrives. First, it's Ryan's parents. His mom carries a massive tray of her famous potato salad. Trailing them is Ryan and several of his friends. Friends who don't live on our street. Friends like Finn.

My heart speeds up a little.

I had a feeling Finn would be coming. It's not a picnic unless Ryan and his teammates are playing a game of baseball in the backyard, and Finn has been officially admitted as a member of the crew.

But before I head outside, I look at my latest poem one more time.

> *The sea is never still*
> *(so they say)*
> *and maybe I've subscribed to that line of thinking.*
> *But when we danced*
> *(cheek to cheek)*
> *(hand to hand)*
> *(almost lip to lip)*
> *I could feel the rhythm resonate in your chest,*
> *and I thought it was the music,*
> *the notes that float out into the night.*
> *But it's something more than that*
> *because there's a song from the water that you've held to,*
> *a song in the water I can't hear,*
> *a song composed of sea and sky,*
> *spray and foam,*
> *whale and man,*
> *shell and stone*
> *(smooth from the tumble in the waves,*
> *edges soft now, it can't hurt).*
> *A song you share*
> *but not with me.*
> *The sea is never still*
> *(so they say),*
> *but I don't believe that anymore.*

Because when we danced
(cheek to cheek)
(hand to hand)
(breath to breath)
I could hear it just a little.
When we danced,
I could smell the sea clinging to your hair,
a trace of it left on your skin,
a rasp rattling in your lungs,
and it's a constant that you cling to
when you pretend that you're clinging to me.

The entry Leta wrote in her diary about the ball at the Crawford house is almost the last one I have on my phone. If I want to write any more, I'm going to have to find a way to sneak up to Caleb's room again. Which doesn't feel like it's going to be easy somehow.

The sound of heavy footfalls on the stairs rouses me, and I close my journal, just in case someone pops into the office. Russ appears in the doorway, dressed in khaki shorts and a button-down shirt that looks like a red-checked tablecloth.

"Just looking for some extra baseball gloves," he says, rummaging through the closet. When he finds them, he grins, and turns to me. "You should come downstairs."

"I know," I reply, my hand on my journal.

"Maybe socialize with the living for a change."

I stay seated, my head turning slowly in Russ's direction.

He's laughing quietly, like what he said was funny, but it fades when he realizes I'm not finding this hilarious. I stare blankly at him, my mouth frozen and my words stuck on the tip of my tongue.

"Anyway," he says, clearing his throat, "everyone's here. Come down and get some food." He leaves with two gloves.

I can't move, even after he's gone. I'm too stunned. I touch the picture of me and Mom and Dad, tilting it toward me so I can see them more clearly, and tears well up and spill over the rims of my eyes.

Outside the office door, the sound of rampant, determined footsteps and Mellie calling, "Mack, Mack, Mack!" makes me wipe away the tears and take a deep breath. I blink up at the ceiling, hoping I can contain myself for the sake of my little sister.

"Mack, look who I found outside!" Mellie whoops with a leap, dragging Finn into the office behind her. She freezes when she sees me. There's no hiding anything from Mellie. "What happened?" Her face crumples a little, and I'm afraid if she thinks I'm crying, she's going to start, too.

"Nothing," I insist, smiling. I put my journal into my messenger bag. "Why would you think something happened?"

"You're puffy and you're fake smiling," says Mellie.

"You okay?" Finn asks, his voice soft and cool.

"Mmhm." I nod, but I feel a lump in my throat rising, and I

can't stop my bottom lip from trembling. I blink back the tears and cover my mouth, pretending to be preoccupied with a few stray pencils on the desk.

"Hey, Mellie," says Finn, letting go of her hand. "Do me a solid and go downstairs and get me a hot dog before those beasts outside eat them all. I can't pitch on an empty stomach. What about you, Mack? You want a hot dog?"

I shake my head.

"Mack doesn't like hot dogs," says Mellie. "She only eats fried chicken at picnics." She thinks for a moment. "The drumsticks are her favorite."

"I'm okay for now," I tell them.

Mellie nods and darts to the door, giving one last glance over her shoulder. Then she disappears down the steps.

"Doesn't matter if I wanted a drumstick anyway," I mumble, swiping at my wet cheeks. "Russ thinks eating more than one of the same piece of chicken is selfish."

Finn takes a hesitant step closer to me, like I'm an animal trapped in a snare and he doesn't want to upset me any more than I already am. "Is this about Russ?"

I shrug. "Maybe? I don't know."

He takes a seat on the corner of the guest bed, his hands folded between his knees, and he leans toward me, waiting for me to tell him more.

"He's just never taken the time to get to know me. And he

makes these snide side comments like he has me all figured out, or that I don't have feelings, and he's wrong, and it hurts."

The tears start all over again, and Finn reaches out, grabbing the seat of my chair and rolling me closer to him. "Hey, hey, hey," he says, his left hand on my knee, and his right tucking a loose strand of hair behind my ear. "Don't cry. Some people you just can't change, right? Please don't cry."

I nod, sniffling, and wipe at my eyes again. "I'm okay," I assure him. "I'm fine. I mean, it's nothing new, right?"

Finn doesn't look very convinced.

"Thanks," I say quietly, suddenly acutely aware that his one hand is still on my knee, the other cupping my face. My body hums as he runs his thumb along my jawline.

"You're welcome," he murmurs, his eyes focused on my lips. "I don't like it when you cry."

I swallow, my breath coming faster. "I'm sorry if I upset you."

"No," he says hoarsely, almost a whisper, and he touches his forehead to mine, his upper lip brushing across my mouth.

"I've got the hot dog with extra mustard!" Mellie shouts as she hops into the room.

Finn springs backward and stands automatically, and I roll back to the desk.

"I hope you like extra mustard." She holds up the plate for inspection.

"Love mustard," he says. "Love it. Thanks." They fist bump.

"Come on, you guys, we have to go downstairs. Finn has to eat now so that he can digest and then play baseball. Ryan said I could have a turn hitting."

"Okay, let's go," I say, standing and following her out the door.

Finn's behind me, and as we descend the steps in an almost line, I feel the faint pressure of his hand on my back. I reach out and run my finger along his wrist. He takes a deep breath.

At the bottom of the stairs, I think if Mellie dashes out the back door, if she just disappears for a moment, I'll have a second by myself with him, a chance to kiss him quickly before we join the others at the picnic table. But before my sister can make it outside, she's greeted by Chloe.

"Hey, Mel-Mel," she says. "That hot dog for me?"

"No," says Mellie, pointing to the stairs. "It's for Finn."

Chloe's eyes follow Mellie's finger to find me and Finn coming down the steps together. "Finn, huh?" she says. Mellie escapes to the rest of the picnic goers. Chloe stands with a playful smirk to her lips. "You and Finnian Pearce, coming down the stairs." She pauses. "Blushing a little."

"Hey, Chloe," says Finn, easing past me and following Mellie outside like it's the most ordinary thing in the world for this to be happening. God bless his natural suavity. "Save you a seat, Mack?" he asks, poking his head back in the door.

"Yeah, be out in a few." I wait until he closes the door and turn to Chloe, my shoulders slumping, and I feel like crying again. "Chloe, about last week," I start. "I'm sorry. I know it was shitty of me to want to stay, and I felt awful, and I had the worst time, and—"

She gathers me into a swift embrace, squeezing me tightly. "You're my bestie," she says against my shoulder. "I was mad. Time passed. You apologized. We're fine." She leans back, looking me in the face. "I'm sorry I left you like that. That wasn't cool. It wasn't even safe."

"It's okay," I say with a shrug. "Finn picked me up."

Her mouth upturns in a knowing smile. "He picked you up, huh?" She peeks over her shoulder, trying to catch a glimpse of him out the window. "But what was it you said Finnian Pearce was? Nothing, wasn't it?"

"Go away," I say, shoving her in the shoulder.

"Chloe!" Ryan shouts from the far end of the yard when he sees us come out the back door together. "Chloe, come play. I'll show you how to catch a baseball."

"And I'll show you how to catch a hint," she calls back, taking a seat at the picnic table. The company all chuckles at this, and Mom passes her an empty paper plate and some plastic utensils.

I take a seat between Chloe and Finn, and when I do, he bumps his shoulder against mine, smiling.

"Feeling better?" he asks.

"Much," I reply, taking a good long look at the table and figuring out what I want to eat first. But before I can decide, a plate lands in front of me, filled with potato salad, baked beans, and, most important, two drumsticks.

I glance up, and Russ pulls his hand back, completely focused on his conversation with his brother, and he takes a sip of beer. I don't miss the little wink he sends my way, though.

CHAPTER THIRTEEN

Leta

1862

Clouds moved in overnight, but the rain didn't start until dawn. Still, Mother insisted on going to sewing circle. She tried to convince me that I'd enjoy myself if I went, but I told her I was busy. I planned on writing something new today, something to send to my editor in Boston, but I can't seem to put pen to paper. The rain drips and dribbles down the window beside my desk, forming shapes and patterns on the pane. But nothing can make me forget about Elijah's going to war.

Or the feeling of my body clasped by Benjamin Churchill's hands.

I want to forget both. I want things to go back to the way they were.

Something taps against my window and draws my attention away from the raindrops and down to the grass below. I push down on the latch, and the pattering of rain infiltrates the garret.

"Captain Churchill," I say. "Get out of the rain, you'll be soaked!"

He grins up at me, his left hand filled with tiny pebbles and his right ready to launch another at my window. "Invite me in, then."

He's a scoundrel. And I can't help myself. "Come in! Get out of the storm."

Closing the window, I dash over to the little mirror I keep hanging near the staircase, making sure that my hair is falling the way I prefer it, and then meet Ben at the front door.

"What are you doing out in this weather?"

"I thought I'd take a walk," he replies, dripping on the wood floor. He runs his hand across his drenched hair and flicks water about the room.

"Annie!" I call down the hallway to our housekeeper. "Put the kettle on. Captain Churchill is here for a visit. Could you take his coat for me and bring it into the kitchen?"

Taking off his coat and handing it to Annie, he ambles down the hall and toward the front room. He sits down at the edge of my father's armchair, staring out over his shoulder as the rain continues to pour.

"By all means," I say, staring at him, "make yourself at home."

"Thank you," he says. "Were you writing?"

"I was until you interrupted me."

"I'm sorry." He folds his hands between his knees and leans toward me.

I emulate his posture. "It doesn't mean that all interruptions are unwelcome."

He tries to suppress a smile as he tilts his head to one side, and I suddenly see him as he was years ago. He was several years my senior, and he ran with a rough group of boys. He'd never paid attention to me except, of course, to aggravate me during math class.

"We were the talk of the town after the ball," he says.

I sigh, leaning back against the sofa and resting my cheek against my hand. "I can't remember a time when the whole town found me that interesting."

"Towns like these are always burdened with their own gossip. You just so happen to be the topic this week."

"Thank you, I suppose."

Annie brings a tray of tea and cookies into the parlor and places them on the table before Captain Churchill. I can't help but notice her cheeks blush when he thanks her.

"That's why I went to sea," says Ben.

"Because Highland was gossiping about you?"

"Because Highland was suffocating and judgmental, and I wanted to be on my own. Away from everyone's expectations. Free to do things that mattered to me."

There's weight to his words. Feelings I never contemplated when I sat down at my writing desk and pretended to be him. My fingers twitch with the urge to write now, and a sad acknowledgment that I may never really know all that he's seen. Keen as my imagination may be, there are depths to Benjamin Churchill, a dark and churning sea deep beneath the surface.

"Haven't you ever wanted that?" he asks quietly.

"Yes," I reply.

"You and I are alike," he says while I try to preoccupy myself with pouring tea, offering him sugar and cream, but he prefers it black. He takes the cup from my hand, refusing the saucer.

The more Captain Churchill talks, the more he frightens me—the more my own feelings frighten me. That I could have created someone from thin memories and a longing I didn't even know I possessed, and here he is. Flesh and blood and eyes like the ocean, sitting in my very parlor, drinking tea.

I take a quick breath and try to change the subject. "What do you think of your cousin going off to fight in the war?"

Ben sips his tea. "I think that's the fastest way to die."

"You're one to talk." I pour my own tea. "You hunt whales for a living."

"But I'm good at it." Outside, a tremor of thunder rumbles the house. "It's not the same as walking in a straight line toward an enemy with firearms waiting to blow you apart."

"Let's stop, please," I say, my teacup shivering in my quaking fingers. "I can't think that way of him."

"Are you fond of Elijah?" Ben asks.

"Of course I am," I say quietly. "He's been my best friend since we could speak. I don't want to lose him."

Ben takes a sip from his cup and stares out the window at the relentless rain. "What do you do on days like today?" he asks. "Other than entertain wandering sea captains who stop by for an impromptu cup of tea?" He smiles. "Write your poems?"

"Sometimes," I say quietly.

"Can I read one?"

I look around the parlor. "Now?"

"Why not?" Placing his teacup on the table, he stands and offers me his hand. "Do you keep them upstairs? In your little writing nook?"

"Yes, but—"

"Are you turning shy suddenly?"

I place my teacup back on its saucer with a resounding clank. "I most certainly am not," I reply. "Come upstairs. I'll show you a poem." I flounce out of the parlor, hoping he's far enough behind that I can sneak in a word with Annie.

She's busy stuffing a chicken for dinner, and as I turn the corner up the stairs, I throw over my shoulder, "Don't tell anyone."

"What was that, miss?" Annie says with a smile. She wipes her hands on her apron and takes a step toward me.

With my eyes, I indicate that I'm referring to Captain Churchill, who is right on my heels.

"Oh," says Annie, suddenly flustered. "Of course not, miss. Surely."

I realize I'm putting Annie in an awkward position, but truth be told, I'm not doing anything with Captain Churchill that I wouldn't with a female acquaintance. I'm simply sharing poetry.

Ben's steps are heavy and slow, like he's casually taking his time, and meanwhile, I sort through my mental inventory of poems. There must be an innocuous one stored among my piles of words—one that I wouldn't mind sharing with him; one that doesn't bare all that I am before his curious eyes.

He waits a good distance away and paces the room while I riffle through my desk, studying my bookcases and opening the occasional trunk lid.

"Ah!" I say, finding a suitable work. "Here. Read this one. I'm really quite proud of it."

Ben crosses the room, one hand behind his back and the other taking the scrap of paper from mine. "Black-eyed Susans," he reads. His mouth twitches into a smile.

When the heat of summer arrives
And the boats all dock in the bay,
That's when she sprouts, all gold and black,
At the height of a glorious day.

No flower is quite as cheerful
Or brings such delight in her bloom.
She spreads her warm glow over hills
In attempt to cast out the gloom.

But when the winds of October
Do finally gust o'er the land,
Fair Susan will shiver and die,
Petals cast to rough surf and sand.

All winter long we will wait here
For the first hint of Susan's light,
And when summer at last returns
She will end all the hardship and blight.

When he finishes, his eyebrows raise, and he nods his head. "Very nice," he says.

I feel stupid. I've written far better poems than my dalliance in coastal vegetation. I don't want him to think my poetry is *nice*. I want him to see himself in it.

"You don't like it," I say.

"No, of course I did. It's very . . . wholesome."

I snatch the paper back from him and hide it among the others in my desk drawer.

"Don't get me wrong," Ben continues, sauntering over to the window and watching the rain stream down. "You have a talent with words. It's just that I thought . . ."

"What?"

"I thought you'd write a little more passionately about something. *Someone*, maybe."

"Like who?"

He shrugs then smiles. "Do you ever write about Elijah?" he asks.

I snort. "You're teasing me now."

"I'm not," he swears. "I'm not teasing you. I'm sorry."

"No," I say, resting my hand on the desk, and I realize it's the only thing holding me upright. "I've never written about Elijah."

He nods, taking a step closer, his eyes falling upon my diary. He stares, and his fingertips brush the cover, but he doesn't move to open it. "Would you ever write about me?" he asks. This time, his eyes won't meet mine.

I can't respond. *I don't write about you,* I'd like to tell him. *No, I've never written about you. I write as if I am you, as if we're two bodies occupying the same soul. It's better than you think. If you look at me, I'll tell you.*

His hand flinches ever so slightly. It's a rough hand, a long scar running from the base of his thumb and disappearing under his sleeve. His hand crosses the desk and lifts two of my fingers. My heart races.

"Miss Townsend!" Annie shouts from the bottom of the steps.

I practically jump out of my skin, clutch my heart, and close my eyes. Ben steps back.

"What is it, Annie?"

"Miss Townsend, the Captain is home. Your father is at the garden gate! What do I do?"

Wordlessly, Ben scurries down the stairs. Touching Annie's arm, he asks, "Is there a back door?"

"Yes, Captain Churchill," she says. "Right over there."

"Thank you, Miss Annie, you're a peach." He seizes his coat from the peg by the door.

She giggles uncontrollably.

"Captain Churchill!" I call to him as I practically tumble down the steps.

He staggers to a stop and pokes his head back into the stairwell.

"What are you doing?"

"You'll see," he promises, and darts out the back door into the rainstorm.

Annie and I both wedge ourselves into the window's cove to look outside. Beside the hydrangea bushes, he stands in the rain, allowing himself to get drenched, then walks the path to the front of the house. Simultaneously, we rush into the parlor, seeking a better view.

"His teacup, Annie, take his teacup!"

She quickly gathers the things from the table and brings them to the kitchen.

At the front gate, I see Ben greeting my father as if he had only then arrived, and together they hurry toward the house.

I whip around, situating myself on the sofa, and as they enter, I take a sip of my tea.

"Look who has stopped by for a visit, Leta," says Father. He removes his coat and Ben does the same.

"How wonderful," I say. "I was just sitting down to a cup of tea. Annie! Won't you bring two more cups?"

"Yes, miss," she calls from the kitchen.

"You're looking well today, Miss Townsend," says Ben.

"I have relentless rain, a cozy fireplace, and pleasant company. What more could I ask for?"

Father and Ben take a seat across from me. Ben nods as Annie pours him his second cup of tea for the day, then he raises it, saucer and all, in my direction and takes a sip.

CHAPTER FOURTEEN

MICHAELA

present day

Now that Chloe is the lead in our local theater's summer production of *Much Ado About Nothing*, she isn't always free when I am. I decide to wait for her to finish play practice, see if maybe she has some time after that, and I stand in line at Highland's local coffee shop, The Good Bean, contemplating the brew of the day, and whether I want regular coffee or some kind of fancy latte with wispy foamed milk.

The girl at the counter waits patiently.

"I'm thinking the latte," I say. "Whole milk. No sugar."

"Be sure to add a little cinnamon," says a voice behind me.

I whip around and come face-to-face with Caleb Abernathy.

"Trust me," he says with a smile.

"And a little cinnamon," I add to my order. "To go." The barista gives me a nod, and I sit at one of the café tables while Caleb decides on his perfect cup of coffee.

I'm not sure whether this should be awkward or not. The last time I saw him, he was . . . preoccupied, and I'm not even sure if he knows it was me who walked in on him. I cross one leg over the other, trying to look casual.

"I haven't seen you around Whaler's Watch lately," he says, strolling over with a lazy swagger, his hands in his pockets. He wears a collared shirt, buttoned all the way up to his neck despite that it's well over eighty degrees outside. The shirt is loud and floral, and I think my grandma has something in the same print. I know he's trying to be artsy, but I can't stop staring.

"Been a little busy," I say, smiling. "I work shifts at the Shellfish Shanty over the summer."

He laughs. "That place? Talk about a heart attack."

"I don't eat there every day," I murmur, shifting uneasily in my chair.

"Where are you headed today with your time off?"

I peer over my shoulder and out the window, catching a hint of Cape Cod Bay glimmering in the late afternoon sun. "Probably down to the beach to write a little."

"Can I join you?"

I shrug. "Sure. I won't be very fun company, but sometimes it's nice to write around other people."

"We can work on our submissions for the statue dedication."

My chest pinches uncomfortably. Maybe it's petty of me, but I want to win. I don't want to work with him or next to him on a competing poem. I can't shake the feeling that the only reason he's even entering this contest is to prove that he's the best. How is it even fair if he's working under the mentorship of the professor who's sponsoring the whole event? He has the advantage.

But he's also going to have a rude awakening.

When our coffees are ready, we head out of the shop and down Main Street, crossing Beach Plum Lane and finding an empty bench facing the bay. The late afternoon beachgoers are still lounging in their chairs, their umbrellas shifted to block the ever-moving sun. I squint to see the words on the page of my journal, and Caleb sits crisscross, scribbling away in his leather-bound notebook.

We sit like this for a while, but he keeps sneaking glances at me. I smile at first, thinking that he's just watching me and trying to be cute, but after three times, I'm not amused anymore. I edge away uncomfortably, trying to think of a reason to get up and leave, to go and write on my own. I don't get my escape until the familiar crack of a bat against a ball draws my attention away from my journal and down the street, past the park.

There's a baseball diamond on the other side, and two teams play in the cool twilight. It's getting dark enough now that the big lights come on over the field, but I still can't see clearly to figure out which teams are competing.

"Hey, I'll be right back," I tell Caleb, and close my journal and throw it into my bag.

"Where are you going?" he asks, shifting his position like he's going to get up, too. "I'll come with you."

"Just across the street for a minute." I smile to let him know it's no big deal. "You don't have to come."

"Oh."

"I think I see my friend over there. I want to say hi. I'll be right back."

"Yeah, it's fine," he replies, but he's back to scribbling at his poem, then crossing things out with exaggerated distaste.

It feels better to be away from him, to be away from my stupid thoughts about him, my bitter resentment toward him entering the contest. I cross the street, through the park and past the pedestal for Churchill's monument, and approach the chain-link fence that's supposed to keep passing pedestrians safe from errant baseballs.

Harwich is playing the Highland Whalers. Well, the summer league of our school team, that is. The same boys who play in the spring for the high school travel the entire Cape during the summer, playing other local teams—players who want to keep in shape and be scouted by colleges, the Cape Cod Baseball League, and sometimes even the major leagues.

The home team is in the field, and I weave my fingers through the chain link, my eyes roving first to the players I know: Ryan, Aidan, and Matt, and then to the pitcher's mound. Finn rolls his shoulders back, bringing his gloved left hand up over his mouth, studying Aidan, who is crouched behind home plate. Finn shakes his head twice, then finally nods, winds up, pulls his right arm back, and launches the ball right past the batter. The boy swings wildly, but he never had a chance of making contact.

Finn ends the inning, the infield coming up behind him and patting him on the shoulder. In the dugout, which is right beside me, I can see a few of them even swat him on the butt. Boys are weird.

I'd say hello, but this is a Finn I haven't met yet; an intense Finn; a Finn who takes what he does a lot more seriously than I ever thought playing a game deserved. I smile down at him, his back to me, as he fills a cup with Gatorade and chugs it down. His coach, several inches shorter than him, gives Finn advice, and he listens, chewing on the rim of his paper cup and nodding occasionally. With a clap on Finn's shoulder, the coach walks away, his attention focused now on the batter.

Finn lowers himself to the bench, taking off his baseball cap and wiping the sweat away with his forearm. I wonder if I should call over to him. It feels awkward. And Ryan is close enough that he would hear me, too, and I really don't want him to make a scene. I just want to say hi to Finn.

Resignedly, I figure I should get back to my bench by the bay, grab my belongings, and see if Chloe feels like doing something after rehearsal. One last glance at Finn, and his eyes drag away from the batter and find mine.

"Mack," he says, standing, then jogging up the three stairs to stand in front of me. "I didn't know you were gonna be here."

"It was kind of unexpected. I was over by the bay writing, and I heard the game going on, so I figured I'd come over and check to see if you were here." I smile. "And here you are."

"Here I am." He looks back at the field over his shoulder. "Did you see me strike out that last batter?"

"It was awesome."

"Yeah." His grin is practically splitting his face. My heart thuds in my chest, over a verbal exchange about fastballs, a conversation that a month ago I would have called mediocre and banal. Boring. Hesitantly, his fingers climb the chain link until his hand is next to mine. "I'm really glad," he starts to say, but his voice grows quiet, and he looks at his feet bashfully. "Glad you're here."

"Pearce!" calls his coach. "Stop flirting with the crowd and get back in the dugout."

"Listen, I have to go," says Finn quickly. "Can you stay till the end of the game? It's the seventh inning already."

"I think so," I reply.

"After, I'll just shower quickly, and maybe you wanna come with me to P-town? Aunt Becky's giving a lecture, and I told her I'd be there."

"Yeah, that sounds great."

"Okay, cool. Meet me over where the Highland Whaler statue is gonna be."

"Okay," I promise him. "I'll stick around and watch the game. Let me go grab my things, and I'll be right back."

"Cool."

I turn into the coming dusk, ready to head back to the bay where I left Caleb, but when I look for him at the bench, I don't find him there. I see him lingering near the pedestal, just where Finn and I are supposed to meet. When he realizes I've spotted him, he shoves his hands in his pockets and ambles back to where we left our stuff on the bench.

I give him a few moments, not really wanting to walk with him or answer any questions he might lob in my direction. When I get to where he waits, I grab my messenger bag.

"How'd you do?" I ask.

Caleb shrugs and shows me a mostly blank page with lots of crossed-out words. "Guess I caught a pretty bad case of writer's block," he replies.

"I'm gonna head out," I tell him, thumbing behind me toward the field.

"To the baseball game?" says Caleb, almost laughing.

I stare at him for a moment. "Yeah, to the baseball game."

"You do you," he says, obviously amused and shaking his head.

"Thanks, I will." And with that, I don't even offer him a parting glance.

———

"You said we were going to P-town with just Finn," says Chloe from the backseat. "You didn't mention dingus over here." She won't even look at Ryan, who sits next to her. After her play rehearsal ended, I asked her to join me and Finn. Even *I* had no idea that Ryan was Finn's tagalong.

"I have a name, Chloe," Ryan grumbles.

"It makes me sick when I hear it."

"Guys, honestly," says Finn, glancing in the rearview mirror. "It's my fault, okay? I invited all of you." He settles back into his seat. "Unfortunately."

There's some traffic getting into Provincetown, and we sit for a little while, trying to turn onto Commercial Street and then find a parking spot on MacMillan Pier.

"I still don't get why Big Mack gets to sit in the front seat," Ryan says from behind me.

"Dude," says Finn, putting on his left blinker and turning into the lot. "Give it a break."

Ryan chuckles, and I turn in my seat, lunging for his leg with my closed fist. "Hey!" he cries. "You can't hurt me! We have some big games coming up."

"Don't tempt me."

"Are you all gonna behave when we get to the library? This is a big deal for Aunt Becky. She's been prepping for weeks now."

"What's she gonna talk about?" Ryan asks.

"Captain Benjamin Churchill," says Finn.

I shiver.

"You okay?" Finn asks, leaning his head toward me.

"I'm good," I reply. "Good."

"I thought you'd be interested because you kept asking about him a while back. Remember?"

"Mmhm," I say with a nod.

Finn finds a tight, faraway spot, and we all climb out of the Volvo.

Ryan groans as we walk toward the library. "I don't even like books."

"Why did he have to come?" Chloe asks.

"Because Big Mack isn't the only one Finn likes." Ryan huffs. "I was there first."

Finn laughs, but I see his cheeks flame red, even in the muted glow of the parking lot lights. He pulls down his baseball cap lower on his head and drops his chin to his chest.

"Besides," Ryan continues, pacing ahead of us, his hands dug into his pockets, "I offered to take you to the movies, but you wouldn't go."

"That's because you're gross," Chloe explains. "If you want

a girl to take you seriously, then you need to act serious. But you just act like an asshole."

Pausing, Ryan turns to her. "So you don't *actually* think I'm an asshole?"

Chloe clears her throat. "I mean . . . I've met worse."

"I'm not gonna lie. I feel really close to you right now, Chloe."

We cross Commercial Street and head east into Provincetown. The library sits on a little hill, and Finn leads us up the lit steps and through the front entrance.

Mom used to take me here when I was little because inside, where the children's books are, there's a replica of a ship. Like books weren't escape enough, there was an actual vessel there, ready to take us away.

"The *Rose Dorothea*," says Finn once we're inside, like he can read my thoughts. But when I look at him, he's staring in awe at the ship. "Pretty amazing, right?"

"Is it a whaling ship?" I ask.

He shakes his head. "A schooner."

I follow Finn up onto a balcony that overlooks some folding chairs, a podium, and a microphone. Below us, a few people holding brochures meander around, quietly chatting and drinking coffee from paper cups.

Aunt Becky takes her place, organizing her note sheets, and I lean my arms against the railing to watch her. She's older than my mom, younger than my grandma, and she's purposeful tonight. Not like when I last saw her, when she was frantically getting ready for a meeting with the bank.

"Hey, Dad," says Finn.

"Hey, buddy." A carbon copy of Finn stands beside him, only older and wearing a suit and tie. He extends his hand to me. "How are you? I'm Finn's dad."

"Michaela Dunn," I say.

"This is my friend from school, Dad," says Finn. "She's helping me with my English over the summer."

"Oh, yeah? And how are you doing?" He hands us a few pamphlets about the night's event.

Finn gives him a thumbs-up. "Mack's been a good tutor. She writes poetry."

"What kind of poems?" his dad asks.

I shrug. "I've been working on a portfolio for a retreat I'd really like to attend at a college I'm looking into."

"She's writing about the Highland Whaler, for the statue dedication," Finn finishes for me.

"Looks like you've come to the right place," says Mr. Pearce. "Becky loves Captain Churchill. She's been researching him since we were in high school. She says there's something poetic about him, a man who's so popular, but can't be traced."

"Like a rumor," I say.

Finn smiles at me.

At that moment, the room quiets, and Aunt Becky is at the podium.

"Thank you all for coming this evening," she begins.

There's an anticipation clenching my chest, in publicly hearing about Benjamin Churchill when I've kept him all to myself these past few weeks, like he's someone who only exists in my imagination.

"We're all here for the same reason," Aunt Becky says, "because we hear about the Highland Whaler. We watch as his football team takes the field every fall. We look forward to when his ice cream stand opens in the spring, and we get our free cup. We wait in line every summer to play mini golf at his course. He's everywhere around here. And yet, he's nowhere."

I grip the railing, steadying myself.

"No one is certain where he was born. Some say Boston, others suggest New Bedford. But those of us who really know are certain he was born in Highland around 1840."

She has a slideshow projected behind her, and she skims through pictures of the time period: ships, coastlines, sketches of whales being violently harpooned. But none of them show any likeness of Benjamin Churchill.

"His feats at sea were well known throughout America and even in Britain. There was no better whaler than Captain Benjamin Churchill. He was the youngest captain on record, at nineteen years old, and certainly one of the richest."

She speaks of his voyages: the far-off ports he visited; the Confederate ship he fought off. But I want to see his face—to see what Leta Townsend saw. I pull a pen out of my bag, click it open, and begin jotting down a few lines on my pamphlet.

"What are you doing?" Ryan asks from behind me. "Taking notes?"

Pulling my pamphlet, I reply, "Writing down words I like."

"Leave her alone," says Chloe next to him, slapping his arm.

"For what?" Ryan asks anyway.

"A poem I'm writing."

He scratches his neck. "I don't get it."

"Color me surprised," Chloe mutters.

"Words are powerful," I try to explain. "So if I'm listening to a story about something that moves me, then the best way for me to process those feelings is by writing them down. Like this." I show him a few lines I've pulled from Aunt Becky's presentation, and the words I've added to make them my own.

"That's really good, Mack."

I take a moment to stare at him. In all of the years that Ryan and I have been forced into each other's company, he's never said anything complimentary to me before. And surprisingly, it's kind of a nice feeling.

"Thank you," I reply.

The presentation winds to a close. Finn's aunt clicks to a black slide.

"Captain Benjamin Churchill died in 1861 while hunting sperm whales in the Pacific," Aunt Becky says.

I laugh through my nose and whisper, "That's not true." Once the words are past my lips, I wish I could grab them and stuff them back inside.

"Hm?" says Finn, leaning over to me. "What's not true?"

"He didn't die in 1861."

Aunt Becky continues. "I have been searching for Benjamin Churchill ever since I was a little girl. And when I had a daughter, we searched for him together. I think it's the thrill of the chase, the hope that what we thought was simply a story, or a tall tale, has roots. That he's not a ghost, an ever-floating idea, but someone we can cling to, someone who matters, and someone who lives on. Thank you so much for spending the evening with me. Good night." She smiles, hands folded, and even offers a little bow.

Finn applauds his aunt, giving her a sharp whistle. With his attention temporarily turned from me, I slip my paper into my back pocket and stand.

"I'm gonna head downstairs. I'm Becky's ride home," says Mr. Pearce. "But you guys should stay in town. Go walk around."

"I could eat," says Ryan.

Outside, a cool breeze seeps in from the bay, carrying with it the scent of salt and dampness, of Portuguese fried dough, someone's cologne, and fried seafood.

"Let's walk up Commercial Street," I suggest.

Ryan nods, and he and Chloe follow behind me and Finn. We pass the restaurants and bars, the drag queens and their six-inch heels, the gift shops and tattoo parlors, and we make it to the West End, where things are a little quieter.

"I'm gonna stop for ice cream," Ryan says.

"You want ice cream, too?" Finn asks me as he begins heading in the direction we came from. "My treat."

"Thanks," I say, touching his upper arm.

Inside the ice cream shop, it smells like coffee and fudge and vanilla and Christmas, even though it's July. Ryan orders a massive cone and then disappears into Commercial Street with Chloe. Finn gets one to match. He watches me as I decide.

"I don't know," I say, staring at the assortment of fudge from behind a thick glass window. "What would you get?"

"It's up to me?" he says, pointing to himself and licking his ice cream cone. He grins and then replies to the girl at the cash register. "Can I get a slice of the maple walnut fudge?"

"Maple walnut?" I ask as she wraps up his order.

"You're not allergic to nuts, are you?"

"No, but maple walnut?"

"Trust me," says Finn. He pays for the fudge and takes the paper bag while leading me back out into the stirring light of Commercial Street. This used to be a town of fishermen and whalers, then artists, musicians, and writers. They're all here, compounded by the rainbow flags, the diverse array of couples, the restaurants, and the inns converted from old captains' houses—the embodiment of summer on Cape Cod all in one crowded street.

"So," says Finn, leaning against the building, "how do you know Benjamin Churchill didn't die hunting sperm whales in 1861?"

"Oh, I see," I say, taking a bite of my fudge. "You buy me fudge." I chew for a moment. "Really, really delicious fudge—"

"Told ya," he says, taking a bite of his cone.

"And you think I owe you an answer?"

"I think it's kinda weird that you think you know when he died. Or when he *didn't*, actually."

I take a deep breath, the maple fudge melting on my tongue. "I wanted to show you something. I've been wanting to show you for a while, actually, but I was being kind of selfish."

"Selfish about what?"

Pulling my phone from my back pocket, I open to my pictures and scroll until I find Leta Townsend's diary entries. "This."

He takes the phone from me with his left hand while crunching on a piece of cone. He studies the picture, and his chewing slows. "Mack," he says, "are these real?"

I nod.

"Where did you find these? This is . . . this is my . . ."

"Great-great-great-grandmother," I finish for him. "Leta Townsend."

"She's talking about Captain Churchill like—like she knows him. Like she's—"

"Like she's in love with him?" I almost choke on the words.

"Where did you take these pictures?"

I shove another piece of fudge into my mouth like that's going to stop Finn from asking me any more questions. "I took them at the Whaler's Watch Inn. While I was there trying to write the poem for the statue dedication."

"Why didn't you show me earlier?" He swipes through each picture, pausing to read as much as he can make out from Leta's scribbles and the poor quality of my photography.

"Because I was being selfish. I thought they were going to be my ticket to winning, like somehow Leta's words were going to reveal something worthwhile in my poems, but now . . ."

"Now what?"

I sigh. "Caleb Abernathy is entering the contest, too. And he already goes to Winslow College, and they're the ones hosting the event. It just feels natural that he would win. I mean, I found the diary in his writing room! He's probably read it, too."

"You were in Caleb's room?" Finn asks, the hand holding my phone sinking with his expression.

My mouth begins working without anything coming out. "It

wasn't exactly his room. It's the one he uses to get work done at the inn."

"And her diary's in there?"

"On a shelf," I say. "At the far end of the room."

"But that doesn't make sense." Finn looks away, staring down Commercial Street where a musician plays a fast-paced song on his guitar. Ryan claps along to the performance, and Chloe taps to the beat. "Leta Townsend never lived at the Whaler's Watch Inn. It was a house that belonged to the Pearce family for decades before they sold it to the people who turned it into the inn. It hasn't been lived in by a family since the seventeen hundreds."

I shrug. "I don't know what to tell you," I say, happy that we're off the subject of me being in Caleb's room. It's like I cheated on Finn, I realize. Only that can't be the issue. I'm not dating Finn. He's never even asked me out.

"You found these, Mack. You write your poem. I won't say anything to Aunt Becky if you don't want me to."

I take a deep breath. "I don't know what I want," I tell him.

He nods. Taking a step forward, he begins weaving his way through crowded Commercial Street, looking back over his shoulder once to make sure I'm following. He reaches his hand out for mine. I stare at it for a moment, contemplating what I should do.

"Well, I know I can't tell you what to want," he says. "But it seems kind of ridiculous to ignore the fact that you could be with someone who doesn't make out with random girls at parties."

My mouth trembles with the words that I'm holding back, things I'd like to say to Finn, but I feel silly even thinking them. Like how I've held on to this belief that he wasn't the kind of person I should ever be involved with, that it would be impossible to have feelings for him, and how I'd hate myself if I did. But I press my lips together and fight them off. I extend my hand, our fingertips brushing briefly.

"Someone who can't stop thinking of you. Not since he saw you on the first day of sophomore year."

"Finn," I say quietly.

"You guys!" Ryan shouts from the opposite side of the street. "You guys! He has a monkey." He points to the musician, and then steps aside to reveal a little monkey in suspenders. "And he dances!" Even Chloe is laughing. Ryan says something to her, and she laughs so hard, I can practically hear her snort. She shoves him in the shoulder.

Finn looks down at his feet and laughs, like he's relieved. "A dancing monkey?" he repeats. "We can't top that."

"Nope," I agree and slip my hand into his, guiding him across the street, safe in the warmth of his grip.

CHAPTER FIFTEEN

Leta

1862

Mother planted black-eyed Susans all along the garden path that leads out to the main road. She said they were striking, with their yellow petals and deep, dark center. I pluck a few of them, hoping Elijah will think the same.

The flowers wilt in the summer heat, dipping over my clenched hand, a flimsy apology for what happened at the ball. A paltry reason not to run away to war.

They're in a sorry state by the time the lighthouse comes into view.

When I was little and still in school, I was determined to be known as the smartest student. I knew that I was cleverer than even the oldest boy in my class, and I think Elijah knew, too. When I was thirteen, and geography was the subject I struggled with most, I found the answers to an upcoming test, and before

I could even think through the consequences, I snatched them off the teacher's desk and stuffed them into my bag.

On the day of the test, I lingered too long near the coats, trying to memorize the answers. Our teacher asked me what it was I was transfixed by, and I didn't know what to say. It was too late. She grabbed the answers from my hand and headed for the ruler on her desk.

But Elijah took a step forward. He told her he was the one who had stolen the answers and that I had warned him not to, but he didn't listen.

The teacher punished him with a thwack of the ruler across the palm of his hand and a failing grade on the geography test. When I later asked him why he would take the punishment for me, he replied, "Because you're more important than any grade I'll get."

My lips tremble even now at the memory.

The path to the lighthouse curves around and up the hill, and when I reach the top, I breathe in the sight: the Atlantic Ocean for as far as the eye can see. Nothing is on the horizon except a sloop, probably on its way to Boston, and endless possibilities.

"Come to see me off?" Elijah calls to me. He stands at the door to the lighthouse keeper's residence, shoving a few more shirts into his rucksack. Cinching the bag tightly, he throws it in a pile near the steps.

"I thought you were leaving tomorrow?" I say.

"Plans changed."

"You didn't tell me."

He pauses, regarding me with curiosity. "I never see you."

My mouth is frozen.

"It doesn't matter," he says, his back to me as he lifts his bag. "What's one day, after all?"

"It matters to me," I say, circling so that I'm standing in front of him. "I thought we'd have more time together before you left so that we could talk things over. What about a proper goodbye?"

"Leta," he says, shaking his head. His sandy hair falls into his eyes. "I'm sorry."

"You don't have to go!" I say, tears suddenly choking me. I want to hold on to him, to anchor him to the ground. "Please. You don't have to."

Elijah's face softens, and he reaches out his hand for mine. "I have to go now. I made a promise."

I sniff and swipe the tears from my cheeks, my hand releasing its grip of the flowers. "It was a stupid promise."

"I think it's best," he says, dropping my hand. "Maybe for all of us."

He begins walking down the hill, and I follow him.

"What do you mean?" I ask.

Elijah sighs. "I mean, there's a war going on, Leta. And

maybe I should send all of my effort and energy in that direction instead of staying here, where . . ." He looks far off to the Atlantic. "Where maybe there isn't a place for me anymore."

"Don't say that." I grab his hand again. "That's ridiculous, and you sound like one of the Crawford girls. You're talking nonsense. You've lived in Highland your whole life! There will always be a place here for you."

He stares down at his feet. "What about you?"

I pause, shrinking back. "What do you mean?"

"Is there a place for me with you, Leta? Or am I to always be your reliable friend?"

"Elijah, I . . ."

But my hesitation doesn't stop him, it only seems to bolster his words. "I'm asking if you love me, Leta. Can you promise me that you'll be here for me if I return?"

"Stop it," I say. "Don't say 'if.'"

"Because I've loved you since you first came running through the tall grass when we were seven, asking me to save that crab from the clutches of the seagull in the surf. Do you remember that?"

I smile despite the return of my blinding tears. "Of course I do," I manage to murmur.

"I love everything about you. Your face, and your heart, and your humor, and your poetry. There is nothing about you that I don't love, even your flaws." There's an openness about Elijah that I love. An honesty in his green eyes that mirror the waves below the cliff.

"Elijah, please don't do this."

But he grabs my hand. "I have to, Leta. I would like to stay, really I would." His breathing is heavy, and his head tilts a little. "Tell me that when I return, you'll marry me."

If I tell him how I truly feel, I'll be sending him to war with a broken heart, so I formulate the words in my head that will save him—the words that will buoy him and relieve him. *Of course I'll marry you. I was waiting for you to ask me. When you return, we'll set a date. I want to be your wife.*

"Elijah, I . . ." I swallow and close my eyes. *Say them, Leta. Say the words.*

He waits.

"I can't tell you that."

His shoulders slump.

"Tell him what?"

Behind Elijah, Benjamin Churchill hauls a net and two spears over his shoulder, then drops them between us.

"Nothing," I say quickly, swiping my cheek angrily, but it takes a moment to realize why. I'm angry at myself for hurting Elijah, and I'm angry at Elijah for putting me in this position, and I'm angry at Ben for existing at all because if he didn't, I would have said yes.

The tears won't stop now.

I would have said yes a month ago. I would have said yes if Captain Churchill were actually dead, if he never existed outside the confines of my imagination. Because now it's all changed. Now I cannot see the world except through his eyes.

"Best of luck, Elijah," Ben says, clapping his cousin on the shoulder. "Show those graybacks what the Yanks are made of."

"Yes," says Elijah.

"And don't worry about a thing here," Ben continues, squatting to rearrange his belongings. "I'll take care of your lighthouse. I'll keep safe what you love." He pulls on a rope, pre-occupied with his task.

On my tiptoes, I reach up to kiss Elijah's cheek. He takes in a sharp breath and squeezes my hand.

"I'll write to you," I promise him.

"Don't waste your words on me," he says with a half-smile. He adjusts his bag over his shoulder and heads down the road.

I watch until he disappears—until that tiny speck of him no longer exists.

"What did he say to you?" Ben asks.

"It's none of your business."

"All right," he replies. "Walk you back home?"

"Yes," I say, crossing my arms over my torso and traveling the gravel path back to town.

We're silent for a long while, and the weight of it is oppressive. I search for something to say to make me forget about

Elijah, to make me think only about Ben. "What's that in your hands?" I finally ask him.

"My harpoons."

"Let me see," I say, reaching for one.

"Careful."

"I promise not to impale myself," I say, holding the harpoon before me and examining the metal tip. It's sharp and certain. "Captain Churchill?"

"Ben," he says.

"Ben," I continue. "Are these your initials inscribed into the tip of the harpoon?"

He grunts, but when I glance over at him, he nods.

"What's the point of having your initials on a harpoon tip? Something that's going to be embedded into the back of some poor whale that you'll soon reduce to oil?" We trail down a steep hill until we're back on the main road of Highland. There's a view of the bay from here, and several neighbors stop and greet us.

"You don't catch every whale you chase," Ben finally says. "Harpoons are something to take with me. Something to leave behind."

"I don't understand."

He turns to me, rather sharply and with mild agitation. "I'm the youngest whaling captain there is. Maybe that ever was. And I've had to prove myself time after time, day after day. If I find a whale, and it happens to escape me, then another captain will capture it, and what will he find?"

I think of a whale. I see the mother and calf off the shores of Truro. Teddy and I had been on a walk, and we found them by accident, only a few hundred yards from shore. They were huge, much larger than the blackfish. The mother skimmed the surface with her huge mouth, and her baby frolicked in the waves beside her. I can still see them now, clear as the shaft of sunlight that slices across Ben's face.

But that's what I found in a whale. I don't know what a whaling captain would find.

"My harpoon tip," he says bluntly.

A little less poetic than what I was thinking, but at least I understand what he implies.

"Mine." He stops in front of me, pointing into his own chest. "With my initials on it. And they'll know they weren't the first. They'll know I existed. They'll know that whale has carried me with it this entire time, and they'll speak of me."

He waits for me to say something, but every thought I have is unspeakable.

"What does it matter?" I ask quietly so that no one passing can hear me. I want to understand. I want him to feel like I'm someone with whom he can confide his thoughts.

He tilts his head to the side in confusion. "What does it matter?" he repeats, almost as if he's surprised by my lack of comprehension, as if he expected more of me. "What do your poems matter?"

"You know that's different," I say. "You know that a poem isn't the same as slaying an animal for profit."

"It's hard to explain," he says, still several steps ahead of me.

"But I'm willing to try to understand," I press.

"I've never had to explain it to just anyone."

It pricks my heart in a particularly sensitive area. I almost stumble over my own feet at his use of the term "just anyone." I don't want to be his "just anyone."

"Captain Churchill," I try again.

Still he walks ahead.

"Ben!"

He pauses and turns back to me.

"I'm afraid I misrepresented myself the other day with the poem I showed you. Maybe you could accompany me home and I could show you another?"

He looks at his harpoon and nods. "Yes, I'll join you."

I lead him down the road and through the garden gate where he pauses among the black-eyed Susans, his face dappled by the sunlight through the oak leaves. He leans the harpoons against the great tree trunk, touches the bark, and lets his hand linger there. My resident fox observes him for a moment before darting back into the woods, but Ben doesn't acknowledge him.

We slip through the back door and into the kitchen. In the parlor, Mother hosts several women for tea, but they are likely to be too preoccupied with local news, the comings and goings of their neighbors, to notice my leading Captain Churchill into the garret.

Upstairs, I open a window to let in some fresh air, and Ben finds a seat on the bench.

"The other day, when you asked to read a poem," I begin, leaning up against my desk, "I showed you one that didn't really matter to me."

"Why is that?" he asks.

"Because I was afraid of exposing some part of myself to you."

"You don't have to hold yourself back from me, Leta."

I nod, grappling with what I'm about to do. "Then I'd like to show you this one." I pull a sheet of paper from the desk drawer and hold it out to him.

Lifting himself from the seat, he crosses the room, taking the page from my hand, and reads it silently.

"I wrote it after Teddy and I saw two whales off the shore one morning. A mother and her young."

His eyebrows furrow, and he doesn't say anything.

I want him to see that I know whales, too—that I can see them as he does.

Two Right Whales in April

In the spring, they must have lingered
Beneath the murky, ink black sea
While ships did sail over dip and swell
Without heeding to their plea.

For every whale must travel far
In search of sustenance, companion, or peace,
And their journey is never ending
Unless the bloodshed soon shall cease.

Ben flips the page, his eyes scanning the words, moving quickly line to line. That is, until he gets to the bottom. I anxiously wait for his reaction, anything to let me know that he feels the same way, that he's seen himself in my words.

"Leta," he says, finally looking me in the eyes. "Why have you signed this poem with my name?"

CHAPTER SIXTEEN

MICHAELA

present day

M ellie!" I call from the top of the stairs.

She's in the living room, constructing an elaborate maze of opened books, and she's driving her ponies through its snaking corridors. She has a voice for each horse, and this last one is frantic, begging not to be forced to enter the Maze of Doom.

"Mellie!" I try again.

"What?" she asks, and under her breath I can still hear the cries of the last pony: "Please, no! Not the Maze of Doom. Take my carrots, anything but this! Ahhhhhhh."

"Melody Louise, look me in the face."

She does and blinks several times.

Standing at the balcony, I place my hands on my hips authoritatively. "Did you touch my journal?"

"Nope."

"Did you touch my messenger bag?"

"Double nope."

"Are you lying?"

"I never lie!" she cries, offended.

I arch an eyebrow.

"I tell fun stories to make real life more interesting." The last pony gallops through one of the book walls triumphantly. "But I wouldn't lie about touching your stuff."

I huff. I wish she had touched my stuff, because then at least that would explain why my journal isn't where it usually is. I had the heart of the poem. It was in Leta's voice, and it addressed Benjamin Churchill, and it was the start of something. I used the diary entries that I had on my phone, and I even filched a line from Benjamin Churchill's letter from the Maritime Museum, the one that Finn showed me that was addressed to "my love," because I know it was Leta. And now it's gone.

"Mellie, go and get your camp shirt on. I'll drive you."

"Okay," she replies, poking the line of books with a quiet little "Boop!" They topple over like dominoes.

"And clean up your mess."

"Ugh, you sound like Mom."

"Thank you."

When we're in the Durango, Mellie makes me shuffle through all the preset stations, making a disgusted face when we come across her father's preference of nineties grunge rock. "Is this even music?" she asks.

I stop the car in front of the weathered cedar shake building at the nature camp. "Last stop; everybody out."

"Thanks for the ride, Mack," says Mellie, unbuckling herself, grabbing her little cinch-tie nature camp bag, and closing the door of the Durango. She waves wildly at me until she spots one of her friends, then runs off.

I pull out of the parking lot and head back to the center of town. I figure I can start at The Good Bean; maybe I left my journal there. But that can't be. I had it when I was on the bench near the bay with Caleb. Propping my phone in the cup holder, I click Chloe's name and put the phone on speaker. No such luck. She probably has a rehearsal or something. I move on to Finn.

Just when it sounds as if his phone is going to ring forever, he answers.

"Finn," I say. "What are you doing right now?"

I can tell by the sound of the wind blowing into the phone's microphone that he's outside. "Just got to the field. I'm about to warm up. Why, what's happening?"

"I lost something, and I wanted your help finding it, but it's okay. I'm headed over to the bay, on the opposite side of Beach Plum."

"No, it's cool. I have some spare time. I'll meet you there."

I park at the bottom of the hill on Main Street, behind the

coffee shop, even though there are signs that specifically warn me that parking spots are for patrons only. If I find my journal, I'll buy myself a celebratory iced coffee.

When I get to the dunes, I catch Finn jogging over in his practice uniform. "What's up?" he calls to me. "What'd you lose?"

"My poem," I reply.

His expression instantly drops. "The one for . . . ?"

"That one."

"Well," he says. "At least it wasn't an earring in the sand."

We travel together to the bench where I sat the other night, trying to collect my words, shuffle them, make sense of them. There's nothing left here. It's been days, and there have been storms and wind, and people who might have tossed my journal in the trash.

"Anything?" Finn asks.

"Nothing," I reply, flopping onto the bench and sighing.

He stands in front of me, his features darkened by the corona of the sun behind him, just like that late afternoon I came here and he was collecting oysters. "When were you even out here?" he asks.

"That night we went to your aunt's lecture in Provincetown," I reply, staring out into the bay. "I should have just stayed at the coffee shop, but then Caleb said it might be nice to write by the water, and—"

"Caleb?" says Finn.

I straighten, realizing what Finn probably thinks. "Yeah, he was writing his poem for the contest, too, so we . . ." I trail off before I can finish.

Finn nods, taking a step backward.

"Where are you going?" I ask.

He nods toward the baseball field. "I have practice," he says quietly. "Coach gets mad if we're late, and I don't think there's anything I can do here to help you."

"Finn, wait." I launch from the bench and trail him, but his legs are longer than mine, and he's set off at a determined pace. "It's not what you think."

He shakes his head and smiles a little sadly. "I don't think anything, don't worry."

"No, you do, I can tell. Caleb just showed up. I didn't invite him."

"But you sat with him, and you worked on poetry together. You couldn't even show me what you were writing when I asked to see, but he shows up and everything's different?"

"I didn't—"

"Is it because I'm not as sophisticated as he is? Because I'm not some elitist faux intellectual prick who gets passed-out drunk at parties in Chatham and makes out with other girls?"

"Finn, I never said that."

"No, I'm just the guy you call when the other one doesn't work out."

My mouth drops.

"Here's what gets me, Mack," he says, pausing in the middle of Beach Plum Lane and turning on me so abruptly that I skid to a stop. "I like you. I have *always* liked you. And not the pretend you—not the person people think they know, or the girl you wish you were, the girl you want to be for Caleb. I like the *real* you. Always have." Finn waits as a Volkswagen curves out and around, passing us slowly, before he continues his trek across the road, cutting through the park and jogging onto the baseball field.

Behind me, a pickup truck honks to alert me to its presence, and I trot off the street, back to the bench on the bay, just like I did the night I saw Finn play baseball.

I pick up my things and wander back to the parking lot where the Durango waits for me. When I get in the driver's seat, I slouch down, cover my face, and start to cry because I broke something with Finn, and I can't remember the words. I can remember bits and pieces, but they're not fitting together like they did when I first wrote it. The only line that sticks with me is the one from Churchill's letter. The hot, crowded air of the truck is suffocating me, and I can't think clearly, so I blast the AC, trying to collect myself.

Pulling out of the parking lot, I slowly cruise down Main Street, passing the baseball field and craning my neck to see Finn. He's pitching to Aidan.

Once I cross Route 6, I know where I need to go. My poem might be lost, but at least I know where I can find the material to help me write a new one. I'm fresh out of Leta Townsend's diary entries, and her words only live at the Whaler's Watch. When it rises from behind the hill of wildflowers, I breathe a sigh of relief.

It's near lunchtime, and people are starting to mill around, admiring the old portraits hanging from the walls. I try to keep out of the way, to wait until Brittany appears instead of setting off and looking for her. In my little downstairs office that over-looks the inlet, I search the shelves of books. But there are just a lot of classics, a lot of tomes on transcendentalism, on nature, on wildflowers of the Outer Cape, and on whales that migrate to our shores each year.

"Hey!"

I turn to see Brittany standing in the doorway, clutching a clipboard to her chest.

"I didn't know you were coming today." She pauses when she gets a good look at me. "Is everything okay?"

I shrug. "Things have been better. I lost the poem I was writing."

"Write another one, then," Brittany suggests. She looks so relaxed in her wide-legged gray pants and silky white T-shirt. In contrast, I'm a mess of nerves and conflicting thoughts.

"It's not that easy," I say, collapsing into the desk chair near the window. "Sometimes it takes a while to really get into the swing of the poem, you know?"

She nods but is just being polite. "Well, look for something to inspire you here," she suggests. "Whatever you find, you're welcome to use. Go exploring. Just don't bother the guests." She pivots out of my office and resumes her place at the hostess station.

I cross my right leg over my left, bobbing my foot up and down and seriously considering what Brittany just said. *Whatever I find. Go exploring.* I leave the office, crossing the hall and then one of the smaller dining rooms until I come to the staircase in the center of the Whaler's Watch. Before I can even take a step up, Caleb greets me.

"Careful there," he says when I almost lose my balance. He cups my elbow for support, but I jerk my arm away. Caleb is the last person I want to be near right now.

"I'm fine, thanks," I tell him.

He nods, grabbing a jacket off a hook near the door, then shoves his hands through the sleeves.

"Are you leaving?" I ask.

"About to run some errands for Brittany's mom. Need anything while I'm out?"

I shake my head. If he's leaving, then I'll have access to his writing room—to Leta's diary. Maybe it's still on the shelf where I left it. I can take more pictures, read the rest of her entries. My fingers tap the wooden bannister with anticipation.

"You writing here today?" Caleb asks.

"I might," I reply.

"How's the poem coming along?"

I shrug, not wanting to give away my all-consuming panic and anxiety. "Pretty well."

"Good, good." He nods. "I'm done with mine."

This causes me to pause. "You're done?"

"Yeah." Caleb grabs for the handle of the door.

"But the other day you hardly had anything written. You had writer's block."

Now it's his turn to shrug. "I did. Now I'm over it. I just sent my poem to my professor a minute ago." He glances up the staircase, like he can see his email taking flight above our heads.

I try to force my mouth into a smile, but it's hard to pretend to be happy for someone who just completed exactly what you set out to do. "That's great," I say. "I'm happy for you."

"Bye." He waves and disappears out the door. I watch out the window as he travels down the sidewalk lined with vibrant flowers to the parking lot and ducks into his car.

His writing room draws my attention. Brittany said I could go explore as long as I didn't disturb any guests, and there aren't any guests staying in Caleb's room. I take one step, still testing my resolve. If I could only snap more pictures of the diary, of the entries I've already read and maybe a few new ones, I could probably write the poem again. I take another step. It's not as if Caleb would ever know I was there. Two steps this time. Above me, a couple bickers quietly with one another, and when they get to the staircase, they clam up immediately upon seeing me. I smile to make it seem like it's totally natural for me to be there, then I hurry my pace. I'm only two steps away from the main hall of the second floor. I can see the door leading to the curving staircase, and almost as though Leta Townsend herself is beckoning me, I lose all sense of hesitation and follow her words to Caleb's room.

It's just like it was when I was last up here: twinkle lights hanging from the windows, Caleb's messy desk across the room, the muted rush of the waves crashing along the shoreline. I approach the bookshelves and breathe a sigh of relief when I find the diary among the misplaced and discarded books on his shelf.

Placing it gently upon his desk, I open to page after page, taking pictures and making sure I don't damage the contents. Once I've snapped every page, I close the cover, accidently tapping Caleb's mouse with my knuckle. His computer screen wakes up, and I know I should turn away, that his emails and writing are private, but I can't. I'm so consumed by the fact that he's already done with this poem and that I have to start over, that my hand finds the mouse and scrolls through the open windows. If I can find what he wrote, maybe I'd know what I'm up against. Maybe I'm making it so much bigger in my head than it even is.

A file on his desktop is labeled "Highland Whaler submission," and I hover the arrow over it before clicking.

I stare at my own words glaring at me on the screen. I shake the feeling of inadequacy and the sudden trembling from my body.

"You piece of shit," I mutter. "You complete piece of shit."

Anger simmers inside me, my brain unable to think clearly and my hands useless; my cheeks burning even though there's no one here to witness my embarrassment. The complete and total embarrassment of ever having found this guy attractive, of ever having thought we had even a strand of similarity, or that he was more interesting or more worthwhile than Finn. I hate myself for that last part the most.

I pivot toward the bookshelves, anxiously searching for what I know must be there, and my fingers find it instantly. My journal, discarded with the other books. He must have stolen it that night at the bay, when I left the bench to go see Finn's baseball game. I wrench it from its resting place then turn back to the desk.

I stare at Leta Townsend's diary—at Finn's great-great-great-grandmother's diary. A small token that might help his Aunt Becky, that will explain who Captain Churchill means in his letter and that will unveil the actual writer of the poems. Without another thought, I grab it along with my own journal, and I leave. I take the stairs two by two, and when I'm safely in my office over the inlet, I stash my belongings into my messenger bag.

"You find anything good?" Brittany asks as I pass her on the way out.

"A few things. We'll see how they work. Thanks for letting me explore."

She smiles. "Of course. I can't wait to see what you write."

I wave as I leave and head home.

CHAPTER SEVENTEEN

Leta

Summer 1862

Caroline and I walk arm in arm down the hill to where the other picnic-goers gather.

"Then what did you say?" Caroline asks.

I adjust the picnic basket I'm carrying so that it isn't crushing my forearm and sigh in a most melancholy and dramatic manner. "I said nothing. I stood there, my mouth working like a fish out of water, and I couldn't even explain myself! I didn't give him any good reason for having used his name on my poetry."

"What did he do?"

A breeze pulls at the loose tendrils of my hair, even though Caroline tried her best to secure it with a pretty braid crown. "He said, 'Excuse me, Miss Townsend, I've overstayed my welcome,' and left."

Caroline stops in front of me. "I want you to know that your poem about the right whales is my favorite," she says.

I blink.

"Every time I read it, it takes me to the beach in the spring. I'm standing, watching as the whales skim the surface of the water. And I feel blessed by their presence."

"Thank you," I say quietly, tucking a loose strand of hair behind my ear. Caroline has never spoken with me about my poetry like this—never claimed a poem as her favorite or told me why it moved her. We continue our journey toward the church in silence.

We have a new minister, Reverend Cartwright. His wife is quite lovely, and they have two daughters and a son who are close to my age. Today, the entire congregation is attending a picnic to get to know the family better. Caroline and I are bringing salads; I chose cucumber salad, and she chose potato salad. When we get to a pleasant little spot under a huge oak tree, the breeze weaving through the leaves, the branches hushing back and forth above our heads, we spread our blanket, and then deposit our contributions on the long wooden table the reverend has brought out from the manse.

"Good afternoon, Mrs. Chilton, Miss Townsend," says Reverend Cartwright when he sees us. "Your salads look delightful."

"Thank you, Reverend," says Caroline.

When I return to our blanket, Susannah and her husband sit with Teddy, their plates already full of delicious treats.

"Aren't you going to eat something?" Susannah asks,

studying me. She's so like Mother, it's often disarming. "There are lots of things to try. You don't want to offend anyone."

I watch as Caroline fills her plate, and my stomach grumbles ever so slightly, but the thought of eating something doesn't sound at all appetizing. I scrutinize the crowd, hoping to find Ben somewhere among the familiar faces.

When my eyes finally fall upon him, he's huddled with a group of young men and a few younger boys, his coat discarded and his sleeves rolled up to his elbows. They're discussing something that looks mildly important if I'm to judge by their expressions.

"What's going on over there?" I ask once Caroline is beside me again.

She nibbles on a chicken leg and observes the group. "It looks like they're going to play a game of baseball."

"I love baseball!" cries Teddy.

Caroline grins. "Well, finish the potato salad I worked so hard to make and ask if you may play."

Susannah shifts uncomfortably on the blanket. "Teddy is significantly younger than even the youngest player over there."

"He'll be fine," I insist. "It's a game, isn't it?"

"I'll be fine, Mother," says Teddy, puffing up his chest. "It's just a game."

I never like admitting that I could be wrong, but once Teddy stands and darts over to the group of boys, I realize just how small he is. He stands up on his tiptoes, trying to be a part of the huddle, then he tries ducking under one very tall boy's arm. I decide that I should go over and appear to be interested in observing the game while keeping a closer eye on my nephew.

"Coming with me, Caroline?"

She looks down at her plate. "Maybe in a minute."

I gather my skirts and find a seat among a few of my friends who are situated near the impending baseball game. They're all whispering to one another about how handsome someone is, probably Captain Churchill, but when I don't engage, my heart too focused on my Teddy, they stop including me in their conversation.

The players take their places on the field, Ben having been elected the pitcher, and he strikes out the first player. He hurls the ball past the batter, who swings eagerly at every pitch. The crowd applauds as they mill about, sampling food and drinking lemonade under the summer sun.

Teddy steps up as the next batter, and even I wince at the sight of it. He can hardly hold the bat upright let alone successfully attempt to swing it at one of Ben's pitches. I clap loudly and cry, "Go, Teddy!"

He glances over his shoulder and waves, then resumes his very serious stance.

Ben takes a deep breath, and I know he'll go easy on Teddy. He must, of course. Teddy's so young, and so small, and so desperate to act like the older boys. Ben pitches just as wickedly as he did for the previous batter. Teddy doesn't even realize that the catcher has caught the ball behind him. He blinks.

"You have to swing, Teddy," Ben calls to him with what I think I perceive to be the tiniest roll of his eyes. "Swing at the ball."

Teddy nods earnestly, lifting the bat and preparing for the next pitch. When it whizzes past him again, he gives it a good swipe, but I'm not entirely certain he's ever swung a bat before.

"Put your back into it!" Ben tries again. With a sigh, he readies himself for what might be his final pitch.

Teddy is determined this time, I can tell by the way he squares his shoulders. He wants to hit the ball, but more important, he wants to prove to Ben that he can. He squints, watching as Ben hurls the last ball toward him, and this time, Teddy swings so hard that the bat goes flying and hits Ben in the shin.

Cursing, Ben grabs his leg, hopping on one foot.

"I'm sorry!" cries Teddy, his hands covering his mouth in shame.

"You're out," Ben finally says, gesturing wildly toward the side of the field. "Out. Off the field. Get out. You're supposed to hit the damn ball."

My nostrils flare at this.

"Could someone come to bat who can actually play the game?" he demands.

I stand slowly. A few of the men laugh, waiting for the next batter, but there are no volunteers. I stride over to the collection of baseball bats, grab one by the handle, and take my place in front of the catcher.

Straightening, Ben's mouth upturns in an amused grin, and when he ventures a look over his shoulder to see if any of his teammates see what he does, he begins to laugh along with them. "Thank you for the entertainment, Miss Townsend," he calls to me. "But really, we're trying to play a game here."

"So am I."

Ben scoffs.

"Throw your best pitch, Captain Churchill. You've only proven you can strike out boys so far."

His teammates roar with laughter. They start to clap.

"Fine," says Ben, his eyes flickering with amusement. "I'm happy to strike you out as well."

I curtsy before him, then raise my bat. At this point, spectators are gathering. Families that were too preoccupied with food and conversation now congregate around the baseball diamond. My hands tremble, but I remind myself I'm doing this for Teddy. I'm proving to him that it's perfectly fine to strike out against such a merciless opponent and to have a good laugh about it later. I'm doing what any good aunt would do.

The first ball Ben sends in my direction zips by me so quickly that there's hardly time for my brain to tell my arms to swing. The sharp call of a strike makes me jump a little. Damn my good intentions. Damn them all the way to hell.

With the second pitch, I swing. I give it a valiant attempt, but I miss entirely.

"It's all right to give up, Miss Townsend," Ben calls once the catcher has thrown the ball back. "No one would blame you."

I breathe deeply. "Throw the ball, Captain Churchill."

He takes his time releasing the ball, and with my eyes closed, I swing the bat.

The crack of wood is so sharp that it splinters in my hand. When I open my eyes, I watch as the ball flies over the heads of every boy on the field.

"Run, Leta!" my father calls from our picnic blanket.

I gather my skirts and make a dash for the plates. Even though the outfielders make a valiant attempt to retrieve my ball, it's gone too far, and I'm already rounding third base when one of them tries to throw the ball back to Ben. Only Ben isn't there. He's waiting for me at home base with the rest of the infield, his hands cupped around his mouth, screaming my name. I slow before I get there, afraid of barreling down the group of boys who jump up and down at my approach. I take a resounding leap into the air and land on home plate, and the entire picnic goes mad when Ben lifts me off my feet and, with the help of one of his teammates, carries me off the field on their shoulders.

When I'm finally back on solid ground, Teddy greets me with a hug and an enthusiastic, "Aunt Leta, you hit a home run!"

"I did!" I cry.

The baseball game dissipates, the players drawn away by the full buffet of food and the shock of the home run by Leta Townsend. I finally feel ready to make a victory plate of delicious lunch for myself when my attention is drawn away from the salads and pickles and cold chicken by the proximity of Benjamin Churchill.

"Well done, Leta," he says quietly, and takes several long gulps of lemonade. "Not many people can hit a home run off me."

"You were being kind," I say, taking a scoop of Caroline's famous potato salad and plopping it onto my plate. "Surely you were going easy on me because I'm a girl."

He arches an eyebrow. "I respect you too much to placate you. I threw my hardest."

"Hm," I muse. "Well, then, I've impressed myself."

Glancing over his shoulder, Ben takes a step toward me, lowering his voice and inclining his head. "After lunch, will you meet me by the old oak tree at the end of town?"

"The one on the way to the ocean?" I ask.

"That one."

I take in my surroundings, hoping that no one has heard his forward proposition. There doesn't seem to be anyone paying attention; they're all engrossed in their own gossip and food.

"I will."

He nods and saunters away, rejoining his friends.

But the thought of our rendezvous haunts me for the rest of the afternoon. Caroline, who has always known me better than I've known myself, attempts to distract me, though she has no idea what she's up against. Teddy regales me with stories of his seashell-hunting adventures, and Fred argues heartily for the Union cause, cursing those damn Confederates any chance he can get.

I think of Elijah.

I wonder what he's doing now. He's been gone for weeks, headed to Georgia. It's not as if I expected any letters from him—why would he bother after the way we parted? But I miss him. I miss going to the lighthouse and finding him there singing sea shanties that should make me blush.

When the sun begins to sink in the western sky, all thoughts of Elijah disappear, and I leave my things on the blanket. The rest of my family is too involved in their own stories to likely notice that I'm gone, and I begin to wander down the hill toward the sea.

The oak tree isn't hard to find. It must be hundreds of years old, reigning over the great glacier rocks that litter the land before the sea claims the sand. Ben leans against its massive trunk, plucking the petals of a black-eyed Susan, hardly even noticing my approach.

When my shadow drifts over him, he looks up and smiles. "You came," he says.

"I did."

He shifts so that now only his right shoulder is propped against the tree's trunk, and he drops the ruined flower to the ground. "We never got a chance to talk about your poetry."

I straighten my shoulders, suddenly defensive. I didn't think he'd even want to discuss my poetry. I was hoping our conversation could revolve around ball games and picnics instead. The wound from my poetry is still too fresh. "We did not."

"I didn't give you a chance to explain why you wrote your poems under my name."

I try to maintain my composure. "I should think that's rather obvious."

"Not to me."

"Well, you never got a chance to explain why you left so abruptly upon discovering this little secret of mine."

"I should think that's rather obvious."

I cannot contain myself. "Not to me!"

"You used my name! You pretended to know the words I would use if I were ever pressed to write such things down. Why, Leta?"

I lower my voice. "Because I thought you were dead, and that I would have free reign over your name. That I could create the man I thought you were, the adventures I thought you might have had, the feelings I thought you could entertain. And once I started, I couldn't stop. Once I started, I was intoxicated by you. I was obsessed."

He abandons his spot by the tree, lessening the space between us. "You weren't intoxicated or obsessed with me. You were intoxicated and obsessed with the man you wanted me to be—the one you created." He reaches out to touch my hand, gently, but then pulls his hand away and takes a deep breath. "That isn't me, Leta," he says, and he almost sounds flustered. "You cannot live the life I have and accommodate that kind of nonsense, that kind of ridiculous, sentimental . . ."

I feel the tears pricking the corners of my eyes.

He reaches out and touches his forefinger to my chin, lifting my face toward his. I draw in a breath. "I want you to be intoxicated and obsessed by me," he says, almost whispering, his mouth so close to mine, I think I can taste him. "But the real me. Not the boy you made up when I was away."

I swallow and pull my chin away from his touch. "And who might he be?"

Ben backs away, touches the trunk of the oak tree behind him, and takes a step toward the sea. "He's the one inviting you down to the beach."

"Now?" I ask.

"Now."

"But it's—"

"Excessively hot and the perfect time of day for a stroll at the water's edge." He holds his hand out to me. "Come with me."

"Fine," I say, my nose in the air. I bypass his hand. "But I need to be home before supper." I trounce down the sandy dirt path to the sea, lifting my skirts above my ankles.

The late heat of the summer afternoon still scalds the scant amount of skin I have exposed. The closeness of the fabric of my dress is exasperating, but I refuse to slow down for Ben to catch up. I venture a glance over my shoulder, and he's plucked another one of the black-eyed Susans, twirling the blossom in his hand.

At the bend in the road, I bear to the right.

"No," says Ben from behind. He's paused in the middle of the fork. "Let's go this way."

"There's no easy access to the shoreline that way," I say.

"I know." He nods in the direction of the narrowing path that leads to the cliffs.

I follow him, and now that he's the one leading the way, I feel slightly panicked, a little desperate. "What beach are you taking me to?"

"The one I found the other day on a walk," he says. "If you want to know the real Captain Benjamin Churchill, then you'd let him take you somewhere." He pauses, both in sentence and in pace. "If you trust him."

"I do," I say.

We trail through the tall grass, past beach plums and through the crowberry until we get to the edge of the cliff that overlooks the great Atlantic, stretching outward before us. Ben spins the flower between his thumb and forefinger once more, then it drops from his hand.

"Over there," he says, pointing to a narrow path that clings to the cliff and down to the beach. "I'll go first."

I follow him, my hands outstretched so that if I lose my balance, they'll find his shoulders as support, but he already anticipates my lack of coordination; maybe he can even sense my fear against the steepness of the cliff.

"I have you," he says, turning so that he scales the path with his back to the sandy cliff face, his right hand reaching for mine.

"I'm fine," I reply quietly, but I cling to his arm, my knuckles turning white.

"I have you," he says again, quietly. "We're almost there."

When we reach the packed sand below, the tide, now so far out, is attempting a return, slowly, so that you can never really tell if it's moving at all.

"Well?" I say as Ben paces ahead of me. "Here we are. What is it you wanted me to see?"

He removes his boots, pulls his socks from his feet, and begins unbuttoning his vest.

"Ben?" I say again.

He discards the vest in the sand and pulls his shirt off over his head.

"Captain Churchill," I say, snapping my gaze away from his bare skin. "What if someone sees you without your shirt?"

He chuckles. "Why do you think I brought you here?"

I venture a peek at him, and my heart begins to race. His back and shoulders are covered in lines of black tattoos, in stretching, cascading designs, some of them solid and thick and others scattered in tiny, persistent dots.

"What have you done to yourself?" I ask in awe of the artistry.

"Come here," he says. "We're going swimming."

"No, I'm not dressed for swimming." I motion to my layers of skirts.

"So I'll help you out of your dress."

"Are you mad?" I turn back to climb the path, but the height of it stops me in my tracks.

"No one will see you," he promises. "That's why we walked so far. After all, I've already bared myself to you." He gestures to his bare chest.

"It's not the same, and you know it."

Laughing, he steps casually into the lapping waves. Farther out past the breakers, the land stretches in a hook, and lazy seals bask in the sunlight, barking and calling to one another.

"Come on," he says, beckoning me to him.

I lean over and pull my shoes from my feet. If I go slowly, maybe I can convince myself that this is nothing. These are shoes and stockings. Bare feet are acceptable. No one would question that. But he must want more. I know it must be something more, otherwise he wouldn't have brought me here.

Ben emerges from the ankle-deep surf and reaches out a hand to assist me.

"No," I say, pulling back.

He looks away. "I'm sorry."

Gathering my skirts, I step hesitantly into the ankle-deep waves. The water is icy cold, and I breathe out in relief. Suddenly the sun doesn't seem so hot. The water quenches my parched skin. I want more.

I cast him a cautious glance. "Help me," I say quietly, stepping back out of the water, reaching my hand over my shoulder and pointing to the line of buttons down my back.

Silently, he approaches me, coming out of the water, and with certainty, he unlatches each button. My dress falls from my body and into the dry sand, and my arms immediately cross over my torso in accustomed modesty. Ben reaches out, gently pulling my arms away and holding on to my hand.

"Step out of your skirts," he says.

I do as he says without question until I'm stripped down to my chemise, corset, and drawers. Goosebumps form against my flesh despite the sweltering heat.

"Now," he says, turning back to the waves. "Come in with me."

"We didn't bring anything to dry ourselves," I point out.

He points up. "We have the sun."

I swallow and take another step into the waves. They swirl about my knees, kicking up sand against my thighs. Several yards in front of me, Ben studies a wave, takes a few steps, then dives below the white foam. When he emerges, he grins and calls for me to join him.

"It's cold!" I shout to him.

"It's perfect." He dips below another wave, and when he resurfaces, two gray seals ease past him, poking their heads up out of the water. He salutes them, and they swim deeper into the Atlantic.

"Why are we doing this?" I ask as we meet one another.

"Why wouldn't we?" He turns and stares at the horizon. "Do you feel that, Leta?"

I look around us. "Feel what?"

"The current," he says. "Do you feel it pulling at you? Close your eyes. Lift your arms. Float. Can you feel it?"

I close my eyes and allow my arms to float at the surface of the water. I lift my feet, surrendering myself to the tide.

"There was never a place on land that was for me the way the sea is," he says. "You can never stay in one place too long on the sea, and I think that's what I love. On land, you're stuck. You inevitably stay in one place too long. And the more time you give a place, the more of yourself you give, the more of a chance you give that place to turn on you."

My hands float on the surface of the waves, and when I open my eyes, I see him watching me. He reaches out his hand, and the tips of our fingers brush against one another. His arm now raised, I can see the side of his solid torso, and running the length of it, the tattoo of a massive sperm whale swims toward his feet.

I can't stop staring at it.

"You hunt these whales," I say slowly. "You tell me I assign them sentimental emotion, and yet you decorate your body with their image."

"They're like a church," he says. "Like God, like purpose. I search the ends of the earth for them, and half the time, they're swimming right beside my ship, like ghosts. When I was a little boy, at night, when I was tucked into the hull of the ship, trying to conjure sleep, I was always certain they were there. Only a wall of wood separating us and their songs weaving through the blackness of my own thoughts."

"And you said you weren't a poet."

"In my own way, I suppose I am," he says, and he cuts the water between us. "Or maybe your presence brings out my eloquence."

He touches my arm, and in response, I reach out and caress his torso, tracing the lines of the whale.

Lifting my chin, he runs his mouth against mine, breathing softly against my lips. And we stand in the waves, body to body, soul to soul, fighting the current that threatens to pull us apart.

CHAPTER EIGHTEEN

Leta

1862

I t's Tuesday morning and the ladies' sewing circle is gathered in our parlor. My mother sits to my right; Caroline, to my left; and we all bear the circumstances silently, sewing and listening to Mrs. Budd rattle on about her niece's engagement.

"I told my sister," Mrs. Budd continues, staring determinedly down at the handkerchief she's creating. "You know what I said? I said, 'If your daughter doesn't marry soon, she'll end up an old maid as certain as Sunday's the seventh day.'"

The other women nod. So does Mother. But Caroline leans back and pinches the sensitive part of my upper arm, and I try to stifle my grin.

"I know, Leta," Mrs. Budd turns on me. I suppose I wasn't that prudent in my merriment. "I know you laugh now. Today, when you're young, and pretty, and have a pleasant figure and a passable personality. But just you wait. If you keep to your independent ways, no decent man will have you."

"Passable," I say with a chuckle.

"Oh, please, Mildred," says Mother, followed by a condescending laugh. "Don't you know that Leta expects a proposal from Captain Churchill any day now?"

The room falls silent.

"Mother," I whisper.

"He's been calling upon her almost every day this week, hasn't he?" She turns not to me but to Caroline to confirm this, and it's infuriating.

"Is that so, Leta?" Mrs. Budd seems startled. "A whaling captain? You know what my grandmother always said about sailors, don't you?"

"I don't, but I'm sure I can venture a guess," I mutter.

"She said they're not to be relied upon! Now you might say that your father is a good man, and indeed he is, but he is the exception, not the rule."

"How fortunate for all of us," I say, yanking my thread through the needlepoint, "that Father was the captain of a packet sloop."

"Indeed. Quite fortunate. And now there's Captain Churchill. He's young, and he's handsome, and you mark my words, he hasn't had his fill of seeing the world yet or of making his fortune. What do you think he'll do at every port he lands in?"

I drop my needlepoint and raise my eyes to Mrs. Budd's. "Find a warm bed and a hot meal, I would imagine," I say slowly. "Because surely you're not impugning a young man's good character."

She clucks her tongue and settles back to her threadwork.

I smile assuredly, feeling more determined than ever to finish my needlepoint.

"Captain Churchill is renovating the old Pearce house," says Caroline, coming to my defense, as always. "We're certain he intends to move there permanently."

"How nice," says Mrs. Budd, refusing to look either of us in the eye.

"He's there now, in fact," Mother chimes in. "The boy never tires. It has such lovely views of the inlet, doesn't it?"

Teddy's swift flight is a sudden blur out the window. He sails up the garden path, clutching a few letters in his hands. The kitchen door slams open, and he appears in the parlor doorway, panting and brimming with excitement.

"Here's the mail, Grandmother," he says, dropping the pile of letters on the side table. Quietly, he leans in to me and says, "There's one especially for Captain Churchill, Aunt Leta." Then he whispers, "From *Boston*."

My hands freeze, and my eyes focus on his. Instinctively, I reach out and snatch the letters, my needlepoint dropping from my lap and onto the floor as I cross the room. At the window, the sunlight illuminates the words. No one seems to notice or care, and the babble of their everyday conversations ebbs and flows while I tear open the letter from my publisher.

"Do you know that he chased that fox out of the chicken house and down into the center of town?" someone says.

Dear Captain Churchill,

"I'm certain he did! I saw it with my own two eyes!"

Recently, I made a special trip to Highland to meet our popular writer of poems.

"No," I say quietly.

When I came to your address and asked a lady in the garden if Captain Churchill was at home, I was directed to a house near the inlet. I met him there. He confirmed that he was, indeed, the famed whaling captain. He looked as a captain ought to, though younger than I had anticipated.

He did, however, inform me that he has never written any poems, never collected royalties for any poems, and does not intend to in the future.

Considering this information, I am no longer confident of your identity. I do not feel comfortable continuing our business relationship, as you have portrayed yourself as someone you most certainly are not.

"You bastard," I mutter.

Until we are able to meet in person so that I may match a face with a name, consider our contract terminated.

Sincerely,
Maxwell T. Jacobs

I crumple the letter, my chest heaving, as I watch Teddy escape out the kitchen door. On the opposite side of the window glass, he weaves through the tall grass toward the bay.

"It's true," Mother says from behind me. "Susannah prefers either Leta or Caroline to watch Teddy while she and her husband are at the general store, but I think spending some time there might do him some good—to strengthen the poor child."

I blink, trying to ignore the tears brimming my eyes.

"Well," Caroline offers, "at least he has Captain Churchill. They can spend the afternoon watching the blackfish."

I turn. "What did you say?"

"The blackfish," says Caroline, cutting her thread with her teeth. She glances up at me. "Teddy said that Captain Churchill has spotted some blackfish, and that Teddy should join him presently."

I'm frozen for a moment, wondering why Ben would ever call Teddy to watch blackfish. His words from our first dinner burn in my ears. *Blackfish. They have the finest oil, which is good for watches. Mr. Nye would pay a pretty penny for it.*

"No!" I cry, sprinting to the kitchen and out the back door.

"Leta!" I hear Mother call after me, but no threat of reprimand will stop me.

I lift my skirts far above my booted feet, and I race down to the bay. The scrape of the yellow seagrass can't hinder me, and the rush of the wind in my ears only encourages me. I know that Benjamin Churchill doesn't watch for blackfish. Watching is passive, and Benjamin Churchill must control. He doesn't wait and observe; he doesn't sit by when there's a profit to be made. He doesn't consider the presence of others, even small boys.

But he sounds the rallying cry, alerting all able-bodied men and boys in Highland to make their way to the shore, armed with lances and harpoons. Because there is no sentimentality in Benjamin Churchill's heart. There is no empathy to spare Teddy's more delicate feelings. Sometimes I'm able to convince myself that there is, that the Benjamin Churchill I created in my head and on the page is one and the same with reality. But I know, when I crest this hill, the sight that will greet me.

Beyond the slope of the late summer grass, Teddy stands among throngs of men and boys who dash along the shoreline, calling and whooping to one another. Out on the bay, boats and small-masted ships move closer, and before them, a group of blackfish slice through the waves, a conglomeration of their sleek black bodies, foam, and spray, the puffs of their anxious breath. The men on the boats shout and clang pots and pans to frighten them and corral them into the shallow water. They're desperate to escape but too disoriented to flee. On the shore, a tall man holds a long knife, rubbing the wooden handle of it against the roots of his white beard. A glint of sunlight bounces off the metal blade.

"Teddy!" I scream.

He turns, his small chest heaving with strained breath. "What are they doing?" he calls to me. "Aunt Leta, why don't they turn around? Why don't they go back out to sea?"

I sprint toward him, sweat dripping down my back, and I grab Teddy's small hand. "Teddy, please, come with me. Let's go home. Your mother will worry."

But he yanks his hand from my grasp and dashes to the sand. "Go back!" he screams at the whales. "Go back home! They'll kill you!"

I chase him over the dune. "Teddy, don't go any closer!"

The men begin to wade into the shallows, readying their tools as the first line of blackfish beach themselves. There is no mercy. Waves of red claw the shore, and the once calm bay boils with the blood of whistling whales.

I gather Teddy to me, lifting him from the ground with some difficulty, and he sobs into my shoulder. The fabric of my dress soaks with tears, but I keep hushing him, running my hand down the back of his head.

"It's all right," I assure him. "I'm taking you home."

When I peek over my shoulder, Ben jumps from one of the boats, knee deep in the crimson water, and he watches me retreat up the dunes.

———

In the morning, Annie helps me dress in my pale blue skirt and favorite white blouse. She brushes my hair and then neatly weaves two braids on either side of my head, pulling them back and securing them at my neck. I am collected and professional and ready to head into town in order to mail my letter to my editor in Boston.

"Mother," I call once I'm at the back door in the kitchen. "I'm heading into town. Do you need anything?"

"No, dear," she replies from the front room.

I gather the other letters I'll be sending along with my own and head out into the open air, almost slamming Ben's face with the door in the process.

"Good morning, Miss Townsend," he says, taking a step back and removing his hat.

"Captain Churchill," I reply, my nose in the air as I pass him.

This, however, does not deter him. "Such a frosty greeting. Might I inquire as to what I have done to deserve this?"

"I think you know."

I pass the rows of hydrangeas and travel down the main road into town, Ben easily keeping pace with me.

"I don't."

In the middle of the road, I turn on him, in awe.

"I could have forgotten the way you treated Teddy at the baseball game. The way you couldn't even lob him an easy pitch. Instead, you chose to embarrass him in front of almost the entire town and then yell at him."

"He wanted to play with us," says Ben with a shrug. "If he wanted to play with the older boys and men, then surely he appreciated being treated like one. Life isn't going to go easy on Teddy. Why should he get used to a coddled existence?"

"He's eight!" I cry.

"But he won't be forever."

I keep walking, letters clutched in my gloved hand. "But it was the whales," I continue. "You invited him down to see black-fish. Did you even tell him that he'd be witness to a slaughter?"

"Pods that size don't often swim by, Leta," Ben explains. "I wasn't going to miss that kind of opportunity just to spare the boy's feelings. Besides, if I didn't call the hunt, someone else would have."

"You could have sent him away."

"He was following me around all morning," says Ben, his arms spread wide. "Chattering away while I tried to do repairs on the old Pearce house. I thought you'd be happy that I included him. I thought you'd be happy that I was trying to bolster the boy instead of treating him like a baby."

"I do *not* treat him like a baby."

Ben stares at me, and when he finally speaks, his voice is quiet: "Sometimes you do."

"You'll excuse me, Captain Churchill," I say, shouldering past him. "I have errands to run in town."

I hear him huff behind me. "Everything I have done since returning to Highland has been for you."

I slow my pace, but I won't stop, still clinging to my anger. "Everything?" I ask, hardly able to contain my disbelief.

He trots to catch up, centering himself in my path. "Everything," he insists. "I went to a ball for you. I learned how to dance. I hurt my cousin—"

"You don't care if you hurt Elijah."

He nods and gives a small shrug. "I do, a little. But that's not the point."

"What, then, is the point, Ben?"

"The point is, I care about you, I—"

I wait.

"I care for you," he tries again, quietly.

I swallow the welling in my chest, control the impulse to cry because those weren't the words I wanted him to say. "If you care for me," I say, "then why didn't you tell my editor that I'm the one who wrote the poems?"

"What would you have had me say, Leta? If you're not ready to tell your editor, then who am I to make that decision for you?"

"You should have told *me*, at the very least."

He nods. "I should have. But maybe . . ." He stops himself.

"Maybe what?"

Shaking his head, he replies, "Never mind."

"Tell me," I say, reaching out and touching his arm.

His eyes lift from the ground between us to meet mine. "Maybe there was some small part of me that hoped it would end. The poetry."

My words fail me. "You don't like my poetry."

"No," he says, "it isn't that. I suppose I hoped that now that you had me, that I was real flesh and blood, that you wouldn't need to pretend to be me." He straightens his shoulders. "To pretend to occupy the innermost recesses of my thoughts."

"Because you don't let anyone into your thoughts," I say bitterly, continuing my walk down the road. Over my shoulder, I toss, "Even girls you care about?"

He takes my wrist, pulling me against him, his face so close to mine. His thumb traces circles on the palm of my hand and his eyes flick over my features only to settle on my mouth. "Because my thoughts aren't a place any of your poems have ever dared to dwell. Everyone has a corner of their heart they keep tucked away, Leta. Even you."

I open my mouth to speak, but I'm not sure how to fill this silence.

"You have my word," Ben finally says, "that I will never keep something from you again."

I nod.

"Do you believe me?"

I nod again.

He lowers his lips to mine and kisses me softly, briefly. "Good."

"Is there anything else you'd like to say to me?" I ask, hoping that this tender moment between us will spur him to admit the entirety of his feelings for me, so that those gossiping geese at sewing circle might finally be silenced, so that I know he means exactly what I think he means when he looks at me this way.

He shakes his head. "No."

I retract my hand from his and take a step back. "I must go into town," I say, turning from him.

"Leta," he says softly.

But he's too late. I've folded back that crumpled corner of my heart.

CHAPTER NINETEEN
MICHAELA

present day

The Highland Whalers played an afternoon game against Brewster today, and now that the crowds have thinned, and the evening approaches, the team is huddled around their coach on the pitcher's mound, listening to his words of inspiration and maybe his constructive critiques.

I sit in the Durango, watching this from one of the parking spots that line the field, hoping that I'll find the courage to catch Finn before he leaves for home. It wasn't something I had been planning all day, which is probably a good thing. If I spent all day thinking about this, worrying about this, I'd have a hole in my stomach. It wasn't until I gave Chloe a ride to play practice and saw the game going on that I thought this might be a good idea. Maybe.

When the huddle starts to disperse, I tentatively open the car door, place a flip-flopped foot on the pavement, and stand up tall so that he can't miss me. He grabs his bat bag off the first base line and heads toward Ryan's Toyota.

"Finn!" I call, raising my hand.

He and Ryan slow as they get to their car, and Finn opens the passenger door.

"Come here," I say, waving him over.

"What?" he asks, but he doesn't move.

"Get in the car."

"I think she's abducting you, man," says Ryan.

"Shut up, Ryan," we both say at the same time.

Hesitantly, Finn paces over to the Durango, placing his hand on the hood and staring at me. "What's up, Mack?"

"Come with me."

He glances over his shoulder back at Ryan, who starts the Toyota and blasts his music. He and Russ have remarkably similar taste.

"I told the guys I'd go with them to the Shellfish Shanty for something to eat."

"Please?" I say quietly.

With one more glance over his shoulder, he motions for Ryan to roll down his window. "I'm going with Mack."

"Ryan?" I ask before the window is rolled back up. "Can you pick up Chloe from play practice for me?"

"Oh, hells yes, I can." Ryan rolls up the window and backs out of his spot.

"She's going to kill you," says Finn, watching Ryan speed down Main Street until he gets to the playhouse.

"Worth it," I say, ducking into the Durango and hitting the start button.

Beside me, Finn throws his bat bag into the back and then clicks on his seat belt. He leans back in the passenger seat as I pull out of the parking lot and begins scrolling through Russ's preset radio stations.

"Is it okay if I . . . ?" Finn asks, whipping out his phone and wiggling it in front of him.

"Sure."

He plugs it in, his playlists coming up on the screen, and he finds one—quiet acoustic music. "Where are we going?"

"You'll see," I say.

We sit at a stop sign, waiting for our turn to make a right, the click of the blinker resonating between us as I turn onto Route 6.

He's not talking to me like he usually does. Our easy conversations are nowhere to be found. I think for a moment about where to begin, but then I automatically start to speak. "When I was little, I wrote all the time. Poems and songs and stupid stories. My mom would tell me that I was definitely my father's daughter."

Finn is quiet, but I can see he's listening.

"My dad was an English professor. He commuted off Cape

238

three days a week to teach what he loved. Mom says he used to read me stories. I don't remember, though, so I just have to believe her."

Finn shifts in his seat, resting his elbow against the window. "Do you mind if I ask how he died?"

"In a car accident. It was an icy morning in January, and a tractor trailer slid off Route 6 right before the Sagamore Bridge. Dad's car hit a tree."

"I'm sorry," says Finn.

"Thank you." I swallow, trying my best to avoid getting choked up. That's not the point of this ride, after all. "Even if I didn't have any memories of him, I had my words, and I wrote everything, and I shared everything. My second-grade teacher actually had a specific time dedicated for me after recess every Friday so that I could read to the class."

Finn chuckles at this.

"It's true," I say, slowing down and putting my left blinker on.

"Is this even a road?" Finn asks, leaning forward to get a better look at the sandy trail we're about to drive down.

"Trust me," I tell him. "I was pretty much used to it just being me and my mom, facing the world together, but I didn't mind when she said she was going to marry Russ. He was nice enough. When they told me they were going to have a baby, and I was getting a little sister, I almost peed myself with excitement."

"Mellie's pretty awesome."

I nod, slowing down as we go over the bumps and gullies in the packed dirt road. "When we had her christening party, and all of Russ's family came, I was so happy they were coming to our house. It felt like Russ came from a *real* family, with aunts and uncles and cousins. It had been me and Mom for so long that I didn't know what to expect. I thought, *Let me write a poem for my new baby sister. This way, I can give her something, and I can show my new family what a good writer I am. Then maybe they'll be as excited to have me in their family as I am to have them.*"

The dunes surrounding us feel like a barren desert with sparse grass and scraggly scrub pine dotting its landscape.

"The day of the christening came, and our house was packed with people, including all my new cousins. I had my poem ready and my new fancy dress on, but I had honestly never felt more invisible. Everyone was enamored with Mellie, of course, and Russ's nieces and nephews, including Ryan, all played with each other, and I guess I can't really blame them. They were used to each other and they didn't know me yet. Plus, Ryan informed them that I was boring and made them listen to stories after recess for too long."

"Typical Ryan."

"Some things never change," I agree. "But I kept trying to find a moment to read my poem and ended up in the kitchen, reading my poem to myself, trying to muster up some courage. And when I poked my head back into the living room, I saw

Mom holding Mellie and Russ standing beside her, and Russ's brother trying to get a picture. My mom said they should go and find me so that I could be in the picture, too."

Finn takes a deep breath.

"And Russ said, 'Let's get one with just *our* family.'"

Rubbing his eyebrow with his thumb, Finn is quiet for a moment. Then he says, "That really fucking sucks."

"It does," I say. "I honestly don't know what happened after that because I walked outside to my swing set in a kind of daze, and that's where Ryan proceeded to rip my poem from my hands and read it out loud to his cousins."

The road widens, and there are outlines of what should be parking spots amid the tall seagrass. I pull into one and put the car in park.

"I'm pretty sure that's when I stopped sharing my poetry. Not in school, of course. Teachers could always be trusted. But it was when I stopped sharing it with people close to me. What I thought was going to cement my place in my new family only made me feel like a freak."

"I'm sorry that I got so pissed the other night," Finn says in a rush. "If you don't want me to read your poem, I get it. I was just jealous."

"Of Caleb?" I say.

"Yes," he replies, looking out his window, unable to meet my eyes.

"I didn't let Caleb read my poem, either."

There's a pause. "Oh."

Opening the car door, I hop out, pulling the legs of my shorts down a little and adjusting the straps of my tank top. "Will you come with me?" I ask, nodding toward the path over the dunes. "Down to the water?"

"Yeah," Finn agrees, climbing out of his side and circling around the back of the truck. He unties his sneakers and takes off his socks, tossing everything in the backseat.

He follows me up the path and over the dunes, adhering to the worn tire tracks left by pickup trucks that people parked at the top. Sometimes families camped up here. Sometimes couples parked there at night to make out. But today, in the late afternoon, we're the only ones around. When the deep navy of the sea appears as we crest the dunes, I kick off my flip-flops, the hot sand scalding the bottoms of my feet.

"Come on," I say, making a dash to the water. The sand grows damp and cold, and soon the chilled water of the North Atlantic nips at my ankles in relief.

"Why'd you bring me here?" Finn asks, bending down to yank his baseball pants up to his knees. When he stands, he shades his eyes with his hand, trying to see more clearly into the water. There's a hook of sand that arcs out into the sea, protecting this little cove where we face one another.

I take a deep breath and reach into the back pocket of my

shorts, extracting a folded piece of notebook paper, soft and flimsy from the multiple times I've opened it and reread it. I hold it up to Finn.

"What's that?" he asks.

Staring at the paper, I take a shaky breath, trying to focus on the words and not the fact that Finn is standing right in front of me, both of us ankle deep in the Atlantic.

"Mack, you don't have to—"

"Yes, I do," I tell him. "Because if I can't read it in front of you, then I can't read it in front of anyone, and you deserve this."

He's quiet, nodding.

"Okay," I say. I bend my knees and straighten my shoulders. "Here we go."

"You've got this," says Finn.

"Maybe don't say anything? No offense. It just makes me more nervous."

He zips his lips, turns the lock, and flicks the imaginary key into the ocean.

"You know what? I'm just going to turn and face the water. You can hear me, right?"

"I can."

"Good." My hands want to tremble, but I grip the paper more tightly. I start to read.

Every tale born from the sea
begins with once upon a time,
the sad ones and the joyful,
the despondent, the sublime.

But this one begs to differ,
Starts with a boy tossed to the sea
And the burden of his story
Has been taken up by me.

What once was just a name,
A distant memory at best,
Now has life and motion,
A beating heart within a chest.

They say he traveled half the globe,
Chased whales over swell and wave.
But no one ever caught him
From his cradle to his grave.

But I'm the one who held him
In one place for a short while
And I'm the one who brought him back
When others' efforts proved futile.

Years to come, when they speak of him,
All talk of me will not be heard
They ache to love a broken boy,
Not the girl whose love he spurred.

Perhaps my heart was not enough or
the weight left him weak and hollow
And it sank him dark and deeper
to a place I could not follow.

I cannot call him back here
For it's a bright and boundless sea,
A sea full of crushing anguish
To blind him to his love for me.

For a little while, it's just the screech of seagulls above us and the trickle of the waves as the sea calls them back over the pebbles and shells that litter the shoreline. I turn to Finn to see his reaction, but he's stoic.

"I tried to figure out what mattered about the Highland Whaler," I say in explanation. "Why he should matter to us, or why there should be a statue of him in the park. And I realized that who really mattered was Leta."

Finn nods and begins unbuttoning his shirt.

"Um," I say as a wave rolls up behind me and knocks the back of my knees. "What are you doing?"

He balls up his jersey and tosses it onto the dry sand. "What does it look like?"

"Stripping," I reply. "It looks like stripping."

"I'm going for a swim." He bends down and takes off his pants until he's just wearing his boxer briefs, and my blush crawls up my neck and occupies my cheeks. "Come in with me."

"But I don't have anything dry to change into."

"So what?" Finn begins wading into the deeper water, and soon it's up around his waist. He's all solid muscle, the pale outline of his uniform, his tan arms and neck, his short black hair, and when he turns to me, he squints one eye. "Come on—come in with me."

I traipse back onto the sand before I join him, folding up my poem and tucking it safely into one of his pockets. I'm not going to lose it again. When I turn back to the ocean, Finn has disappeared under a wave only to pop up again, raking the water from his head and waving me in. "Let's go!" he calls.

"It's really cold, Finn." I reach up over my head and pull off my tank top, then wade into the water in my bra and shorts.

"Toughen up. You're a born Cape Codder. This ocean's practically in your veins."

"It's warmer in there," I mumble.

He reaches out for me, grabbing my hand and rushing me the rest of the way. "There we go," he says when we face one another, the water at our stomachs and sometimes higher when a wave rushes in. "It's like ripping off a Band-Aid."

I gently splash him, and he spits the water out in an arching stream. Then his eyes settle on me, watching me. He presses his lips together.

"What?" I ask quietly, suddenly feeling bashful.

"Thank you for reading that to me," he says.

"You're welcome." I turn to look over my shoulder and up at Highland Light.

"No, don't look away," he says, grabbing my hand. "Please don't look away. Look at me."

I do as he asks, but it's almost painful. Just as painful as it would have been for him to watch me when I read my poem.

"It meant a lot to me, and I know it wasn't easy."

"It's easier to share things with you than it is with most people," I say with a laugh.

"That's what I want," he says. Then, "If that's what you want."

"Since sophomore year?"

He grins, slapping the water with the palm of his hand.

"You never even talked to me sophomore year!" I say with playful accusation.

"That's because you never talked to me."

"That's because you hung out with Ryan. Guilty by association." I pause and keep thinking. "And because it felt cliché to like you. Every other girl in our grade had a crush on you, and I didn't feel like becoming just a name on a long list of admirers."

"You were never just a name," Finn says quietly, looking down as if he can see his feet below the surface of the water.

I float closer to him, the current pushing us together, and I lift almost weightlessly as a wave rolls past. "Well, you're more than just a fastball," I say, hardly any space between us now. His eyes drift over me and his fingertips caress my jawline, the sea dripping in rivulets from his hand, down my neck, across my collarbone.

"I'd like to kiss you now," he murmurs.

"I'd like you to kiss me."

"I was hoping you'd say that," he says, then his mouth is warm against mine, warm in contrast to the cold water. The kiss makes me dizzy, makes me aware of every inch of my body. His free hand inches down my back and presses my hips against his. Reaching up, I wrap one arm over his shoulders and my opposite hand rests against his pounding heart. I kiss him harder, kiss him so he knows I mean it. When we both finally need a breath, he rests his forehead against mine, his chest rising and falling.

"I have something for you in the truck," I say, but then kiss him again because his mouth is so close. When we part, I start to head back in toward the shore.

"I don't really want to go to the truck." He holds on to my hand and stretches my arm all the way back to him. "Stay in the water and play."

"You'll like this, though."

"But I *really* like this."

I turn back and arch an eyebrow.

"Fine. You ruin all the fun, Mack."

We traipse back to the Durango, Finn buttoning his jersey

as we go and me wringing out my wet hair. In the trunk, I find a discarded beach blanket and drape it over the driver's seat before climbing in. My teeth chatter despite my best effort to keep them still.

"Hey," says Finn, running his hands up and down my arms. "Here, I have a hoodie in my bag."

He turns in his seat and grabs his sweatshirt. It's big and gray and has Highland Whalers in burgundy letters across the chest. Pulling it over my head, I ease out of my wet bra underneath and toss it on the backseat.

"You can keep it," he says. "Maybe wear it to one of the playoff games in the fall when it gets cold at night." Then he scratches the back of his head. "You know, if that's what . . ." He clears his throat. "If that's what this is."

I want to burst out laughing. The most handsome, most athletic, most sought-after boy in school needs reassurance. From me. "If that's what *what* is?" I ask.

He smiles, his eyes darting away from me then back again. "This," he says, motioning between us. "What we just . . . I dunno." He crosses his arms over his chest and sighs.

"I'm teasing!" I say, reaching out and pulling his face toward mine. I kiss him again. "I'm teasing."

"I can't tell," he says. "I'm bad with sarcasm, obviously." He intertwines his fingers with mine and leans back in his seat. "So, what do you have for me?"

I lean over his lap and open the glovebox, retrieving my gift for him. I don't even feel bad about it. "This," I say, handing him Leta Townsend's leather diary tied neatly with a faded, tattered ribbon.

"What's this?" he asks, pulling the loose knot free and opening the pages. He reads for a little bit then his mouth falls open. "Mack, is this . . . ?"

"Yes, and it's complete with entries all about how in love with Benjamin Churchill Leta was."

"Did you take it from the Whaler's Watch?"

"With permission," I reply, but now I feel a little guilty about it. Like I stole something for Finn. "Sort of."

"Mack, this doesn't feel right."

"Well, it should!" I feel myself explode. "Caleb stole my fucking poem and submitted it as his own, so I should at least be able to take the diary that rightfully belongs in your aunt's museum. Leta is your relative; these are her words, her poems. They belong to you."

"But won't Caleb know?" he asks. "If you took this from the Whaler's Watch, and he's been researching all of this, too, then won't he know the diary is missing?"

I shift uneasily in the driver's seat, pushing down on the brake and hitting the button to start. "His sister told me to use whatever I found."

"Where did you find this?"

"In the room on the third floor where he does his writing."

Finn sighs. "Mack, you know what he's going to think."

"I don't care what he thinks."

Finn closes the diary and turns his attention to a fly stuck on the inside of the car. He watches as it fumbles and hits the glass, then he presses the button, rolling the window down. The fly takes a moment to recognize its freedom then zips away. "You should submit your poem and take what's yours, Mack."

I scoff. "If we both used the same material, how am I supposed to prove that it's mine?"

Finn reaches into the pocket of his jersey and withdraws my folded poem, opening it carefully, as if it's just as precious as one of Leta's entries. "Not all the same material," he says, and he points to the final stanza. *"For it's a bright and boundless sea,"* he reads. "That's from Churchill's letter."

I stare at the words.

"The letter that's in the Maritime Museum."

CHAPTER TWENTY

Leta

1862

That was amazing!" Teddy cries. He grips my hand as we leave the train station and stream through the crowded streets of Boston.

This is a world away from Cape Cod, and Teddy has never been in a city before. I want him to ask me where the seagulls are, or the sea breeze, the clean scent of pine and sea carried across the dunes. I want him to miss Highland as much as I do, to validate how lost I feel here. But he doesn't. He's too enthralled with this new place to remember why he loved the old so much.

"Don't dart anywhere, Teddy," Caroline tells him. She adjusts her hat and straightens her shoulders while we wait for a horse and carriage to pass. "This isn't like Highland. We don't know our way around, and we don't want to lose you."

"I promise, Aunt Caroline."

"Good boy."

I stare at the map in my hands, trying to decipher street names that are lost in the paper's crease. "I think," I begin, then squint ahead of me, as if that will help me see more clearly. "I think we need to head up Dorchester."

"You lead the way," says Caroline.

I falter a bit. I'm not used to leading the way. I usually have Father around, or one of my older sisters, or Elijah to help me.

My heart winces at the sudden thought of him, and before my mind gets carried away with ludicrous notions of cannon fire and gunshot wounds, I bury his image.

"Leta, wait," says Caroline. "Isn't this the place?"

I pause and look above me to find a rather innocuous building, but the sign hanging from the door, creaking in the wind reads JACOBS & SONS PUBLISHING.

"Yes."

"You goose," says Caroline with a snicker. "You practically walked right by it! You're off in the clouds."

I felt so sure about this encounter this morning. I picked out my green dress with the black trimming and matching hat, and I looked so smart, even Mother commented on my appearance. But now I'm a child playing dress up.

Caroline comes to my side, snaking her hand around my waist. "What will you say?" she asks quietly.

I swallow hard. "I'll say what I need to."

Gathering my skirts, I climb the stairs and enter the building.

The curtains are drawn, and inside the air is stagnant and reeks of over-cologned men. There's one sitting at a desk, his spectacled eyes focused on the papers before him. He hardly glances up when he hears the bells jingle as I open the door, and when he does, he casually returns his attention to the business before him.

"Excuse me," I say.

"Yes?"

"I'm here to see Mr. Jacobs."

The man clears his throat, removing his glasses and cleaning them with a cloth from inside his breast pocket. "Is he expecting you this morning?"

"Not quite," I say. "You see, I—"

"You wrote a story? Something you'd like him to consider?"

"Not exactly. I—"

"Mr. Jacobs does not consider unsolicited work, so unless he specifically asked for something, he'll not make the time for you. Thank you, good day."

My nostrils flare, and I straighten my shoulders. "I know for a fact that he'll want to see me."

The man snorts in amusement. "Do you? And how might you know that?"

I offer him a knowing smile. "Because I'm Captain Benjamin Churchill."

He drops his glasses.

"Boston was *amazing*, Mother," says Teddy when Susannah comes to pick him up in the evening. He's exhausted from our trip, and he slept the entire train ride back, his thumb close to his lips, but never actually in his mouth, because he's too old for that now.

"Was it?" Susannah asks. She bends to kiss the top of his head. "You can tell me all about it before bed."

"I wouldn't quite say amazing," I admit, standing at the kitchen door. The cool breeze seeps in and carries with it a trace of the sea and the soft clashing of wind chimes. "But it was eye-opening."

"Well, what did you say to Mr. Jacobs?" Susannah asks me, running her hand through Teddy's hair.

I shrug. "I told him what happened—that I was the Captain Churchill who had been writing poetry for the journal and not the man he encountered here. He pressed me for a handwriting sample and asked me several questions only I would know. He was thoroughly convinced."

"What will you do now?"

"He wants me to write the poems in my own name. He told me I never needed to pretend to be a man to get published. My words speak for themselves."

Susannah smiles and takes a deep breath. "They must." She's about to leave but then turns back quickly. "Oh, Leta, I almost forgot. A parcel for Mrs. Charlotte Pearce came today at the general store. Do you think you could deliver it for me? It's the opposite direction of home." She hands me a brown package.

"Of course. I'll go now while there's still sunlight left."

I walk Susannah and Teddy to the end of the garden, and when we part, my nephew waves to me. He turns every so often and waves again. I keep checking back until he all but disappears into the coming dusk.

Mrs. Charlotte Pearce lives only a mile from home, and I don't mind the evening stroll. It gives me a moment to bask in my own accomplishment, to think of all the things I'll say to Benjamin Churchill.

"I don't need any useless proposal from you," I say aloud as I pass a lumbering turtle in the yard. "Today I have proved that I am dependent only upon myself."

A fox scurries across the road ahead of me.

"You, sir," I say, jabbing my finger into the air. "*You* are not a gentleman. Any feelings I may have felt are long gone. Long gone."

When Mrs. Pearce's house comes into view, I curtail my verbal assault on my imagined foe and touch my hair to make sure everything is in place. I knock gently upon the wooden door.

"Oh, Leta!" cries Mrs. Pearce when she sees me.

"Good evening, Mrs. Pearce. I've brought a parcel for you."

I smile broadly, but her eyes well up with tears. "Mrs. Pearce, what's the matter?"

"Come in, child, come in, and look who's here!"

If she's crying over Ben visiting her, I will not be surprised, but I will be abrupt. I won't stay any lengthy amount of time trying to force conversation with him.

And sure enough, when I come to the end of the hall, he's perched on the edge of a rocking chair, his hands folded and dangling between his knees. When he sees me, he stands, and his eyes widen, but he doesn't acknowledge me further.

"Good evening, Captain Churchill," I say, and quickly avert my eyes. I hold out the parcel to Mrs. Pearce. "I only came to drop off this package for you, so I'll be on my—"

But when I round the corner of the room, I breathe in so sharply that I feel like I've dragged a rough knife across my own throat.

"Hello, Leta," Elijah says. He struggles to stand, gripping a cane awkwardly, but when Ben crosses the room to help him, he waves him away. "I'm fine," he mutters then glances at me.

I swallow the urge to cry and force a smile. "Hello, Elijah."

"I'm really fine," he assures me, taking a stilted step in my direction. "Just a shot to the hip, and I probably won't be as fast as I once was."

I nod, covering my mouth with my hand.

Elijah stares for a moment and smiles. "It's good to see you, Leta."

I meet him halfway across the floor and grab his free hand, pressing it against my lips, and my tears fall on his calloused knuckles. I squeeze my eyes shut, but a sob wrenches free from my throat, and before I can stop myself, I throw my arms around his neck and cry into his shoulder.

Behind me, I barely hear Ben say, "I should go home." I'm too caught up in the feeling of Elijah's heart beating through his shirt.

"It's all right," Elijah whispers across my ear. "I'm right here."

CHAPTER TWENTY-ONE

MICHAELA

present day

I s baking considered a craft?" Chloe asks from her folding chair beside me. She crosses one leg over the other and dangles her foot over her knee while taking a sip from her reusable water bottle. We're relaxing under the shade of the Highland Youth Theater tent on the green lawn of the park, surrounded by other local craftspeople trying to sell their wares below the heat of the August sun. There are jewelry makers, women who've sewn baby blankets, a guy who makes cute pet apparel, and even a homemade fudge stand. Somehow, Chloe persuaded me to help her sell tickets to their production of *Much Ado About Nothing*, which opens in less than a week, but it hasn't been all bad.

It's nice to be outside on such a gorgeous day, working for a good cause and getting to hang out with friends. My best friend seems oddly distracted by the antics of the Highland Whalers baseball team across the park, as they attempt to sell baked goods to offset the cost of their playoff trip to Boston at the end of the month. Ryan has become a mix between a carnival barker and a general heckler, but he keeps getting people to come to the stand and buy cupcakes and brownies and pies.

"I guess it's not technically a craft," I reply. "Why, you hungry?"

She shrugs, twirling one of her long braids.

"I'll go over. I told Finn I'd try one of his brownies."

"He made the brownies?" Chloe asks.

I stand. "He made them last night. I had to walk him through it over the phone."

"The directions come on the box."

"He's new to baking. I'm trying to encourage him."

I cross the park, squinting in the sudden brightness of the sun, and when Finn sees me he stands, ready with a little paper plate and a brownie. "Okay, try one," he says. "Tell me how I did."

Beside him, Ryan chuckles. "No one's buying any of Finn's brownies since they saw Coach take a bite and do a sneak spit into his napkin."

"Bite me."

I reach for the plate. "Lemme try. I mean, it's a brownie. How bad can it be?" I take a large bite to show just how solid my support of Finn's baking is, and I immediately regret it.

"Good, right?" he asks, eyebrows raised, watching every painful chew.

I press my lips together and try to swallow. "So, so good," I say between excruciatingly dry and excessively flavorless bites.

"She's lying," says Ryan.

"I can speak for myself," I say. Then, "Can I have a bottle of water?"

Finn collapses in his chair in defeat.

"It's okay," I assure him after a few gulps of my drink. I lean down and kiss his cheek. "It was your first time. You'll get the hang of it."

Ryan doubles over with laughter, and I realize what I just said.

"Ew, Ryan. Don't be gross."

"It was your first time. You'll get the hang of it, Finn." Ryan can't get a hold of himself.

Sorry, I mouth in Finn's direction.

He shrugs. "I'm used to him."

"Chloe wants a baked good, but I'm not sure I'm going to bring her a brownie," I say, hoping to change the subject to something Ryan's more interested in.

Ryan immediately says, "I made something good. Tell her to try this." He hands me a plate of cherry cobbler.

"You made this?"

"Yeah, of course."

I arch an eyebrow. "Your mom made this."

"Tomato, tomahto." He considers this for a moment. "Don't tell Chloe that. I want her to think I'm a gourmet."

"Sure thing." I turn to Finn, who stares out into the park at something or someone, his arms crossed, his eyes narrowing. "You okay?"

"I'm fine," he replies, his attention flicking back to me. I peek over my shoulder, trying to find the source of Finn's glower. Caleb and a few of his friends are making their way from tent to tent, being too loud, laughing and shoving, and making an overall spectacle of themselves.

"You want me to get us tickets for Chloe's play next week?" I ask Finn softly.

Finn still stares beyond me, but replies, "Sure."

"Michaela!"

I cringe at the sound of my name coming from Caleb's mouth. Out of the corner of my eye, Finn stands slowly.

"Don't make a scene," I murmur to him.

"*Me?*" he asks, his hand on his chest. "Make a scene?"

"I know, but I'm asking you right now not to escalate anything."

Before I even realize he's beside me, Caleb slings his arm around my shoulders, his friends flanking on either side of him. "Michaela, fancy meeting you here." He smells faintly of sunblock and alcohol. "What are we raising money for? The poor?

Shelter dogs? The environment?" He blinks a few times. "Ah, sports. Refuge of the weak-minded and intellectually incapable."

"Is he for real?" Ryan asks me.

I shrug out of Caleb's loose embrace. "There's a water stand down that way a little," I say, pointing. "I feel like you need to hydrate."

"I came prepared," Caleb replies, reaching into his back pocket and revealing a little flask. "Want a sip?" He waves it in front of my nose.

"No, thanks," I reply, taking a step back.

"It's good," he says. "I've got plenty."

"She said no," says Finn, edging his way around the table.

"She can speak for herself," says Caleb, trying without much success to bring himself up to Finn's height.

"I know she can." Finn looks down at him, then tilts his baseball cap up farther on his forehead. "She tried. You pushed."

"Guys, let's just get back to work, okay?" I try. "Chloe is waiting for this cobbler over there, and . . ."

Caleb, his eyes still locked with Finn's, comes to my side. "I'll come with you."

"I'm fine, actually," I say. "I'm surprisingly capable of walking across the green and delivering baked goods."

"Here," says Finn. "Let me help." He takes the plate of cobbler from me, but before we can escape, Caleb knocks it out of his grasp.

"Oops," he says, feigning innocence and covering his mouth with his hand. His friends laugh insanely behind him, but it wasn't as funny as their reactions would suggest.

Behind Ryan, Aidan and Matt stand up, and their presence makes me uneasy. They feel like wolves prowling a rival pack. Today was supposed to be about sunshine and fun and crafts, and suddenly it's much darker than that.

"Dude, come on." Finn bends down to scoop up the cobbler with the plate.

"What's your deal?" I ask. "Go drink some water, honestly."

"What's my deal?" Caleb repeats. "Maybe I'm just sort of irritated that every chance you get, you choose to spend time with *him* instead of me. I don't get it, Michaela. I honestly don't get it."

"You don't get to be irritated with me," I tell him, but my knees are feeling weak and my stomach is churning with every word.

"I can be whatever I want," he says. "Just obviously not physical enough to catch your eye. Maybe I need to grunt and throw a ball around to make you pay attention. Hit things with a big wooden bat. Like that's not evidence of deeper issues lurking beneath this guy's subconscious." He thumbs in Finn's direction.

I can feel myself bristling. "Stop it."

"You really need to go," says Finn.

Caleb lifts his nose. "I can stay. It's a public event."

"You're shit-faced."

"Fuck off." He shoves Finn in the shoulders. Not hard. Not enough to hurt. Just enough to set Finn slightly off-balance. More of his teammates stand now.

"Caleb, stop. This is ridiculous."

"Come on," says Caleb, shoving Finn again. This time it's Caleb who wavers with the force of his effort.

"Let it go," says Matt behind Finn, only I'm not sure if he's warning Finn or Caleb.

Finn is gentle, I think. Finn is thoughtful and kind. I look up, trying to interpret his face, but he's stoic and unreadable. "Come on," he says softly to me.

Before we can escape, Caleb calls after us, "Good, go. Take your little slut with you."

That's when Finn pivots, teeth clenched, and grabs Caleb by his shirt, slamming him against the shingled wall of the windmill. Two cedar shakes fall from its frame like chipped teeth from some broken mouth.

"Don't talk about her that way," says Finn, then he releases Caleb's shirt and turns back to me.

But this has the opposite effect on Caleb. It doesn't frighten him, it doesn't pacify him, and it doesn't make him back off. His chest heaves three times and he charges at Finn, the two of them collapsing to the ground. Only Caleb is too drunk to realize that

Finn's got the advantage, in size and in territory. Once Caleb has him down, he only gets one hit in before Finn flips him on his back, punching him solidly in the face. Letting out an excruciating wail, blood spurting from his nose, Caleb moans pathetically. Finn backs off, standing slowly, his teammates surrounding him and hovering over Caleb, who curls in on himself like a dying beetle. His friends try to help him to his feet, but he's too busy sobbing.

And it happens quickly, too quickly for me to process. There's a crowd that's formed, people yelling at the baseball players, calling for Finn's coach. Finn's teammates try to tell his side of it, but it looks worse than it is. It looks like Finn started it. It looks like Finn finished it. His coach is beet red, flustered and angry, spit flying from his mouth with every word he barks at Finn. He says a lot of things, but mostly, "This isn't how a Highland Whaler acts. This isn't how he acts when he's out in the community. Gather your stuff and go home. I'll deal with you later."

Finn nods silently, easing past Caleb, who is sitting on a chair surrounded by old ladies who are trying to get his nose to stop bleeding.

"Finn," I say, scampering after him. "Are you okay?"

He stalks toward where his car is parked on the side road, his tongue darting out to check his swollen, split lip. He winces as fresh blood trickles down his chin. "I'm fine," he says quietly. "I have to go home."

"Let me come, let me drive," I implore, scooting in his path, trying to stop him, but he eases by me.

"It's okay, Mack. I really need to be alone right now, though. I can drive."

"You're upset."

He pauses as he opens the driver's side door, his chin to his chest. "Yeah, I'm upset." He ducks inside, starts the engine, and pulls away.

Chloe jogs up behind me, her hands on her hips as we watch Finn's car disappear down the hill. "Shit. I just wanted a brownie."

———

Finn doesn't text me all day, so right before bed, I decide that maybe I should be the one to text first. But I don't know what to say. I don't want to bring up the fight if he doesn't want to talk about it or if he feels like it was my fault.

I decide to text, **Good night.**

I watch the screen expectantly, waiting for the dots to show up to let me know he's typing. After a minute, they do. Then they disappear. Another few minutes pass, and they pop up again, this time for a while. And then disappear. I huff.

Finally, he replies. **Night.**

I toss my phone onto the pillow beside me and roll onto my back, staring up at the lazy whirl of my ceiling fan. I'm not going to sleep now, obviously. I want to do something productive, something to relieve my anxiety, and while writing a poem is the first idea that comes to mind, it isn't going to work tonight. Rolling out of bed, I throw on a pair of shorts and trot down the stairs, through the living room, and into the kitchen.

The pantry, as always, is fully stocked, and it doesn't take me long to find the huge Tupperware containers where Mom keeps the flour and sugar, a brand-new tin of cocoa powder, chocolate chips, and even an unopened package of Double Stuf Oreos. This is basically gold in my house.

I organize my ingredients and measuring cups on the counter, set the oven to 375 degrees Fahrenheit, and get to work. Finn might not be able to make edible brownies, but I sure as hell can.

Mom says that cooking for someone shows that you care— that you want to take care of them. Mom said when she and Dad were in college, she used to make him cookies when he had to stay up late and study for exams.

I start to mix the batter, adding the dry ingredients to the eggs and sugar in the bowl, and suddenly Russ comes in through the back door. Behind him, the night is dark and unsteady, a jagged rain falling from the sky, a wailing wind carrying in a storm. He lifts his hat, a Highland Whalers baseball cap, from his head and hangs it on a peg by the door.

"Are you baking?" he asks, checking the clock. "At almost eleven o'clock at night?"

Without looking up from my bowl, I reply, "I'm stress baking."

"I see." He makes his way to the counter and eyes the package of Oreos. "Do you need this whole thing?"

I shake my head. "I need sixteen of them."

"Good." He opens the wrapper and grabs two for himself, then leans against the counter and watches as I pour the batter into a greased baking dish. "Wanna talk about it?"

I stare at him incredulously. "You want to talk about it with me?"

Russ shrugs. "Sure."

It takes me a minute to identify the unsettling feeling that's rising inside. As I scrape the excess batter out of the bowl with the spatula, I realize that I actually wouldn't mind talking to Russ right now. That it's kind of nice to have him standing here, interested in what's bothering me. Maybe it would be helpful to unburden myself to a willing ear. I start placing the Oreos in rows throughout the batter, then push them down until they're covered.

"I'm okay," I hear myself say, turning away and attempting to appear preoccupied with cleaning up splattered batter. If I told him the whole story, I'd have to talk about how guilty I feel, how much I actually care about Finn, and Russ and I have never discussed those things. "I don't think you can help." I open the oven door and slide the tray inside.

Nodding, Russ takes another Oreo and makes his way through the living room and up the staircase.

I sigh. Maybe it's a little too much to open up to Russ about this. Not yet, especially when I'm not even sure if Finn is mad at me or at his coach's reprimand. I just hope he'll see these brownies as the perfect peace offering.

———

Finn doesn't text me in the morning, and I convince myself that this is fine. I can simply show up at his house, brownies arranged in an aesthetically pleasing manner and sprinkled with powdered sugar, and hand deliver them while wearing my favorite jeans and white T-shirt.

By lunchtime, though, when I pull into the Pearces' drive-way, I'm overcome with apprehension. His mom's car is parked out front, and if Finn doesn't want to see me, if he rejects me, then I'd really prefer no one witness that. But I'm here now. Time to get it over with.

I only knock once before Finn's mom opens the door, and she smiles kind of sadly at me.

"Hey, Mrs. Pearce," I say, holding up my Tupperware con-tainer. "I brought Finn some brownies."

"Come in, sweetie," she says. She's dressed in workout

clothes, one earbud in and the other in her hand. "I was just about to go for a run, but I think Finn will be happy for some company." Then, quieter, "He hasn't left his room all morning."

I look at the clock above the mantle of the fireplace. It's 12:36 in the afternoon. Finn likes to get up before eight, do his morning run, and go to the batting cages with Ryan most mornings.

I don't want Mrs. Pearce to think that I'm the person who got her son in trouble. So I begin cautiously. "Did Finn tell you . . . ?"

Mrs. Pearce nods. "He did. I'm sorry that happened to you. Finn was really upset."

"Oh."

"Go upstairs and see him," she says, glancing up the steps. "There's also some cold milk in the fridge to go with those brownies when you're ready." With one more smile, she jogs out the front door.

Hesitantly, I put my foot on the first step, craning my neck to check for any signs of life, but the second floor is silent. By the time I get to the top, I poke my head into each of the three rooms and finally find Finn in the last one, curled up on his bed and facing the far window, still in what I think must be his pajamas—joggers and a Highland Whaler T-shirt.

I step through the door, the jamb creaking under my weight. "Finn?"

He shifts on his bed, and I wonder if he's asleep. Then he manages a "Hey."

"Are you okay?" I deposit my container of brownies on his desk under a poster of Derek Jeter that's tacked up haphazardly and torn in the bottom left corner.

"Yeah." His voice is croaky and dry.

Gently, I place a knee on the far corner of his bed, then the other, and wordlessly I crawl over to him, trying to spoon him, but he's too big to make that a total success. I nestle my nose between his shoulder and neck, and slowly he reaches back and takes my left hand, pulls it across his chest, and rests it over his heart. He holds it there.

"What's the matter?" I ask, and I follow my question with a kiss between his shoulder blades.

"Coach took me out for two rotations."

Pitchers don't pitch every day, maybe once a week, so if Finn's out twice, then that means he won't pitch again for almost three weeks, and—

I stop myself from jumping to conclusions.

"Finn," I say as he takes a deep breath. "Does that mean you won't pitch during your playoff game?"

He nods.

"This is all my fault."

Lifting his body from the crumpled comforter, he turns so that he's facing me. Dark circles rim his eyes and his hair is messy and matted in places. "It's not your fault. I started it. Coach said I was lucky he didn't throw me off the team."

"But you're their best pitcher!"

Finn smiles sadly and shakes his head. "Doesn't matter. They have a zero-tolerance policy for violence. He said the only reason I'm still around is because the rest of the team told him what Caleb said."

I reach out and run my fingers through his hair, my hand finally settling at the top of his jaw bone, just below his ear. "Thank you for standing up for me."

His eyes are suddenly clouded, his brows knitted together. "You don't have to thank me," he says, his voice soft. He focuses on my mouth and leans over and kisses me, his hand cradling my cheek, and it takes me a hot second to realize that this is the first time I've kissed a boy on his bed. And not just any boy, but Finnian Pearce, who is honest and sincere (which are similar but not the same), and smart despite how he protests, and beautiful (so beautiful that sometimes I find myself staring at him, wondering where he even came from, how is he even real?), and poetic when he doesn't mean to be, and strong when I can't be.

I raise myself up on one elbow, my hand grasping the collar of his T-shirt, coaxing him onto his back. My left leg intertwines his, and his hand finds my waist, gripping it, stopping me. "What's the matter?" My breath still comes fast.

"You don't have to thank me," he says again, his dark eyes so focused, so serious. "But you have to make it up to me."

"I'm trying to."

He shakes his head and rolls himself off the side of the bed, pacing to the window.

It's cold over here suddenly, and I feel oddly exposed despite being fully dressed. "I don't understand."

"Caleb wants what he wants," says Finn. He intertwines his fingers behind his head, his elbows jutting out, and the cut lines of his stomach peek out from under his shirt. "Yesterday he wanted you, and when you said no, I sent the message home."

I'm waiting for the punch line.

"But you let him get away with taking your words. Taking what wasn't his. He gets a free pass every fucking time, and you need to show him you're not going to stand for it."

I roll onto my back and cover my eyes with my hands. "It's not as easy as that," I say.

"Not as easy as what?" He crawls back onto the bed, stretching out beside me, his hand on my stomach. "Not as easy as being punched in the face?"

I peek out from under the palm of my hand and regard the cut that splits his swollen lip, the bruise that blossoms across his cheek like a plum.

"I want you to go to the poetry ceremony for the Highland Whaler, and I want you to read your poem."

"Finn, that won't work."

"Why won't it work?"

"Because it's too late! Caleb already submitted the poem and the deadline has passed."

"But it's *your* poem. So you show up the day of the ceremony when everyone else is gonna be reading, and you read the poem you wrote. Tell them you missed the deadline, but you still want to enter. Bet they won't turn you away."

"That's not easy. It's more than just saying it's my poem, that I wrote it. It's calling him a liar in front of a crowd, and that's uncomfortable."

He watches me for a moment. "I'll be right next to you. I won't leave you alone."

I close my eyes, hoping if they're closed he won't see the tears brimming along the edges. But too late. One sneaks past my lashes, tumbling down my cheek. Before it can leap from the precipice of my chin, Finn's thumb is there to wipe it away.

"No crying," he murmurs.

"Okay."

"Look at me." He pulls my hands from my eyes. "I've got you. I'll help you. I'm not going anywhere."

I nod. He kisses me.

When I get home, Russ is busy power-washing the front of the house, and he doesn't pay any attention as I slam shut the door of the Durango and head for the tire swing in the back. It's been my place of refuge for as long as I can remember. I can still fit in it, but it's getting more and more difficult to bend my legs getting out without falling on my butt. Now that I'm here, swinging, my attention focused on the throng of black-eyed Susans that run the length of the woods out back and beckon me down the path to the sea, I'm not thinking about getting up yet. I'm thinking about confronting Caleb.

From the front of the house, Russ trudges through the fallen pine needles and over the knobby roots of the yard until he's standing at the back porch, pretending to be preoccupied with the power washer. He's never been good with social cues. He would never realize that I'd like to sit alone with my guilt, dwell on the fact that it's my fault Finn is out for two rotations, and that he's going to miss the playoff games in Boston, where there could be scouts. Maybe from the Cape Cod Baseball League. Maybe from the major leagues.

"What's Finn up to today?" Russ asks without facing me. This is something he does—asks an innocent-sounding question when he already knows the answer. Ryan for sure told his dad about what happened. And his dad naturally told Russ.

"I'm sure you've heard."

He's quiet for a moment before he says, "I heard he's out for two rotations. Didn't hear why."

"He tried to fix something he shouldn't have."

Russ clears his throat. "For you?"

"Is that so impossible to believe?"

His shoulders slouching, Russ sighs. "I didn't say that, Mack."

"It's implied."

"Don't put words in my mouth."

My chest tightens at this, and he makes me want to scream. "Then what *did* you mean?"

"I didn't mean anything," Russ tries. "It just seemed like you felt a little sad back here, so I figured . . ."

"That it's my fault he's off rotation?"

"Jesus, Mack."

"Just do us both a favor, Russ. Don't try to be a father to me when it's not what you've ever wanted."

"I tried, at one point, Mack. I tried to be a father to you. But you—"

"Oh, please."

Russ bristles at this. "You kept running! And you're right, I gave up. I gave up. I figured I could never get another man's daughter to love me like she'd love her father. So I thought maybe I could have my own. And I did. And I loved her. I do love her."

My bottom lip starts to tremble, and I swipe angrily at the tears that keep coming. "I'm not asking you not to love Mellie. I'm not even asking you to love me. I'm asking you to leave me alone." I extract myself as gracefully as possible from the tire swing and make my way to the porch steps, ready to go inside.

"Wait." I pause and turn. Russ nods, running his hand through his thinning hair, and then he faces the picnic table and sits down. "I, uh," he begins, staring out at the path that leads through the woods. "I found that notebook you left in the kitchen. The one with all your poetry."

I don't trust him. I want to sit down across from him and let him tell me whatever it is he has to say, but I don't trust him yet. "I'll clean it up," I say. "I'm sorry I left it out."

Russ shakes his head. "No, that's not what I mean."

"I'm applying to the Winslow College of Fine Arts," I tell him. "You can't stop me."

He laughs quietly. "Geez, Mack, I'm not trying to stop you. Put your wall down for a second, would you?"

I cross my arms over my chest.

"Come here," he says, motioning to the bench across from him. "Sit down a minute."

I take a few steps toward him, then straddle the bench. I'm sitting, but I'm not necessarily staying. "What?" I ask.

He folds his hands on the table before him. "I read one of your poems. I hope you're not upset, but it was out in the open, and the title kinda caught my eye."

I blink a few times. "You read one of my poems?"

Russ nods.

"Which one?"

"The, um," he says and scratches the back of his neck. "The

one about Highland Light. The one you wrote about how it's been a beacon for hundreds of years. Every sailor that passes it can feel safe."

I remember that one. The one I wrote when I read how Elijah Pearce went off to fight in the Civil War. And I wondered what would happen to the light, but the answer was always right there. Highland Light is still standing. When the sun finally sets and the stars twinkle above me, Highland Light is the only other glow in the night.

When I finally speak, my words are quiet, like I don't want anyone else to hear that I'm seeking Russ's approval. "Did you like it?" I ask.

He nods. "I did. I liked it. I thought to myself, this girl really does have a way with words." He chuckles then. "It's like, when I read it, I could hear my dad, you know that?"

I shake my head.

"My dad loved lighthouses. We once spent an entire summer trailing the East Coast and stopping at every lighthouse he had on his itinerary. He was convinced I needed to know the history of each one, and damn did I hate every minute of that trip."

I smile down at the bench before me.

"But you know what?"

"What?"

He leans forward, like he's sharing a secret with me. "I wish

I could do it all over again. I'd appreciate it more this time. I'd appreciate him more."

I press my lips together.

"He died when I was sixteen. I know how it is, Mack. I do." He wrings his hands together, almost nervously. "I guess I wanted to tell you that. To say thank you. For the poem."

I don't reply.

He nods, like he understands my lack of response, and he pushes himself away from the picnic table, pacing to the back door.

"You're welcome," I say quietly, but only when his back is turned to me.

Russ pauses, shoving his hands in his pockets, and nods. "If you really want to go to that poetry workshop in the fall, I'm okay with that. Maybe if you help a little with the cost, with your tips from the Shanty or something, it would be all right. Does that work for you?"

I stare at him in disbelief and then nod. "Yes. Yes, I can do that."

"Okay, then." He disappears into the cool shadows of the kitchen.

CHAPTER TWENTY-TWO

Leta

1862

Mother insisted that I attend the dinner party in Elijah's honor at the new minister's house. She told me that Captain Churchill would most certainly be in attendance, and I would want to give him every opportunity to make me an offer of marriage.

Only I haven't spoken to Ben in days. I haven't seen him since that evening at Charlotte Pearce's house, and practically the moment I walked through the door, he escaped out the back. With all those people in attendance, I don't want them staring with expectant eyes, not when I don't even know what to expect.

My only saving grace is that when we arrive, no one is interested in me. And even more perplexing, no one is interested in Captain Benjamin Churchill. They're all enamored with Elijah. For the first time in his life, people want to know his story.

People want to hear about the war with the South. They want to hear ever gory detail of his wound.

Even the Crawfords are besotted with Elijah, and I'd like to think it comes from an almost genuine place—that they've realized the error of their ways and are attempting to make it up to him.

I slip away from the crowd and follow Caroline and Fred to the punch bowl in the dining room.

"Poor Elijah," says Caroline over the rim of her glass. "Inundated with all those people who never spared him a second while he tended the lighthouse."

"He never used to want the attention," Fred scoffs.

"He pretended he didn't want the attention," I say quietly. "But everyone wants to be liked. Everyone wants to be thought of."

Behind me, someone clears his throat.

"Captain Churchill," says Fred, stepping past Caroline and me and extending his hand. "Grand to see you here. A glass of punch?"

"No, thank you," says Ben. He glances my way. "Hello, Leta."

"Captain Churchill," I say. "I wasn't sure you'd make it this evening," I say, attempting to maintain our show of civility.

"I wanted to see you," says Ben.

My throat tightens. He won't play along with me. I should have known better; Ben doesn't play games. He'll be honest, not caring about anyone within earshot, and he'll speak what's on his mind because it's the truth. There's a sanctity to the truth, and he worships at its altar.

"Well," I say, offering him a broad smile, "here I am. You'll excuse me, won't you?"

I ease out of our conversational knot, hoping to find someone, anyone, to speak to. Someone who will keep Ben at bay.

"Leta," says Elijah.

I turn. This is perfect. Ben never approaches me if I'm with Elijah. My friend steps toward me, using the cane he brought for the evening.

"How are you feeling?" I ask.

"I'm feeling decent enough," he replies after a swig of his punch. His eyes don't meet mine, but rather they follow his cousin around the room. "What's going on with you and Ben?"

I smile. It's the most honest smile I've given all day. "It doesn't matter," I say, touching his arm. "Simply a misunderstanding."

Elijah doesn't return my expression, though. "What happened?"

I stare at Ben, who pretends to listen to my mother discuss the new wallpaper she plastered in the minister's house. And the words sort of spill from my mouth. "I don't think that he trusts me," I say.

Elijah's face scrunches in confusion. "In what way?"

"With his heart," I say quietly. I cast my eyes downward.

"Something I fear he keeps very much to himself, something he cannot share. I'm like everyone else to him. I'm someone not to be trusted. And I thought for so long that I was much more."

"Leta," says Elijah slowly.

"That's what happens when you create someone from nothing, isn't it? It's easy to pretend they love you. It's easy to know their innermost thoughts, because their thoughts are your thoughts."

Elijah doesn't answer me this time.

"It's no matter," I say, draining the last of my punch. "Perhaps I should have known better."

People begin to gather in the parlor, taking seats constructed in a semicircle around a piano. Reverend Cartwright's youngest daughter seats herself at the instrument while the guests are encouraged to find a chair to enjoy her recital. Elijah sits beside me to the right and Caroline and Fred to my left.

I make a concerted effort to avoid Ben, but despite my best attempts, he takes a seat directly behind me. I venture a glance over my shoulder. He's brought with him a glass of whisky that dangles precariously in his right hand between his knees, and when Miss Cartwright begins to play, he taps his finger along the rim to the beat.

"May I speak with you, Leta?" he asks. He leans in, his breath playing with the loose tendrils of hair around my ear.

"I'm trying to enjoy the music, Captain Churchill," I say.

"I'll only be a moment."

"I won't be rude and leave my seat."

He clears his throat, and the sound of his chair inching closer causes Miss Cartwright to stumble over a few notes.

· "Very well," says Ben. "I'll say what I need to say right here."

My eyes dart to my right, but Elijah shows no sign of having heard Ben. Caroline, though, inclines her head ever so slightly, her eyes focused on the piano before us.

"Whatever makes you happy," I whisper. I glance around, but no one seems to notice our conversation except my sister. And I don't care if she hears.

"When I was a boy," he says, "I snuck aboard the whaling ship that my brother left on, because I couldn't bear to lose him, not after our father went to jail. Edwin was all I had. So I followed him around the Earth, chasing the leviathan."

My hand begins to tremble. I'd like to think I know where this story is going, but I don't dare hope it.

"My brother would tell me all the best ways to take a whale—the tried-and-true methods of the master whalers—and I'd listen intently. He told me that the best way to secure a large whale is to first harpoon its young. Because every whale will fight to the death to protect its young."

My lungs constrict, and even the deepest breath won't loosen the grip of anxiety.

"And I asked him, isn't that cruel, Edwin? Is it cruel to hunt an animal so dedicated to its child? To use that against it? He laughed at me." Ben takes a breath. "He laughed at me, and I swore at him, and I threw my shoe at him, like you, and I begged him to stop, but he called me sentimental and ridiculous. Because industry has no room for sentimentality, Leta. That's what he told me."

Before us, the piano thunders and crescendos, and the music swirls around us.

"I told myself that it was all right. Edwin could say those things, but I had never seen him harpoon a calf. It's one thing to speak the words, but it's another to follow through. He never followed through."

Beside me, Caroline shifts in her seat, trying to hear the story more clearly without making it obvious that she's listening at all.

"On a clear afternoon, one of the crew spotted a pod of sperm whales. They are powerful creatures," he says. "I've seen one ram the side of a ship in retribution for the bloodshed of his family. But when the water is calm, and their backs break the surface of the sea, water running in eddies down their crinkled skin, they're peaceful. Gentle." He takes a deep breath before continuing. "There were several females and their calves. My brother manned one of the three whaling boats that sped out to take them. As I watched from my perch on the ship, I saw him harpoon one of the young. His mother, you see, she wouldn't have it. And before I knew it, she had struck Edwin's boat with her massive flukes, splintering the whole thing and sending every man and boy into the churning sea."

"Edwin never resurfaced. I begged the captain to stay, to wait. Maybe my brother swam away? Maybe he escaped? But the whales moved on, and so did we. That's what you do on a ship. You are in constant movement, never resting, never staying in one place."

I incline my head ever so slightly, to invite him to tell me more.

"And maybe it's taken me well over a decade to say that story out loud. Maybe I never imagined meeting someone who would encourage me to speak such a thing. But I have."

The music quiets, a lullaby now, something that drifts between each person, whispering soft words in our ears.

"And I have never told that to anyone else. Not a soul until tonight."

The audience applauds Miss Cartwright's performance. Ben takes this opportunity to pretend as if he's one of the appreciative spectators, standing in reverence, but when he abandons his seat, he doesn't bother to clap. He straightens his jacket and exits the room.

"Wait!" I try to call after him, but he's too far to hear me, my words are drowned by the applause.

I follow his dark coat down the main hallway of Reverend Cartwright's house.

"Ben!" I try to call again. I break through the back door and out into the gardens. Ben stands among a throng of sunflowers—heads bowed at the coming night. He looks like one of them.

Slowing my pace, I catch my breath and dig my knuckles into my hips. "Are you all right?" I ask.

"Yes," he replies. "Why did you follow me?"

"Because you—" I begin, but I collect myself. "Because I care about you."

He stares at the ground, but his eyes slam shut, as if he's in pain. "Yes, but . . ."

I take a step forward.

"But do you love me, Leta? Because caring for me and loving me are two separate things."

"They are," I agree.

He laughs. "Don't toy with me."

"I'm not."

"Don't forget me because Elijah has returned. Don't discard me because you feel guilt over the way you've treated him."

The words fly from my mouth: "Don't you dare launch those accusations my way. He's come home barely in one piece, and you dare to accuse me of tossing you aside? After what transpired at the bay? With the blackfish? After what you said? Don't you dare." I jab his shoulder with my forefinger, and my tears are uncontrollable.

His chest heaves with pent up rage, but I'm not sure if it's because of me. I'm never sure of anything when I'm with Ben, and I'm growing weary of the sensation. But his eyes plead with me. They beg me not to give up.

Without hesitation, I reach out my hand and brush his cheek. "What else can I do to prove myself to you?"

"Nothing," he says, shaking his head, and looking to the ground. Suddenly, the space between us disappears, his hands reach around my waist, and he pulls me into an embrace. He kisses me urgently.

Half of my brain wonders if we're visible from any windows of the house, if anyone is paying attention to us. But something inside me that is very much not my brain doesn't care. I clutch at the lapels of his jacket, struggling to be as close to him as possible.

He pulls away from my mouth, his eyes still closed, and his hands grasp mine gently. Softly now, his lips brush against mine. Then he lifts my wrist and places a kiss there.

"Ben!"

The sound of his aunt's voice yanks me from our flirtation. Suddenly the darkness isn't enough to hide us, and the light from the half moon is blinding.

"It's all right," Ben whispers against my ear. "It's only Aunt Charlotte."

"Ben!" she calls again from somewhere far off. "I'm ready to go home now."

"No," I say, searching again for his mouth. "Don't go."

He cups my face with both his hands, and his kiss lingers a little longer than it ought to. "I have to take her home," he says.

Retreating a few steps from me, he calls out, "I'm coming, Aunt Charlotte." Our hands are still entwined, and he stretches my arm to its full extent. "Come inside," he says, his head motioning for the door. "It's too cold out here, and you don't have your shawl."

I touch my fingers to my lips to check if the memory of our kiss is still present. In this moment, he's still here; I can still taste him. He smiles.

"Come here," he says.

In the house, people continue to eat and drink, mingling about and taking part in conversation, and it looks as if Miss Cartwright is getting ready for another performance.

Mrs. Pearce says her goodbyes to my family. Elijah assures her that he will manage on his ride home with the help of Father and Fred. She kisses his cheek then takes Ben's offered arm.

"Mother," I say, pressing my hand to my forehead. I flutter my eyelids dramatically.

She glances up from a conversation with Susannah and Mrs. Cartwright. "What is it, dear?"

"I have a headache. I'd like to go home to bed."

Ben pauses at the front door, his face caressed by the soft light of the whale oil lamps. It's enough to highlight the stubble on his cheeks.

"Well, Leta, that's rather inconvenient right now," says Mother. "We can't up and leave Reverend and Mrs. Cartwright's get-together—not when they've promised fireworks at midnight!"

"I can't stay another minute," I say. "I don't feel well."

"She does look rather flushed, Janet," says Father.

"We can take her home," Mrs. Pearce offers, appearing beside me. "Come here, child." She reaches for me without leaving Ben's side. "We'll get you right to bed."

"Oh, wonderful," says Mother, pouring herself another glass of punch. "Thank you so much, Captain Churchill. Feel better, dear." She waves at me while turning back to Susannah and Mrs. Cartwright.

"Miss Townsend," says Ben, extending his other arm.

I latch onto it and without anyone noticing, he whispers in my ear, "What are you doing?"

I smile up at him while he escorts us to the door.

The ride home in the buggy is uncomfortable, and I think that if I really did have a headache, this wouldn't aid in making the ailment disappear. I stare at Ben's back as he guides the horse down the gravel road and toward the sea. Beside him, his aunt continues to fall asleep, slumps against his right arm, and then rouses herself awake with each bump.

Ben peeks over his shoulder at me. "Are you all right back there?" he whispers.

"Perfectly so," I reply, wrapping my shawl tightly around my shoulders and taking in the view of the Atlantic. The moon is high, and its reflection ripples along the surface of the water, interrupted by each crashing wave.

"Oh, careful there," says Ben, gripping his aunt with his free hand while holding the reins in the other. She's drooped down on the bench, and he nudges her gently. "Aunt Charlotte, wake up," he says. "It's time to get you up to bed."

She nods as the buggy slows before her house. Jumping from his perch and giving the horse a good pat on its hindquarters, Ben rounds the side of the wagon and assists his aunt down. He looks up at me expectantly.

"Will you wait here?" he asks. "I won't be long. I'll help her upstairs and settle her in."

I nod. "I'll be here waiting."

He's gone for some time, and I stare up at the window in the high gable. The room illuminates, and I see the shadow of Mrs. Pearce. Downstairs, the screen door creaks open then slaps shut. Ben appears with a wool blanket in his arms.

"For you," he says. "Come sit up by me."

I agree to this, stepping down from my seat in the buggy with his assistance and then up onto the bench beside him. He spreads the blanket across both our laps. I lean against him, my cheek resting on the soft upper part of his arm, and he clicks his tongue to urge the horse forward.

"It's cold tonight," I say, and my insides tremble, though I'm not sure if it's because of the cool weather or my proximity to Ben.

"Stay close," he says, reaching his arm out and collecting me against his side.

Snuggling deeper into the blanket, I rest my chin upon his shoulder, my mouth perilously close to his earlobe.

"If you cause us to go off the road," he says, a shiver overtaking his body for a brief moment, "I'm not taking any responsibility." His voice is soft and raspy, and with the thin light of the moon, I can vaguely make out his eyes, drowsy with the late hour and the whisky.

I giggle.

"Are you laughing at me?" he asks.

"*With* you," I say, squeezing his hand in mine. "I'm laughing with you."

"You're a beautiful liar."

"I'm the epitome of honesty." I stare off into the night sky. "Tell me what you've been doing at the old Pearce house. No one's occupied it for years."

Ben shrugs as I link my arm through his. "Aunt Charlotte's husband left it to Elijah, but Elijah much prefers the cramped confines of the lighthouse, so he offered it to me. At first, I said no. But then I thought, what if I had a place I wanted to return to? A place to anchor me here? Then maybe the sea wouldn't be so appealing, and I wouldn't jump from expedition to expedition, and I'd long for some place on solid ground."

"Do you think that's true?" I ask, my voice burdened with hope.

"I suppose we'll find out," he replies, turning to look at me. "Do you want to see what I've been doing?"

I sit up straight. "Now?"

"Why not? It's not even nine, and as we both know, the fireworks don't start until midnight."

"All right, then. Take me."

At the fork in the road, he encourages the horse to the left, following along the inlet, rattling over the wooden bridge and up the dirt path to the old Pearce house. He's cleared out all the brush that had grown with a century of neglect. There's a new door on the front, fresh bricks holding up the fireplace, and wooden stairs leading to the entrance.

"I'm not finished yet," Ben says, hopping off the buggy and reaching up to help me down. His hands on my waist and mine on his shoulders, he gently places my feet on the ground. "It's a work in progress." Staring up at the house, he gestures toward the building. "Would you like the tour?"

"How could I resist?"

He leaps up the steps ahead of me and opens the door,

allowing me to step inside first. "I'm afraid I don't have much lighting," he says, standing beside a round table with a marble top. He lights a glass lamp. "This will have to do for now."

I take his arm as he leads me through the empty hallways, showing me the gutted kitchen, the desolate dining room, and the little study in the back with two walls of windows that overlook the inlet. The light of the moon won't make for a dazzling firework display, but it floods the little room, the space between me and Ben, and reflects in his eyes.

"You would like to write there, I think," he says, but it sounds more like a question, so I nod in response. "And up here," he continues, stepping out into the hallway and pointing to a wide staircase, "there are the bedrooms. There are so many. I don't think I know enough people to invite over to fill them."

I smile at him as he takes my hand and leads me to the second floor, past room after empty room, until we get to a door at the end. "Are you going to show off your linen closet now?" I ask.

"Oh, it's not a linen closet," he replies, opening the door to reveal a winding set of stairs. Moonlight drenches every step. "Follow me." He leads the way, his lamp held out before him.

At the top of the stairs, a huge room opens before us, with multiple windows facing the sea. In the center is a mattress with blankets and pillows strewn across it, a few books piled to the side, and Ben bends to try to neaten things up. "Sorry," he says. "I've been sleeping here."

"Until you ready one of the downstairs rooms?" I ask.

He places the lamp on the floor. "No, I think I like it here best. I could use a real bed, of course." He scratches the back of his head and chuckles quietly.

I circle the room, taking in the details. "It's such a big room for one person," I say. "I'd feel so lost in it."

"It's bigger than the cramped cabins on a ship, I'll grant you that," he says. "At least when I'm here, I wake up to the sea. It's not so far away."

I watch him stare out at the water, at the shimmering path of light the moon creates on the surface. "You love the sea," I say quietly.

He nods, still staring.

"Maybe the sea is why you cannot look at me that way." I say it, and at first, I meant it to be funny. But I realize, once the words are between us, that I mean it.

"The sea couldn't possibly compare . . ." he tries.

"It's all right," I assure him. "I wasn't accusing you."

"Leta, I've never had to stay in one place for very long," he says, stepping toward me. "There's never been a reason to. But if there was one, you know that it's you. You know that it's always been you."

I shake my head. "I don't know that."

He studies me in the low lamplight, takes a step back, staring at his feet and licking his lips. "If you married me, you wouldn't be happy."

"Let me be the one to decide that."

"I'd be away for years at a time, and you'd be here—"

"I could come with you."

His head snaps to attention. "What?"

"I could come with you on your whaling expeditions. It isn't all that outlandish, you know. I've heard of captains' wives, even their children, joining them at sea."

He smiles and shakes his head. "You won't like it. You love the blackfish, and killing a whale ten times its size is nothing you'd want to witness, Leta. If whales could scream, we'd all be deaf. You don't know what you'd be in for."

"That's the point!" I cry, grabbing both his hands, pretending as if I didn't hear the part about the whales screaming. "If I want to write poetry, what better place than at sea? Sailing to far-off ports, meeting people of importance instead of being trapped here at sewing circle with my mother and sisters."

His chest rises and falls steadily, but he doesn't say anything.

"It would work," I say, kissing the tops of his hands. "And we would never have to be apart."

"You are remarkable, Leta Townsend," he says quietly, running his hand along my cheek. "That you would give up everything just for a chance to be with me."

I tilt my face up to his, and he kisses me fervently. His fingers wind through my hair, pulling out the pin holding it in place so that the coils spill out across my shoulders. Carefully, I sneak my hands under his coat and begin unbuttoning his shirt.

"Leta," he says, touching my wrist with gentle fingers. "We don't have to do this." But his lips find mine again, and neither of us want to turn back.

"Then tell me to stop," I say.

He shakes his head wordlessly, and as he lowers me onto the mattress, I turn and blow out the lamp.

CHAPTER TWENTY-THREE

MICHAELA

present day

I t's October 2 and a near perfect Saturday morning in Highland. In the park, the leaves are tinged yellow and orange, and a cool breeze promises an even cooler afternoon. People are trickling in, filling up the folding chairs that have been organized around a makeshift dais beside the veiled and completed statue of the Highland Whaler. I stand before him, waiting.

"I wonder what he looks like," Finn says beside me, then takes a bite of funnel cake that he got from one of the food trucks lined on the street. He licks the melting powdered sugar from his thumb.

I stare at the cloth over the statue. Finn and I had googled Benjamin Churchill, and after scrolling through lots of other men with the same name, we finally stumbled upon the image we sought. It was a photograph taken in London in 1861, just before he returned to Highland—and Leta. He was very handsome, very serious.

"Give me a piece of that," I say, reaching up for the chunk of funnel cake Finn just tore off the side. It's delightfully flaky and sweet, but when I eat it, my stomach roils. Not exactly a soothing feeling right before you're about to go onstage and basically accuse someone of plagiarism. I scan the crowd for Caleb and find him in the fourth row beside Brittany and two old people who I assume are his parents. He has his arm around a girl who looks familiar, but I can't place her immediately.

"Come on," says Finn, nodding toward the table of judges, all of them professors from Winslow College. "Now's your chance. Let's do this." He grabs my hand, and we make our way through the crowd toward them.

I stand in front of the table, trying my best not to be rude, because what I'm about to ask is going to require a lot of leniency on their part. One more peek over my shoulder at Finn, and he gives me a thumbs-up. I take a deep breath then clear my throat.

"Excuse me?"

Two of the professors look up from their conversation.

"Hi," I say, offering a smile. "My name's Michaela Dunn, and I was wondering if it was too late to submit my poem? Has a winner already been chosen?"

A tall black man wearing exactly what a college professor

ought to stands and offers me his hand. "Dr. Mayweather," he says.

"Nice to meet you."

"We haven't chosen a winner yet. We're having all participants read their poem and then we'll pick the winner at the end of the afternoon."

I nod. "I know I'm late. But it's really important to me to read my poem here today. I spent the entire summer piecing it together, and it's ready, and it's mine."

Dr. Mayweather smiles and nods, then turns to his colleagues. "What do we think?" he asks.

Both of the judges shrug in agreement.

"All right, Miss Dunn. Thank you for your entry." He takes the copies of my poem and gestures for me to take a seat.

"How'd it go?" Finn asks once I return.

"I'm in."

He kisses my cheek.

We head toward the chairs, walking past Caleb and his family. I try to turn away before I catch his eye, but when he sees me, he sits a little taller in his seat, whispers something to the girl beside him, and stands, stretching. With a casual swagger, he makes his way over to where we're standing.

"I swear to God," Finn mumbles, finishing his funnel cake, "if he says one wrong thing, I'm gonna—"

"Not get yourself kicked off the baseball team," I finish.

He takes a deep breath through his nose. Finn missed his two rotations on the travel team just before school started, and I watched him sit on the bench in the dugout—his elbows resting on his knees, his chin on his folded hands—and how he studied the other pitchers like a stalking predator. But he doesn't take things sitting down. When the scout from the Cape Cod Baseball League showed up in September, Finn squared his shoulders, stood at his full, daunting height and strode over, his arm extended.

"My name's Finnian Pearce," I heard him say. "I'm off rotation until next week, but I would really like the opportunity to pitch for you."

The scout, still shaking Finn's hand, grinned back. "Oh, I've heard of you, son." Then he agreed to come back, just to see Finn pitch a later game.

I knew he was scared. He told me so before the game. He held me for a long time, his chin on my shoulder, before he joined the rest of the team, and maybe they assumed we were like all the other new couples, and that we couldn't stand to be apart, to keep our hands off each other, but I knew better than that. I knew the difference.

Caleb eventually trails his way around the seating area until he appears before us, hands in his pockets, all casual ease and elegance. "Hey, Michaela," he says, and he spares Finn a passing glance. "I'm kind of surprised you're here."

I smile. "Why's that?"

Running his hand through his wavy hair, he shifts away from me. "I don't know, I guess I just assumed with everything that went down over the summer . . ."

Finn stands up straighter.

"You losing your poem and everything, I mean," Caleb clarifies. "I'm glad you were able to come up with something."

"I'm good like that."

"Good luck," Caleb says and walks away.

My family is in the very front row: Mom, Russ, and Mellie, who dangles her feet back and forth because her legs are too short to touch the ground. Beside Mellie is Finn's Aunt Becky, and she and Mellie are having a very intense conversation.

"You okay?" Finn asks quietly as we make our way to our chairs, his hand on my lower back.

"Mmhm," I assure him, taking his hand and squeezing it. "It looks like they're getting started." I lead him to our seats, the two on the end, and sit beside Mom. She reaches out, running her hand through my hair then rubbing between my shoulder blades.

"You don't have to do this, you know," she says quietly. "We're sending you to the workshop. You can show them what you're made of then."

"It's not about Winslow College anymore," I say. "It's the principle of the thing."

Mom nods and squeezes my shoulder. "Good."

Dr. Mayweather takes the stage, adjusting the microphone so that it reaches him.

"Good morning," he begins. "My name is Dr. Kenneth Mayweather, and I'm the chair of the creative writing department at Winslow College of Fine Arts. I also happen to be a native of Highland and a longtime admirer of the gentleman we're here to honor today."

The audience applauds.

"It's a funny thing, to try to commemorate a human we've never known," Dr. Mayweather continues. "A human with so much mystery swirling around him."

The crowd is silent, and I suspect it's because they all think they know Captain Churchill. Of course they do. He plays mini golf and sells ice cream; his name christens a street near the bay; and a cartoon version of him charges the football field almost every Friday night at the high school.

I glance up at Finn, who watches Dr. Mayweather with curiosity. Finn's never been tricked by all of that. I touch his knee.

"But that's what, I think, poetry is for. We've had so many beautiful submissions, and we have so many young artists entering their poems today, that perhaps together, we'll dig to the bottom of Captain Churchill, a possible poet himself. Our first reader is Miss Elise Weinberger, and her poem is entitled 'The High Seas.'"

Everyone claps, and Elise takes to the stage to read her poem. It's long and modern sounding, not entirely bad, but it has more to do with the ocean than it does with Captain Churchill. Once she's finished, she bows briefly, and the panel of judges from Winslow College, all situated to the left of the stage, take turns asking her questions.

"Miss Weinberger," begins a bespectacled woman with perfectly white hair. "How much did you know about Benjamin Churchill prior to this dedication?"

She shrugs. "Nothing, really."

"What steps did you take to ensure that your poem was well-informed before presenting it?"

Elise smiles. "I wanted my words to be as free from outside influence as possible. Therefore, I did no research on Captain Churchill whatsoever."

Dr. Mayweather smiles and blinks a few times. "No further questions. Thank you for your contribution."

A few other entries follow in the same manner, each person reciting lovely poems, poems with feeling and heart, but none of them pretend to *know* Captain Churchill. They could have been placed on a plaque for anyone who once loved the sea, for anyone who once called Cape Cod home. The entrants all receive the same kinds of questions from the judges, and they all give the same kinds of responses.

Until Caleb crosses the stage.

There's part of me that waits for Caleb to recite some other poem. A part that really wants to believe that he realized the error of his ways, found the light, and wrote something for himself.

"Mr. Abernathy is a student of mine," begins Dr. Mayweather, "therefore I'll be abstaining from scoring his submission. What is the title of your entry, Caleb?"

Caleb smiles. "My poem is called 'From Away.'"

I sigh. At least he came up with his own title.

But when he begins, they're my words he spews, my words that make the audience smile. My words that cause Finn to weave his fingers through mine and to clasp my hand reassuringly. They're my words that cause the audience to clap longer and louder; my words he answers questions about. He provides answers that are as vacant as his reading of the poem.

"Mr. Abernathy," begins Dr. Mayweather, "I appreciate that your poem is obviously in the voice of someone involved with Captain Churchill. What spurred this inspired decision?"

"I spent a lot of my time writing this poem in the Whaler's Watch, which is one of those places in Highland where Captain Churchill is rumored to have stayed."

"It wasn't an inn when he was in Highland," I mutter to Finn.

He links his pinkie with mine. "You're gonna get your turn."

Caleb continues, "So it was easy to imagine someone beguiled by him during his stay."

"I don't even think he read the diary," I whisper.

Finn nods silently.

"Some of the lines you include," says Dr. Mayweather from his chair, "well, it's difficult to pick just one, but I think I was most moved by the final few, about the bright and boundless sea."

"Thank you," says Caleb.

"Can you elaborate on that? What moved you to write these lines?"

He shrugs again. "It sort of came to me. I think once you immerse yourself in the setting, then it's easy for the words to flow through you."

"What a load of affectatious bullshit," I whisper.

Caleb leaves the stage, and he's followed by two more poets before it's my turn. It feels like they read forever, their words inching over my skin. By the time it's my turn, I feel dizzy with anticipation, shivering and regretting wearing the lightweight shirt with the big bow tied loosely at my collar that clearly isn't warm enough, as I feel chilled with apprehension.

"Our next reader is a last-minute but welcomed addition," says Dr. Mayweather with a smile. "This is Miss Michaela Dunn."

The audience claps, and Finn gives me a whistle.

"Welcome, Miss Dunn," says Dr. Mayweather. He has a reassuring smile. I think he's genuinely happy to hear my poem. This will all change momentarily, but for now, I'm letting it calm me. "What do you have prepared for us today?"

"I'd like to read my poem, 'A Bright and Boundless Sea.'"

His face twitches ever so slightly, enough to let me know that he finds this questionable, but he doesn't say anything, only nods, then shuffles his papers so that my poem is in front of him.

My voice wavering, I start to read my poem. The same poem I shared with Finn that day near the Atlantic. I read the poem in Leta's voice, the way I think she'd speak to Ben. I read the words that helped me make sense of a person broken in our town's history—a person reassembled in its present. The same way he was broken in his existence, and maybe that's what Leta was trying to do. Reassemble him. Only you can't reassemble people like toys or like a puzzle. The pieces are too delicate, too fluctuating. I finish, and I exhale, and the audience claps tentatively, unsure what it means now that I've just repeated the same poem Caleb read moments earlier.

Dr. Mayweather clears his throat as his colleague writes something fervently and shoves a paper in his direction. He reads what she's written and nods.

"Miss Dunn, I feel a little confused. You just read the same poem that Mr. Abernathy read."

"I did," I reply, clenching the piece of paper in my sweaty hands. It's become soft with folding and refolding.

"To what end?"

My eyes find Finn's brown ones, and he nods once. It's all I need. "Because I'm the one who wrote it."

The audience begins to whisper, and Caleb chuckles to himself. The girl next to him scoffs and crosses her left leg over her right.

"I wrote the poem," I say again.

"Miss Dunn," says the woman beside Dr. Mayweather, "you do realize that you're making a startling claim. Are you implying that Mr. Abernathy stole your poem?"

"I'm not implying anything," I reply. "I'm telling you plainly that's what he did."

Dr. Mayweather nods. "May I ask you a few questions about the poem, Miss Dunn?"

"Yes, sir." I stand up straight but remember to bend my knees like Russ told me, so I won't faint.

"As I posed to Mr. Abernathy, what inspired you to write a poem from someone else's rather personal perspective on Captain Churchill?"

I nod at this easy question. "The poem's narrator's name was Leta Townsend," I tell him. "She lived in Highland in the eighteen-sixties, and she was in love with Captain Churchill. I'm not entirely sure that her love was reciprocated quite as eagerly, but I think he loved her, too. He might have loved her if he could."

Dr. Mayweather nods. "What makes you think he couldn't love her?" he asks.

"The last few lines of the poem," I say, tucking a stray piece of hair behind my ear. "For it's a bright and boundless sea . . . to blind him to his love for me." I take a step forward. "I wrote that line inspired by something that I found in a letter from Captain Churchill to an unknown recipient. The letter is in the Maritime Museum, which is run by Ms. Rebecca Pearce." I gesture toward Aunt Becky and she stands, giving everyone a wave. "I wanted to make sure I used it in my poem, because that made Captain Churchill relevant to me. That's how I made sense of him. Love isn't an easy thing to put into words, but he tried to do so for the girl who offered him her poetry."

"What do you mean?" he asks.

"Leta Townsend wrote poetry under the name of Benjamin Churchill. It wasn't the captain who wrote any poetry. Leta wrote several poems, first in his name, and then eventually in her own—after she married Elijah Pearce."

Dr. Mayweather nods. "Thank you, Miss Dunn. We'll be sure to look into this further."

I step off the stage and Finn is there to greet me. My legs want to give out. I want to collapse and cry, and without even having to say it, Finn already knows, his hand firmly around my waist.

"Come on," he says quietly. "Have a drink of water."

Finn stands beside me, sipping from his plastic cup and staring over my head.

"Stop watching him," I say.

"He just sits there, like a tool, laughing and making these faces like you're—"

"Please," I try again.

"Sorry," says Finn, putting down his cup to adjust the bow at my neck. "You're getting all floppy over here."

I look up.

"You killed it up there. If they don't believe you, then fuck them. You know what you're worth."

"That was beautiful, baby," says Mom, coming up behind me and kissing my cheek.

"I loved it," says Mellie, squeezing her stuffed animal. "I don't know what it was about."

"That's okay," I say, reaching down and holding her hand.

"Nicely done, Mack," says Russ, giving my back a light, affectionate pat.

I'd like to call it a day, to slip back home, grill something outside while the sun is out, and when the night falls, build a fire in the pit and just sit and talk. But I'm in too deep now. Our little circle is soon interrupted by Dr. Mayweather. "Excuse me, folks, would you mind if I borrowed Michaela for a moment?"

I follow him to the dais again, where Caleb, Brittany, and Aunt Becky wait. Aunt Becky holds Captain Churchill's letter safely housed in a binder, sheltered by a glossy sheet protector. It took a lot for her to agree to take the letter out of the Maritime Museum, but she believes in the truth, and she believes in preserving history.

"Miss Dunn," Dr. Mayweather begins, "we appreciate what

you've brought to our attention, and we're determined to get to the bottom of this right away."

Caleb rolls his eyes. "She stole my poem, isn't it obvious?" he says, gesturing at me. "She's the one guilty of the crime she's blaming me for."

I stare stoically at him.

"Mr. Abernathy, please," says Dr. Mayweather, holding up his hand and closing his eyes. "Miss Dunn, you seemed to know a lot about Captain Churchill and this Leta Townsend. Where did you find your information?"

"She stole it!" Caleb cries.

"You're not going to speak for me," I say quietly, and I hope no one notices how I'm shaking. "I was invited to write at the Whaler's Watch by Brittany."

Dr. Mayweather turns to Brittany, and she nods to validate my claim.

"While I was there, I met Caleb. He showed me a room at the inn where he was writing a creative nonfiction piece about Captain Churchill. There were books scattered all around the room. One of them happened to be Leta Townsend's diary, and I used my phone to take pictures of the entries." I retrieve my phone from the back pocket of my jeans and show them the pictures I took.

"You see?" says Caleb.

"There aren't any rules that say I can't use what I find,"

I reply. "And at the time, you weren't even writing a poem. Anyway, I met up with Caleb at a coffee shop a couple weeks later, and we walked down to the bay to write together. I got distracted—"

"By him," says Caleb, gesturing at Finn again.

"You're going to leave him out of this. You've screwed up enough of his life already."

I turn back to Dr. Mayweather. "I got distracted when I saw my friends playing baseball and went to say hi. I left my things with Caleb, and I think that's when he took my work. I can't prove that, though. What I will admit is that I went back to his writing room at the Whaler's Watch and saw that Caleb had submitted my poem. That's when I took Leta Townsend's diary and left. Brittany told me to use anything at the Whaler's Watch as inspiration, so I did." I look at Brittany now, and I feel bad for dragging her into all of this. "Maybe I took what you said too far. I'm sorry for removing the diary, and I'm sorry for giving it away when it wasn't mine to give."

"Is this true?" Dr. Mayweather asks Brittany.

She nods, her gaze flitting to Caleb. "It's true," she says. "I encouraged her to use the resources at the Whaler's Watch."

"And when I did, I made the connection between the letter I had read at the Maritime Museum and Leta's diary."

Aunt Becky opens her binder and reveals the letter. Putting on his glasses, Dr. Mayweather inspects the document, his eyes darting quickly over each word, and once he's finished, he sighs in a satisfied sort of way.

"Caleb," he begins, "I am truly sorry you felt the need to stoop to this level. We'll have to discuss this more later. Right now, I need to announce the award."

I exhale, almost crying, and Caleb throws his hands in the air.

Without any words, Aunt Becky embraces me, and from all the way at the buffet table, I hear Finn exclaim, "Yes!" Mellie whoops with joy (even if she doesn't know why).

"My friends," says Dr. Mayweather once he's behind the podium. "We most definitively have a winner, and it is my privilege to bestow this honor upon Miss Michaela Dunn, author of 'A Bright and Boundless Sea.' Miss Dunn, thank you for your thoughtful portrayal of Captain Churchill. Your words will live on as the dedication to his statue. We look forward to seeing you at our poetry workshop at the end of the month."

I'm motionless with relief, my hands covering my mouth, my family surrounding me, Finn lifting me off my feet. We step back as two men beside the statue lift the sheet that hid the final creation. Captain Benjamin Churchill stands, feet apart, clasping two harpoons. His stoic face is turned in the direction of the sea.

CHAPTER TWENTY-FOUR

Leta

Autumn 1862

I can't stop cleaning. As Caroline prepares pies for the bake sale, I'm on my hands and knees in the kitchen, side by side with Annie, scrubbing the floor near the hearth. I've scrubbed every room all morning, trying to forget something that lingers on the cusp of my thoughts, something that leaks through my consciousness no matter how hard I clean, no matter how my parched skin cracks with the effort.

"Really, Leta," says Caroline. She has flour smeared below her left eye, but she doesn't know it. She's bent over a pie dish, trying to crimp the edges of the crust as best she can, but baking has never been Caroline's favorite domestic activity. "You said we had enough cherry preserves for two pies."

"I thought we did," I reply, sitting up and wiping my hands on my apron.

"Miss Leta, you look right tuckered out," says Annie, leaning back on her heels. "Why don't you go and sit down, and I'll help Mrs. Chilton with the cherry pie."

I *am* tired, and I ache. My back aches, my stomach aches, my breasts ache.

"When it's all finished, and you're cleaned up a bit, you can bring one over to Captain Churchill," Caroline suggests. "He's home today, isn't he?"

"I think so," I reply, lifting myself from the floor. "He went to New Bedford for a few days because a friend of his sailed in. I thought he might be home yesterday, but I haven't heard from him."

"He's probably busy," Caroline suggests, her hands on her hips as she admires her pie.

The warm, sweet scent of baking pies infiltrates the house, winding up the stairs behind me and sneaking under my bedroom door even as I get dressed. Caroline has conquered the cherry and has moved on to pumpkin, and the spicy aroma of cinnamon and nutmeg keeps the chill of the cold drizzle at bay just outside my window. As I button my blouse, my gaze falls upon my diary, my incomplete poetry, and the words I've left unwritten for several weeks. In less than an hour, my house will be filled with the sewing circle ladies, gathering the pies and expecting me to join them on their excursion to the church to set up for the bake sale.

My hand rests on the leather binding, and I gather the diary to my chest before heading down the stairs.

"Do you have a pumpkin pie for Captain Churchill?" I ask. "I'll meet you at the church after I drop it off."

"Fresh from the oven," says Caroline proudly. She wraps it in cloth and places it in a basket. "Give Captain Churchill our regards."

"I will," I say, mustering a smile. But I don't feel like smiling. There's an apprehension in going to visit Ben today that I cannot place. Maybe it's our lack of communication over the past few days. He told me he was going to visit his friend in New Bedford, but he never told me when. I had to hear from Elijah that he had already left and that he would be back in three days' time. That meant yesterday.

As I travel the lane to the Pearce house, my hand over my hat to hold it securely against the wind gusting off the sea, a pinprick of trepidation pinches my heart. I deeply breathe it away, more determined than ever to rid myself of negative thoughts by only thinking optimistically.

Ben is always pleased to see me, and he is always pleased about pie. And if he's been working on renovating the house before our wedding, then he'll have worked up an appetite and be even more appreciative. A little beam of optimism working its magic already.

"Leta!"

I pause in the road, turning to see Elijah heading toward me, his cane in his left hand and his right hand waving. His walking is becoming easier with each passing day.

"I was headed to your house," he tells me. "I'm glad to have met you on the road."

"What perfect timing," I say, lifting the basket on my arm. "I was about to bring Ben a pie. You can share it with us."

"Is he home?" Elijah asks as we continue our journey together.

"I think so," I reply as the peak of the roof rises into view behind the sharp seagrass.

I offer Elijah my arm, but he shakes his head. "Thank you, but it makes me more unsteady. I'd rather walk on my own."

"You're getting so much better," I tell him. "Are you still in pain?"

"Sometimes," Elijah admits. "Getting out of bed in the morning hurts."

I nod, shifting my basket higher onto my arm. I stare off at the ocean, watching as seals pop their heads out of the water and disappear below a wave's swell.

"Are you well, Leta?"

Immediately, I smile. "Of course. Why would you ask?"

Elijah shrugs. "You look pale today."

I mirror his shrug, hoping my nonchalance will be enough to convince me as well as Elijah that I'm perfectly fine. I don't want to admit that I feel faint on our walk, or that the smell of the pie makes me want to heave. By the time we reach the door, Elijah takes it upon himself to knock, and I'm grateful. The effort of carrying the basket has made me oddly weak, and I struggle to catch my breath.

"I wonder if he's working outside," Elijah muses, looking up at a second-story window.

"It's too cold and wet," I reply. "He wouldn't want to work outside in this weather. Perhaps he's in one of the far rooms."

"Should we go in?" Elijah asks.

I nod as he tries the door, but it's locked.

"Here," I say, placing the basket on the ground and kicking a rock to the side. "He hides the key under here." I hand it to Elijah, and the door clicks, opening with a tired yawn.

"Hello!" Elijah calls as we step inside. "We've brought pie."

It's quiet and damp inside, a sad gray gloom cloaking each room.

"Ben?" I call, but I already know he won't reply. I can't feel his presence in the house. I can't hear the familiar sound of his footfalls above me.

I carry the basket into the kitchen and place it on the worn wooden table. Fruit sits in a ceramic bowl in the center, arranged in a pleasing pattern, but when I take an apple, it's rotten on the inside, the skin bruising with the pressure of my touch.

Elijah continues his search of the house, slowly of course,

but I admire his determination. I leave the pie on the table and gather my skirts, traversing the hallway, peeking in each room, which is an exercise in futility because he won't be in any of them. I don't know why I pretend. I climb the stairs, one at time, conscious of every floorboard creak, every scurry of little mouse feet that reminds me I'm not completely alone. Still holding my diary close to my chest, I journey the length of the upstairs hall until I reach the door at the end. In the short amount of time Ben has been gone, a dust spider has built a tidy web in the corner. I step by it, leaving it undisturbed, and climb the stairs to his room.

Everything is neat and orderly, as if his belongings expect him back at any moment. His bed is made, a pile of his laundry folded on the corner of the mattress. His fiddle lays upon his pillow, the bow beside it, like he'll return home soon and place it comfortably below his chin, ready to coax a tune from its strings. The curtains are pulled aside so that I have a clear view of the Atlantic, cold rain pelting the window. I cross the room to his closet, slowly opening the door to find a few of his shirts on the shelves. Lifting one, I press it to my face, breathing deeply. A few feet away, placed in the middle of his desk, a white folded square tries to capture my attention. I stall as I walk slowly and delay opening the letter for a minute or two.

I place my diary in the corner of the desk, my hand resting on the paper.

I open it despite myself.

My love,

You know I'm not good with words, not like you. I won't try
to bury my meaning in flowery statements or artful turns of
phrase. I respect you too much for that. I have left for New
Bedford, and from there I am to captain a ship called the
Inevitable bound for the Arctic to hunt bowhead whales. I
could not refuse this offer, and I could not, in good conscience,
take you with me. I know how willing you were to give up what
you have in Highland for our life together, but that wouldn't be
right. What you gain would not be equal to what you lose, and
I care too much about you to let you make that decision.

Since returning to Highland, I have tried to be the person
you thought I had become, the person you thought capable of
writing your poems. I have tried to be a person deserving of your
love. But in truth, what you want from me I cannot give, and
your love for me is too much to carry. I am not strong enough.

Know that this decision has not been easy, and writing this
even less so. I hope that when people look for something that
is left of me, all they'll find is you. Maybe this is the legacy
I've been searching for, or maybe the call of the sea is too
much for me to ignore. It must be a powerful thing, this bright
and boundless sea, to blind me to your love for me.

All my love,
Ben

I stare at the letter for some time, one hand on my stomach, and I'm hardly even aware when I begin to cry. Tears stream down the length of my nose, across my lips, and drip onto the letter, splattering across inky words.

"Leta?" Elijah says quietly from the top of the stairs.

I'm so tired. I'm so tired of putting on a brave face, as if this is a perfectly acceptable end to whatever it was I shared with Benjamin Churchill. I'm so tired of pretending to be someone I'm not. I'm tired of the fact that whenever I was myself, I hid behind his name. I clench my eyes shut, bending at the waist, and I try to stifle the sob that wrenches from me.

"Leta, don't," says Elijah, the sound of his footsteps and the clunk of his cane making my ears ring and my head spin. His hand on my back makes me wretch, my breathing coming too quickly, my heart beating out of control.

I stumble to the window, pulling down on the handle and pushing it open until the cold, fresh air fills my lungs. I suck in breath after breath, trying to calm myself, but the scream that rips from my throat is irrepressible. It echoes over the inlet, a flurry of birds scattering into the air.

Pushing myself away from the window, I turn back to Elijah, swiping angrily at my eyes, trying to stop the tears.

"Look what he's done to you," Elijah says tenderly. "Has he destroyed you, Leta?"

Slowly, I raise my eyes to his, and I almost laugh. "Has he

destroyed me?" I repeat. "He has wounded me, but he has not destroyed me. Not yet at least."

Elijah shakes his head in bewilderment. "I don't know what you mean."

I lift the letter again. "He will have destroyed me in about eight months' time."

I wait for Elijah's reaction. I wait for his horror, for his surprise, for his reprimand for allowing myself to be so vulnerable to the advances of someone like Benjamin Churchill. For his shock, like everyone else's, when I tell him that I was the one who wanted it first. I was the one to make the first touch, to raise the suggestion, and that Ben gave me a way out. I chose not to take it. I wanted him instead.

Elijah lowers his head and steps toward me, his hand stretched out between us, offering me solace, offering me an alliance. "You are not destroyed," he says. "You've done nothing wrong."

I choke on my own cry, shaking my head and turning away from him. "You are too good, Elijah. You have always been too good, and I don't deserve your friendship."

"Stop it, Leta."

"No, it's true. I have been blind for so long."

"You have been my friend since I was able to define the word. The best I can do is return the gesture, Leta."

"Your friendship is appreciated," I tell him, taking a deep

breath, my hands on my hips, and I stare up at the white-washed ceiling. "But I don't know how it will save me from this."

Elijah nods. "Maybe we'll save each other."

"You shouldn't say this," I tell him, his devotion and kindness overwhelming me. "You should despise me, you should want nothing to do with me, you—"

The smallest movement stops me from saying anything more. Elijah reaches out his hand and touches mine, then he stares at the union of them. He tilts his head to the side and furrows his brows, and nods. "You," he says, and he squeezes my hand, "you don't get to tell me what I should or should not feel."

I don't argue with him.

"I know what you wanted, Leta. You wanted a fantasy. You wanted someone who didn't exist. You wanted the boy you constructed for yourself, out of words, and sea, and sky, but he could never be that for you. I might not live up to that ideal, either, but I came back to you, and I love you. You only have to decide if that's enough."

I take his hand in mine and raise his knuckles to my lips. "I will work to deserve you," I tell him. "I will strive to be the girl you fell in love with."

"You're still that girl," he says. "You have always been that girl."

CHAPTER TWENTY-FIVE

MICHAELA

present day

M ack."

"What's even more fascinating," Mr. Fink continues, and at this point, fifteen minutes into the period on a Monday morning, he's bouncing off the walls, explaining a bunch of important things he's collected for our next unit, "is that jellyfish have been around longer than sharks! Even dinosaurs!"

"Mack, hey?"

I hear Finn. I know he wants my attention for something, but it feels rude to turn around when your teacher is so enthusiastic about his lesson.

"We're not even beginning to tap the surface of what we know of the ocean, and it's right there." Mr. Fink points out the window in the direction of the Atlantic. "What will we learn about it this year?"

"I need gum, Mack."

Leaning back, I begin rummaging through my bag, searching for any abandoned sticks of gum. "It's not even nine in the morning. Why do you need gum?"

"To stay awake. Chewing keeps me conscious."

"Now," Mr. Fink continues, pacing the front of the lab, "to make sure that you don't fall asleep on me this morning, we're going to get up and rotate around the stations I've set up throughout the lab. I've been lucky that my friend and colleague from the university was able to obtain a few samples from a bowhead whale that was taken by native hunters in Canada." He leans back on his desk. "Find yourself a lab partner and pick your station to begin. You'll find your observation sheet waiting for you there."

"Dibs on Finn," I say before Ryan can even open his mouth.

"Take him," he replies. "He's only gonna slow me down."

"You're such a piece of shit," says Finn, standing and stretching. He's wearing jeans that are snug in all the right places and a baseball T-shirt with long sleeves in dark blue and the chest in gray. "Where do you wanna start?" he asks. "How about at the bones?"

We wander over to the tray holding what's labeled as the "vestigial hindlimb."

"These are found in the lower portion of the whale," I read

from the laminated explanation paragraph. "Remnants from when they were four-legged and walked on land."

"That's pretty epic," says Finn, lifting the bone. Next to the tray on the lab table is a diagram of the skeleton of a bowhead whale. "What's next?" he asks as the station beside us opens up.

I'm busy jotting down notes, but he moves on, and Mr. Fink continues explaining the different items he has for us to study.

"The eye of the bowhead whale," he says, "is one of the best ways to determine how old a creature is. And this whale," he says, a grin overpowering his words, "how old do you think this whale was when she was taken?"

"Seventy-six," Ryan calls from across the room.

"Try higher," says Mr. Fink.

"Ninety-two," I say.

He shakes his head and crosses his arms over his chest.

"One hundred and five," Finn tries.

Other numbers are called out, but Mr. Fink keeps waiting until the room goes silent.

At our station, the artifact for our consideration is triangular and sharp. I'm not sure if I'm allowed to touch it, but I can't help myself. I run my fingers over the smooth surface and try my best to read what's been etched into it. It's almost like I knew it would be there. Like the letters would be clear, and they'd be waiting for me the whole time.

I raise my hand slowly, eyes still focused on the harpoon tip.

"Care to venture another guess, Michaela?" asks Mr. Fink.

"I think the whale was close to two hundred years old."

Mr. Fink grins. "Good observation, Miss Dunn."

"How'd you know that?" Finn asks me.

I stare at the harpoon tip in front of me. "Was this found in the whale? When they killed her?"

"It was," says Mr. Fink. "It was embedded in her blubber. A genuine Yankee harpoon tip. And by analyzing the whale's eye and aspartic acid, the scientists were able to determine that the whale died at two hundred and three years old."

"But when was she harpooned with this?" Finn asks.

"I'm afraid that's more difficult to determine," Mr. Fink admits.

"In 1863," I say.

No one says anything, and I pull myself away from the magnifying glass I'm using to study the harpoon tip.

"There's no date on that, Miss Dunn."

"No," I say. "There isn't. But there are two letters engraved on the tip." I extend the magnifying glass, and both Mr. Fink and Finn peer through it to study the harpoon.

"LT," says Finn.

"LT," I repeat.

His eyes meet mine, but I can't hold our gaze for too long. My vision is blurred by my tears, hot, unexpected, overwhelming. I touch the inscription.

"But that can't actually be . . ." says Finn.

"I think it could be," I say. "'*When people look for something that is left of me, all they'll find is you.*'"

CHAPTER TWENTY-SIX

MICHAELA

present day

I lean forward in front of my mirror, applying multiple coats of mascara for a defined and dramatic look to complement my smoky eye shadow. Behind me, Mellie babbles on to Finn about how to give a riveting speech.

"I dunno, Mellie," he says, sitting in the papasan chair in the corner of my room. He rereads his speech, tapping his pencil against his lips. "I think this is pretty good. I don't want it to sound like I didn't write it, you know?"

"You want to wow the crowd, don't you?" Mellie insists. "Like I did with my Mayor of the Third Grade Acceptance Speech."

"You *would* be the mayor," I mutter, blinking to make sure there aren't any clumps in my lashes.

"Sorry that you don't have my charisma, Mack," says Mellie with a hair toss, and she exits the room.

"Oof," says Finn, leaning forward and lifting himself from the chair. "She throws some serious shade."

"She's not wrong," I say, standing over my bed and staring at the three jackets I've picked out to wear this evening. It's the opening of the Captain Churchill exhibit at the Maritime Museum, and Finn is wearing a suit with a skinny black tie because he's one of the guest speakers.

"I just wish she hadn't asked me," he says, shuffling over to the bed and tossing his speech onto one of my pillows. He dramatically face-plants onto my display of jackets.

"Hey, watch it," I say, crawling over to him and shoving him in the shoulder. "I ironed all of these, and I don't feel like doing it again."

"Sorry," he mumbles, standing up, his shoulders slouched and his chin jutting out like a sullen child.

I smile, kneeling on the bed in front of him. "Look at you, you're a mess," I say.

"No, I'm not," he protests, even as I fix his tie.

"You have to look put together tonight. For your aunt. When you take the time to get dressed up for someone else's event, especially when you're not actually looking forward to it, it means you care."

"I care," he says, his face a little bit closer to mine. He smells like a little too much cologne and spearmint gum.

"You can't chew gum when you're giving your speech," I tell

him quietly once I'm finished fixing his tie. My hands remain on his chest.

"I won't."

I tilt my face upward to his, and his lips meet mine.

"Let's not go," he says against my mouth. His hands run up my arms. He makes me shiver.

"But I ironed."

"Well, I want to make you wrinkly."

"That sounds weird."

"You know what I mean," he says.

"Michaela!" Mom's voice floats up from the bottom of the steps.

Finn rests his forehead on my shoulder in dismay. "What is it?" I shout.

"There was a package at the front door for you. It's on the kitchen table."

"Okay."

"I should head out anyway," says Finn, shrugging into his suit jacket, and he looks so handsome, I want to grab him again and pull him up against me. "I want to mentally prepare before anyone arrives and freaks me out."

"Even me?" I ask.

"Never you," he smiles, and kisses me one more time.

"See you a little later," I say, holding his hand until we're forced to let go.

He taps the top of the doorframe on his way out.

In my solitude, without any distractions from a sassy sister or enticing boyfriend, I pick a navy-blue jacket with gold buttons and filigree that reminds me of a fancy naval officer's uniform. I almost pair it with my anchor earrings, but don't want to overdo the nautical theme. Pearls are still nautical but understated. With an application of lip gloss and a spray of perfume, I grab my wristlet and I'm out the door and down the steps.

"Chloe will be here in a minute," I say, passing the kitchen, where Mom unloads the dishwasher. "I'll see you later, probably after eleven."

"Wait, hold up," Mom calls. "Don't you want to see what came for you?"

Mellie sits at the kitchen table, knees up on her chair, waiting patiently. "I asked if I could open it for you, but Mom said no." She pushes a large cushioned package toward me and drums her fingers on the table impatiently.

I tap my phone's screen and see that there's still five minutes before Chloe is supposed to pick me up. Which in Chloe time means at least seven. I grab a pair of scissors from the junk drawer and slice open the top of the package.

"Did you order something?" Mom asks, peering over my shoulder.

"Not recently."

"You have a secret admirer!" gasps Mellie.

I arch an eyebrow in her direction.

"I won't tell Finn, but whoever this person is, Finn is better."

"It's just a package, Mellie," I say, reaching in and retrieving the contents. I wrestle two leather bound books from inside, several letters tied together and protected by a plastic bag, and one note scribbled on lined notebook paper. "Oh, my God." I cover my mouth with my hand.

"What is it?" Mom opens the bag of letters, gently taking one out.

Michaela,

I think this is my apology. I'm sorry for the debacle surrounding the poetry contest. After you won, I did some serious thinking — about writing, and traveling, and feelings of inadequacy. I'm taking a break from Winslow College, and I don't know when I'm going back. I think I need to take some time for myself, you know? But I hope you have fun at the workshop at the end of the month, and I hope you find something to write about from Leta's words. I think you'll know what to do with them.

—Caleb

I drop the note and snatch the diary from Mellie's hands.

"Hey, I was reading."

"I can't believe it," I say, delicately turning the pages. "These are more of Leta's diaries."

The honking of Chloe's car horn from outside makes me jump.

"I'm taking these with me," I say, gathering the letters and the diaries and placing them back in the envelope. "Love you." I kiss Mellie on top of her head and Mom on the cheek as I dash out the front door and across the lawn to where Chloe sits in the driveway, waiting.

"You brought reading material for the ride?" she asks once I'm buckled in and she's backing out onto the street. "It's a six-minute drive. I've timed it."

"I just have to look over a few things." I click on the dome light above our heads.

"I can't drive like that."

"That's just a myth."

Chloe continues to drive (quite well and without distraction) down Route 6, and when she slows and puts on her left blinker, I grab her forearm.

"What?" she practically yelps. "What is it? What happened? Coyote?"

The thing is, what I've just read, I can't tell Chloe first. It has to be Finn. He needs to be the first one to know. Before he makes his speech.

We speed up Route 6, thick pine forest on either side of the highway, and before us, a slice of the lighthouse's beam of light, guiding sailors away from the treacherous shores of Cape Cod. It's there one moment and gone the next, but even when it disappears behind a grove of tall trees, I never doubt its presence.

When we arrive at the museum, there are throngs of people waiting to get inside, to climb the lighthouse, to see the newest exhibit, which aims to prove that the legend of Benjamin Churchill was something more than a tall tale told at sea. His footsteps resonated here, and now they will again.

Chloe and I, arm in arm, navigate the perimeter of the little dwelling attached to the lighthouse. There have been additions over the years, rooms added on to accommodate tourists and history enthusiasts. Finn told me that after his great-great-great-grandfather Elijah returned home from the war and married Leta Townsend, the community came together and built them a much larger house that now sits down the street from the lighthouse. A home big enough to accommodate their growing family. But they only ever had one child.

I keep looking for Finn, the urge to tell him everything I know brimming inside me, but there are so many people, I don't know where to look.

"Ooo, cheese," says Chloe, pausing at the refreshment table.

"You stay here," I say as I finally spot Finn across the room. "Cheese up. I'll check back with you in a bit."

"Cheers!" Chloe raises her cheese and cracker in the air.

Finn's busy introducing himself to guests who paid a lot of money to get into the opening night of the Churchill Exhibit. He tries to greet everyone in the room. It's tough making it through the crowd, but I persist, clutching tight the envelope full of Leta Townsend's writing, until I'm stalled by the exhibit itself. A massive portrait of Benjamin Churchill presides at one end of the room—stoic and handsome, serious and a little sad. Below his image are pictures of him in New Bedford surrounded by sailors, and behind them, the last ship under his command, the *Inevitable*, waits to begin her journey. There are interactive videos of historians discussing the perils of whaling, and biologists outlining the threats these whales still face today.

Perhaps more important is the even larger portrait across from his, of Leta Townsend, and below, a sign that reads THE POETRY OF BENJAMIN CHURCHILL. Her poems are everywhere, printed on resin displays in large, easy-to-read fonts. They've even recorded someone reading them, and those who are visually impaired can listen instead.

"You're here," says Finn. "I was getting nervous. I'm supposed to talk soon, and I don't think I'd be able to if you weren't—" He stares at me, his brows furrowing. "What's the matter?"

"I need to tell you something, before you speak."

He takes my hand, our fingers entwined, and he leads me

through the room until we reach the back exit and slip away from the chatter inside.

Over our heads, the bright moon illuminates our faces enough to be clear, and the path we travel ushers us to the observation deck at the edge of the cliff. Below, the Atlantic bashes the shoreline.

"What's up?" he asks.

I kiss him and he slips his hands into my back pockets, his mouth traveling down my neck and finally settling on my collarbone, just under the lapel of my jacket.

I pull away for a moment, shaking my head, and extend the envelope containing the diaries and letters. "Caleb sent me this today."

"Caleb?" he says, his eyes widening. He takes the envelope, removing one of the diaries.

"I want you to have all this. I want to donate it."

He unfolds one of the letters. "Leta's writing? Are you sure?" he asks.

"I mean it." I take the diary and carefully flip to the very last page. Tucked away against the back cover is a letter Leta wrote to Ben but obviously never sent. It's the letter Finn has to read before all the other ones. Before his speech. "This one is most important," I say, pointing. "I want you to read it."

His eyes dart out to sea, then up to the lighthouse, and he smiles. "Now?"

"Finn, you're not actually a Pearce."

He laughs a little. "Then what am I?"

"Leta Townsend might have given her son the last name of Pearce, after her husband. But her husband wasn't the baby's father and the proof is right here." I carefully touch a few lines to support my claim: *I have never doubted Elijah's affection for our son. He treats him as his own, as if they, too, are made of the same flesh and blood, and for that, I must love him.*

"Mack," says Finn, his voice hardly a whisper.

I smile at him. "I spent my whole summer searching for the Highland Whaler," I say. "And it turns out he was next to me all along."

Finn runs his hand through his hair and turns his back on me. "Mack, I don't even know what to say."

"I was looking for some way to figure out how this person from the past was supposed to be relevant today. Like it was some puzzle to get past the gatekeepers."

Finn leans his elbows on the railing separating the observation deck from the cliff.

"I didn't realize that everything we do now echoes far ahead of us. Every step, every word. We could search for evidence that Benjamin Churchill lived all we want, but you're it, Finn. You're his walking legacy."

Finn laughs again, almost nervously, and looks over his shoulder at the museum, at the people milling about inside.

They're waiting for him. "As it turns out," he says, turning back to me, "when we look for something left of Benjamin Churchill . . ."

"All we'll find is you."

He takes a deep breath and kisses me.

CHAPTER TWENTY-SEVEN

Leta

Spring 1864

My husband said it was true. Our nephew was there, on the *Inevitable*. He saw it with his own two eyes!" Mrs. Budd says from the front room, her voice carrying so clearly that it's almost ear-piercing.

In the kitchen, I pretend to be preoccupied with changing little Ollie's diaper, and Elijah watches with interest.

"You changed him an hour ago," he says quietly, leaning on the frame of the back door.

"I can't go in there," I say. "There are certain days when I can handle Mrs. Budd's blather, but today is not one of those days. Besides . . ." I grin down at my baby, his wide, almost toothless smile interrupted by a few giggles. "Now he's fresh and clean for your trip into town." I lift Oliver and stand, giving him a kiss on his pudgy cheek.

"The whale was charging the boat," Mrs. Budd continues

with dramatic intonation. "And there was Captain Churchill standing bravely, his harpoon held high, but it was of no use."

Elijah and I both pause, but I won't let anyone see how this affects me. Not even Elijah, from whom I never hide a thing. I kiss Oliver again and place him into Elijah's arms.

"Just flour?" Elijah asks.

"Please," I say, and stand on my tiptoes to kiss him. "I'll meet you at home."

He bounces Ollie up and down as they depart, telling him all about the journey they're about to embark upon, and I watch them through the kitchen window as they head down the road and disappear around the bend.

I sigh, glancing over my shoulder and down the hall into the front room where my mother and several of the ladies from town sit sipping tea. They think it's fine to discuss Ben in front of me because I'm married to Elijah. They think because I'm married and we have a child that Benjamin Churchill must not exist for me anymore.

But he does. On nights when I wake from the chill in the bedroom, even though Elijah is sound asleep beside me, my first thought is of Ben. The breeze evokes his lazy smile, or the call of gulls brings him here again, with me, and I'm no longer so cold.

When his son crawls across the sand and toward the lapping waves of the Atlantic, I see him there as well. Before it's too late, I scoop up my baby into my arms, safe where he belongs, and the sea will not take him. It's already taken too much from me.

"That whale couldn't be stopped," Mrs. Budd continues. "Protecting its young, they say."

My hands are slightly trembling, and I take slow steps down the hall so as not to be heard. I wait at the corner, still hidden from view, and beside me a grandfather clock ticks dutifully. Every second inches over my skin.

"He stood there," says Mrs. Budd, "the final harpoon poised above his head, but he couldn't throw it. He couldn't kill the beast. Its back was splintered with the whalers' first attempts, but when it came to finishing off the leviathan, Churchill let it take his life instead."

No one sees me cover my mouth. No one sees me clench my eyes shut or my chest heave with the pain of this news. No one sees me retreat down the hall, out the back door, or up the hill where the entire inlet lay before me, waking from its winter slumber.

No one sees when I break into the old Pearce house—the house that would have been mine. I smash a window with a fallen branch, snapped with the weight of early, wet spring snow. I reach around and unlock the door, winding through halls, climbing the stairs, and retrieving Ben's fiddle from his bed.

It is as unblemished and as perfect as when he left it, and I delicately run the pad of my finger over the strings. There is only one place where this fiddle belongs. Tucking it under my arm, I march to the shore.

The sea is slate gray, reflecting the hue of the sky. In the height of summer, I remind myself, it will be a royal blue, a foaming green, a deep, murky black, and the whales will return. With every step I take, the wind chokes the breath out of my lungs. My boots sink in the damp sand, the fiddle clamped under my arm.

I drop to my knees some yards from the water's edge, and the fiddle falls from my grip. A few grains of sand cling to the strings and worn wood, lodging themselves into the cracks of the tired wooden body. The salt that saturates the air covers my chapped face.

I begin to dig.

I dig a hole large enough to bury an abandoned fiddle, one deep enough so that it won't be washed away too quickly, and when it is, I won't know any better. When a wave splashes at my ankles, my skirts clinging to my feet, I realize the tide is coming in, so I turn and throw a handful of sand at the lingering white foam. I dig wildly, like my life, my sanity, depends on it. I claw at the hole, sand spraying everywhere and matting my hair, encrusting my fingernails and covering the fiddle. With every handful of sand, the ocean fills the hole. I grab the fiddle and scream at the gray water until my throat is raw with exertion.

I wade in, knee-deep, and throw the fiddle into the waves.

"Take it!" I scream to him. "Take it back! I don't want it! I don't want you! I never—" I drop to my knees in the middle of my rage. "I never asked for you."

The fiddle floats for a moment until it fills with water, is swallowed by a wave, and sinks slowly, saturated, like his body must have, into the ever-darkening sea below.

CHAPTER TWENTY-EIGHT

MICHAELA

present day

My alarm is acutely more painful on a Saturday morning, blaring loudly in the blackness of my room. Blindly, I reach out to silence my phone, rub the nighttime crust and bleariness out of my eyes, and swing my legs over the side of the bed.

I shiver as I turn on the lamp on my nightstand, its soft glow trying its hardest to warm my little room. Checking my phone, I see it's almost six. Finn will be here any minute, so I throw on a bra, a pair of leggings, a hoodie from the Shellfish Shanty, thick wool socks, and a pair of Hunter boots. I toss my hair into a sloppy ponytail, brush my teeth, and I feel prepared. One pit stop at my desk to grab the letter and the corked glass bottle I bought at the thrift shop on my way home from school yesterday, and I'm out the door, pushing my arms into my winter coat as I head to the driveway.

Finn's waiting in the Volvo, its headlights turned off. "Hey," I say, opening the door and sliding into the passenger seat. He greets me with a kiss and a bag containing two double mocha muffins. Two steaming coffees sit in the cup holders between us. "You really know what love is, don't you?"

He grins as he backs out of the driveway and heads down the street to Route 6. "Oh, yeah? What is it?"

"It's waking up before dawn when it's twenty-three degrees outside and greeting me with breakfast and hot coffee so that we can go and do weird things at the ocean."

"That sounds on-brand." We coast down Route 6, going slower than usual because somehow the darkness and the cold make you want to move slowly. I nestle more deeply into my winter coat. "You got everything?" Finn asks, glancing over at the contents on my lap.

"I've got it all. I just need a pen, so you can sign the letter."

He leans over and clicks open the glove compartment. "Should be something in there."

I fish around and retrieve a purple ballpoint pen. At first, I'm aggravated that I didn't think to bring the pen I wrote the letter with. Now, when Finn signs it, his name is going to stand out from everything else. But maybe that's the way it should be. I settle back into my seat, taking a bite of my muffin.

When we get to the parking lot below Highland Light, we take out the letter and flatten it on the hood of Finn's car. He comes around to my side, takes the pen in his hand, and signs his name at the bottom.

"There," he says, standing back. "Now it's official."

"Let's do this."

Hand in hand, we walk down the wooden stairs of the cliff and onto the damp shoreline. There's silence except for the roar of the waves, and the ocean is roiling and churning this morning. We stand far enough away that the waves won't hit our feet when they creep up the sand.

I hand Finn the glass bottle, and I unfold the letter.

"Gonna read it out loud?" he asks.

"Of course."

"All right, I'm ready."

We both face the water and wait for the first glimmer of sunrise on the horizon. When it peeks just below the clouds, I clear my throat:

Dear Captain Churchill,

Leta used to write you letters before you came back, when she thought you were dead. When everyone thought you were dead. She'd scribble down all her deepest thoughts, and she'd roll them up and place them in a bottle, then launch them out to sea. When you really did die, she wrote one final letter, and even a poem for you, but she never sent it. We thought it was important you knew what she had to say, that we sent you her poem. These are the most important points:

1. You had a son with Leta. His name was Oliver.

2. Your cousin Elijah loved him.

3. Leta went on to write many more poems under her own name.

4. We think she missed you.

5. You are remembered.

Sincerely yours,
Michaela Dunn & Finnian Pearce
(your great-great-great-grandson)

Words Composed of Sea and Sky
by Leta Townsend

Why not wander down the cliff
Where the laughing gulls do cry?
Far along the shore
Past the lighthouse's lure,
We take to the wind, we fly.

Why not strip all we carry
Shirt and skirt, false hope and lie?
Frolic in the tide
Our young hearts abide,
Away from curious eye.

Why not tell of your burden
'Til your solemn tales run dry?
Sing me your story,
You could not bore me,
Words composed of sea and sky.

When I finish reading, I look at Finn, but he's staring out at the waves. Wordlessly, I roll the letter into a scroll and take the bottle from Finn's hands. "You ready?"

He squints down at me and nods. "Mmhm."

Plugging the bottle with the cork, I ask, "Do you want to do the honors?" I offer it up to him.

He lets the bottle rest in his right hand for a moment, then he strides to the water's edge, winds up, and hurls the bottle far out into the waves. As the sun's rays stretch over the sea, the bottle dips and bobs on the current, until it all but disappears against the sky.

THE END

ACKNOWLEDGMENTS

First and foremost, to my agent, Liza Fleissig, who has believed in my voice even when I couldn't find it myself. You have championed my writing from the very beginning, and I'm thankful that I gathered up my courage at the conference and sat down in front of you. Truly life-changing.

Thank you to my editor, Julie Matysik, who helped this dream become a reality. You have shaped this story into something I didn't realize it could be, and I'll always be grateful for that. Thank you to the team at Running Press Kids who have made this book a dream come true.

To Jess Rinker and Joe McGee, your friendship, your insight, and your support has meant more to me over the years than I can express. You have helped me become the writer I am today, and this book would not have been possible without either of you.

To Donna Galanti, who has been my critique partner, and more important, my friend, for so long and through so many manuscripts that I can't even begin to count years or words. You are my biggest cheerleader, my support when I'm feeling like a fraud, and my voice of reason when things start getting crazy. Thank you for your friendship and sharing your stories with me.

To my friends, advisors, and cohorts at Vermont College of Fine Arts, especially Heather Hale, who keeps me accountable through our check-ins, and Liz Garton Scanlon, who helped me find the poems in my story even when I was certain there were none.

Thank you to my colleague Brian McGowan, who taught me how to string a fiddle.

To the Captain Bangs Hallet House Museum in Yarmouth Port, Massachusetts, and Highland Lighthouse in Truro, Massachusetts. You keep history alive, and your insight into the life of a whaling captain and a lighthouse keeper was invaluable. Thank you to the Center for Coastal Studies in Provincetown, Massachusetts, which answered so many questions about whales and the coast of Cape Cod that I can't even keep track. Your work is vital, and I thank you for the animals you protect.

To McCarter Theatre in Princeton, New Jersey, for introducing me to my love of storytelling. Benjamin Churchill first appeared to me when I was thirteen years old, coming home from having seen a production of *A Christmas Carol*. He hasn't left me since.

Thank you to Kathryn Craft, who has given me so many lessons on what it means to be a writer. The comradery I have found in your house on cold winter afternoons has been vital in my growth as an author. And to Marie Lamba, who convinced me that I wasn't a fraud and I would be fine if I just took a leap and signed up for a writers conference. I did it! I made it!

To Kate Lutter, who took me under her wing and invited me into the world of writing.

Thank you to my teachers, Cherylann Schmidt, who first showed me that my words were powerful, and to John Smith, who was the first person who told me that he knew he'd hold my book in his hands. I hope I've made you proud.

To my dad, who read to me every night; my mom, who took me to the library each week; and Tyler, who read my stories for me out loud. I love you. To Arrow, who is the best dog in the world. Good boy.

This book would not have been possible without all your help, friendship, guidance, and love.